# DREAM GIRL

# DREAM GIRL

A NOVEL

# LAURA
# LIPPMAN

*wm*

WILLIAM MORROW
*An Imprint of* HarperCollins*Publishers*

DREAM GIRL. Copyright © 2021 by Laura Lippman. All rights reserved. Printed in the United States of America. No part of this book may be used or reproduced in any manner whatsoever without written permission except in the case of brief quotations embodied in critical articles and reviews. For information, address HarperCollins Publishers, 195 Broadway, New York, NY 10007.

HarperCollins books may be purchased for educational, business, or sales promotional use. For information, please email the Special Markets Department at SPsales@harpercollins.com.

FIRST EDITION

Library of Congress Cataloging-in-Publication Data has been applied for.

ISBN 978-0-06-239007-3 (hardcover)
ISBN 978-0-06-311502-6 (international edition)

21 22 23 24 25  LSC  10 9 8 7 6 5 4 3 2 1

*For those with whom I have shared various*
*paradises, including but not limited to:*

Andre Dubus III

Denise Duhamel

Beth Ann Fennelly

Tom Franklin

Ann Hood

Major Jackson

Christine Caya-Koryta

Michael Koryta

Dennis Lehane

Laura McCaffrey

Campbell McGrath

Peter Meinke

Jeannie Meinke

Stewart O'Nan

Trudy O'Nan

Tom Perrotta

Marina Pruna

Michael Ruhlman

John Searles

Les Standiford

Kimberly Kurzweil Standiford

Sterling Watson

Kathy Watson

David Yoo

## GERRY DREAMS.

In a rented hospital bed, high above the city, higher than he ever thought possible in stodgy, low-slung Baltimore, Gerry is asleep more often than he's awake. He floats, he rouses, he drifts, he dreams. He tosses, but he cannot turn. He is Wynken, Blynken, and Nod, casting his net over the glittering lights of downtown, deceptively beautiful at night, a city where someone might choose to live, no longer a city where one gets stuck, not at night, not in his dreams.

There is no clear demarcation between Gerry's dreams and his fantasies, his not-quite-asleep and his not-really-awake. His brain chugs, stuck in a single gear, focused on one thought or one image. Tonight he feels he is revolving, ever so slowly, like the old restaurant on top of the Holiday Inn. Then he finds himself hanging from the minute hand of the clock in the neighboring Bromo Seltzer tower, a Charm City Harold Lloyd, slipping, slipping, slipping.

Someone is waiting on the sidewalk below, arms outstretched. It's a woman, but he can't see her face. He lets go and—he wakes up.

Or does he? Was he really asleep, is he ever really awake these days? He spends all his time in this bed, his leg suspended, a nurse attending to his needs, although not very cheerfully. He supposes he should not expect anything more than competence from someone who makes a living wiping adult bottoms and emptying bedpans.

Is it the medication? It must be the medication. His sleep has never been like this before. Maybe he shouldn't take the medication. Does he need the medication? Is he at risk of getting hooked on the medication? Museums are stripping the names of opioid heirs from their buildings, yet here is Gerry, late to every trend as usual. Just like his hometown.

From downstairs, he can hear the faint hum of the night nurse's television show. It weaves itself into his thoughts, a soothing murmur. Tonight's program seems to be a talk show. It sounds like Johnny Carson. It cannot be Johnny Carson. Except—there is some weird channel, something called MeTV, a jumble of older programs from Gerry's youth. Is the nurse watching MeTV? Is her TV— HerTV—different from HisTV? If it were really MeTV, wouldn't it be tailored to one's specific preferences? Johnny Carson, *Mannix, Columbo, Banacek*. That would be Gerry's MeTV, which was really his mother's TV. MomTV.

And then "The Star-Spangled Banner" would play when the local stations ended their "broadcasting day." Nothing ever ends anymore. Gerry misses endings.

He will ask the nurse tomorrow about his pain meds, what exactly he's taking, what he's risking. After the surgery—there had been no time to brief him before, given the nature of his injury—he had been given a pamphlet titled "Your Role in Pain Control." The unwitting couplet is stuck in his head.

**Your** *role*
*In pain control*

*Your* **role**
*In pain control*

*Your role*
*In pain* **control**

It's more Rod McKuen than William Carlos Williams, but it has a sort of bare-bones charm. The words, said over and over, become ridiculous, as all words eventually do. What is Gerry's role in pain control? Isn't the human condition a cradle-to-grave attempt to gauge one's role in pain control? To whom has Gerry caused pain and to what extent did he control it? He makes a mental list.

His first wife, Lucy. If only she hadn't been so jealous.
His third wife, Sarah.
*Not* his second wife, Gretchen.
Not Margot, no matter how she pouts.
His mother? He hopes not.
His father? Who cares?
Tara, Luke?

*I've got a little list.* Nixon had a list. Are people really nostalgic for Nixon now? That seems a bridge too far. His mother hated Nixon. He remembers her screams in the night. *What happened, Mama?* Someone shot Kennedy. *No, Mama, they shot JFK.* They shot Bobby! It's happening again, it's happening again, her voice rising in hysteria.

Everything is happening again.

*There was a letter,* Gerry tells himself. *There was definitely a letter.* That was the indirect cause of the accident, a letter, a letter from a person who does not exist, who never existed, no matter what others believe, claim, insinuate. Only no one can find the letter now. No one knows anything about the letter.

He's pretty sure there was a letter.

"Mr. Andersen, you need another pill."

The nurse, Aileen, looms over him, glass of water, pill in hand. By day, when he is more lucid—well, relatively more lucid—he has checked the label: she is following the dosage meticulously. Still, he's skeptical of the medicine. But what is his role in pain control? Should he ask for less? Does he want less? How would he rate his pain on a scale of one to ten, as the pamphlet encouraged him to do? He feels as if he's in a lot of pain, but he's had a serious injury, so it's hard to rate what he's feeling now.

A seven. Gerry gives himself a seven.

But is that the pain in his leg or his heart? Is pain the problem or does it mask the problems he doesn't want to face, the dilemmas that haunt his dreams, the fear and regret, the people he let down? The dead—his mother; Luke—are kind at least. The living, however—he feels as if the living are enjoying his current discomfort a little too much, assuming that anyone knows what happened to him, and almost no one knows. Still, the living have been waiting a long time for Gerald Andersen to have a comeuppance, although this is more of a comedownance.

"Your medication, Mr. Andersen. It's very important that you take your medication."

He has no choice. He swallows.

# PART I

# DREAMS

*January 30*

GERRY ANDERSEN'S NEW APARTMENT is a topsy-turvy affair—living area on the second floor, bedrooms below. The brochure—it is the kind of apartment that had its own brochure when it went on the market in 2018—boasted of 360-degree views, but that was pure hype. PH 2502 is the middle unit between two other duplex penthouses, one owned by a sheikh, the other by an Olympic swimmer. The three two-story apartments share a common area, a most uncommon common area to be sure, a hallway with a distressed concrete floor, available only to those who have the key that allows one to press PH on the elevator. But not even the sheikh and the swimmer have 360-degree views. Nothing means anything anymore, Gerry has decided. No one uses words correctly and if you call them on it, they claim that words are fungible, that it's oppressive and prissy not to let words mean whatever the speaker wishes them to mean.

Take the name of this building, the Vue at Locust Point. What is a *vue*? And isn't the view what one sees from the building, not the building itself? The Vue is the view for people on the other side of the harbor, where, Gerry is told, there is a $12 million apartment on top of the residences connected to the Four Seasons Hotel. *A $12 million apartment in Baltimore.*

Nothing makes sense anymore.

This apartment cost $1.75 million, which is about what Gerry cleared when he sold his place in New York City, a two-bedroom he bought in the fall of 2001. How real estate agents had shaken their sleek blond heads over his old-fashioned kitchen, his bidet-less bathrooms, as if his decision not to update them was indicative of a great moral failing. Yet his apartment sold for almost $3 million last fall and, as he understood the current tax laws, he needed to put the capital gains, less $250,000, in a new residence. Money goes a long way in Baltimore, and it was a struggle to find a place that could eat up all that capital without being nightmarishly large. So here he is at the Vue, where money seems to be equated with cold, hard things—marble in the kitchen, distressed concrete floors, enormous industrial light fixtures.

"Impressive," his literary agent, Thiru Vignarajah, says, standing in the foyer, or what would be a foyer in an apartment with walls. "But did they mention it was in Baltimore, Gerry?"

"Very funny, Thiru. You know why I bought down here."

Eight months ago, Gerry had been assured by doctors that his mother had less than two months to live. Her only desire was to die in her home, Gerry's "boyhood" home. Gerry, ever the dutiful son, figured he could grant that wish. Two months passed. Then three.

At month four, the doctors admitted they were fallible and that his mother might live longer than expected—not at home, not forever, but she could remain there for the foreseeable future (which, of course, is an oxymoron; the future cannot be seen). Gerry decided that buying an apartment in Baltimore would solve all his problems. His New York apartment sold quickly, despite the kitchen and bathrooms, and he snapped up this place, fully furnished, from the CFO of some smoke-and-mirrors tech company who was going through a bad divorce.

His mother died on December 31, three days after he closed on the Baltimore apartment. A soft, gentle woman, she had spent much of her life yielding to others, but when she really wanted something, she was stubborn. She wanted to die at home, with Gerry under her roof. So she did.

Now four weeks later, Thiru, always the full-service agent, is here for what he insists on calling the memorial service, which consisted of picking up Gerry's mother's ashes and taking them to Petit Louis for lunch. Not that his mother ever ate at Petit Louis, but back in the 1960s and '70s she chose the old restaurant in this location, Morgan Millard, for every milestone occasion. Gerry's graduation from middle school, Gerry's scholarship to Gilman, Gerry's acceptance to Princeton. Her birthdays. Once, only once, Gerry had persuaded her to breach her loyalty to Morgan Millard, insisting that they dine in New York on the day his second novel was published. He had taken her to Michael's; she had seen a famous anchorwoman, then pressed Gerry to approach the blond bobblehead and ask her to feature him on her show. Gerry had declined.

At Petit Louis, a perfectly respectable French bistro, he could not help wondering if Thiru was judging it. Gerry actually prefers this restaurant to its New York counterparts, Odeon and Pastis. It's not so much of a *scene*. He prefers quite a few things in Baltimore, or maybe it's simply that it seems important now to keep a running list in his head of things that are better in Baltimore than New York. *Movies:* it's almost unheard of to encounter a sold-out movie here. *Weather:* the winters are a tad milder, shorter. Grocery stores? The Whole Foods on Smith Avenue is just as awful as the one on the Upper West Side, so that's a push.

Thiru proclaimed himself charmed by Petit Louis, by all of North Baltimore. He seems less charmed as they approach Gerry's new home in Locust Point, a working-class neighborhood that is allegedly gentrifying, with the Vue as exhibit A. Thiru is uncharacteristically silent as they pull into the garage, leave the Zipcar in its designated space, take the elevator to the main floor, where Gerry picks up the mail from Phylloh at the front desk. Thiru does brighten at the sight of Phylloh, a curvy girl whose ethnicity is a mystery to Gerry, although he knows that he must never inquire how she has come by those eyes, that skin, that hair. Would Thiru be allowed to ask? Is it wrong to wonder if Thiru would be allowed to ask? The modern world is forever flummoxing Gerry.

He turns the key and pushes the button marked PH, although Gerry will never call his apartment a penthouse, never. "You can go straight to the apartment from the garage, of course," he says. "If you have the key card."

"Of course," Thiru says.

Thiru's bright eyes continue to appraise everything. It's almost like being in the room for the unbearably long periods when Thiru has one of Gerry's new manuscripts.

"Can you imagine what an apartment like this would cost in New York?" Gerry asks. Tacky to talk about money, but Thiru knows to the penny how much money Gerry has earned. He had to certify Gerry's net worth when he bought the New York co-op in 2001.

"Yes," Thiru says. "But—then it would be *in* New York, Gerry."

"I'll be back," he says. "I need to stay here a year to two years so I don't lose too much money when I resell. And then I'll downsize, maybe try another neighborhood. I was getting tired of the Upper West Side anyway."

"Is real estate appreciating here, then? I thought the city had been rather, um, challenged in recent years. There were those riots? And the murder rate is rather high? I feel as if I read a piece in the *Times* about it not that long ago."

"Millennials are drawn to Baltimore," Gerry says, parroting something he heard, although he can't remember from whom. "It's the most affordable city in the northeast right now. Real estate has been a little soft since, um, Freddie Gray."

He does not add that it's a fraught choice in Baltimore, whether to refer to the events of 2015 as the *riots* or the *uprising*. Gerry can't bring himself to use either term.

"Hmmmm." Thiru begins pacing the top floor, not bothering to ask if he can look around. He is a tiny man with an enormous head, only eight years older than Gerry. But the two men have been together for forty years, since Thiru read one of Gerry's stories in the *Georgia Review*, and the age gap remains significant to Gerry. Thiru has longish hair that he wears in a brushed-back, leonine mane. The once blue-black hair is silvery now, the peak has receded, but there is still quite a bit of it, thick and shiny. His suits are bespoke. They probably have to be, given his height. He still terrifies Gerry on some level, although their relationship has outlasted seven wives (three for Gerry, four for Thiru).

"Are you working on something, Gerry?"

"You know I don't talk about my work in progress."

"Fiction."

For a second, Gerry assumes this is an accusation, not a question, but that's probably because it *is* a fiction that he is working. He hasn't written for months. Reasonable, he thinks, under the circumstances, although he was able to write through every other difficult period of his life.

"Of course. What else? You know I have little patience for literary criticism right now. Most American writers bore me."

"I thought with your mother gone, you might consider that memoir we talked about."

"*You* talked about. The memoir is a debased form."

"But it's such a good story, the thing with your father."

"No, Thiru. It's sad and banal. And I used what interested me about the situation for my first novel. I have no desire to revisit the material."

"It's just that—your publisher would like you to sign a new contract, but they are entitled to know what you're working on."

"And when I have finished a new book—*the* new book—we shall. I don't like advances, Thiru. That's what undercut my second and third novels, that's what made *Dream Girl,* and everything that followed, different. I won't take money up front for an unwritten book. I can't—"

He stops, fearful that he is about to say the thing he doesn't want to say out loud: *I can't write anymore.* It's not true. It can't be true. But given the circumstances of his mother's death, how can he not worry about receiving a similar diagnosis one day? This thing runs in families.

"Well, the view is really something," Thiru says, his admiration sincere. "In fact, I'm not sure I could work with such a panorama spread out before me. I like the fact that you can see the working part of the harbor, not just the fancy stuff."

"This used to be a grain silo," Gerry says. "The site of the building, I mean."

"Good thing you're not gluten intolerant."

*Ha ha, funny, Thiru.* Gerry gives him 15 percent of a smile.

His agent peers down the staircase to the darker rooms below—Gerry's office, Gerry's study, Gerry's bedroom. The intention was to make guests almost impossible, with the medium-size bedroom used as his office and the third, smallest one dedicated to the overflow of books that didn't fit in the study or the upstairs shelves. If Margot should propose visiting—doubtful, someone like Margot would never be drawn to Baltimore—he will be able to tell her there is no proper spare bedroom, only the so-called study with its pullout sofa bed. He hopes it is understood that Margot is no longer welcome in his bed.

"That's—interesting."

"It's called a floating staircase."

"Oh, I'm familiar with the *concept*. But wouldn't it make more sense in an open space, where it could be seen? Rather wasted here. It's like staring down a mouth. A mouth with big gaps between the teeth."

"I didn't design the apartment," Gerry says. "And I needed something in move-in condition. Most of the furniture was part of the staging and I asked to keep it. The only things I brought from New York were my Herman Miller reading chair, my desk and desk chair, my books, and the dining room set."

Thiru's eyebrows, thick and furry, make a perfect inverted V on his forehead, then quickly relax. Gerry decides that Thiru's teasing is a form of envy. It's a beautiful apartment and Baltimore, which he fought so hard to escape, feels serene after New York. Maybe this is all he needs to get back to work, a change of scene. A change of scene, no more Margot drama, no more suspense over the quality of his mother's end of life. He will be able to write again. Soon.

"Anyway, I've brought some things that came to the agency—the usual fan mail"—Thiru grins, because Gerry's mail runs to anti-fans—"and speaking requests, some for quite good money."

Thiru hands Gerry a manila folder of envelopes. He notices one is addressed in cursive, an undeniably feminine hand, so perfect that he suspects it's a machine posing as a person. But it's postmarked Baltimore and the return address is vaguely familiar. Fait Avenue. He's filled with warmth and then—his mind goes blank, he cannot remember the person, someone who provokes nothing but affection, who lived on Fait Avenue. This occurs more and more, this blankness. He knows, technically, what has happened. His frontal cortex has seized up and will not be able to provide the information that Gerry wants, not now. Later, when he's relaxed, it will come to him easily. But for now, the memory is locked, like a phone on which one has tried a series of incorrect passwords. This is not a sign of dementia. It's not, it's not.

Thiru insists on taking an Uber to the train station, as Gerry's new assistant, Victoria, has yet to return from her errands. Gerry doesn't own a car, unless one counts his mother's beloved wreck of a Mercedes, parked in his deeded space until the estate clears probate and he can take legal possession to sell it. For himself, he has decided to make do with Zipcars, Ubers, and the occasional water taxi.

"I look forward to seeing what you're working on," Thiru says. Again, a perfectly normal thing to say, especially given that Gerry, for almost forty years now, has always been working on something. He's not the most prolific writer—only seven books total—but thanks to *Dream Girl,* he doesn't have to be.

He has, however, always been a disciplined writer, working every day from eight to twelve and three to six. Lately, he can't write at all and it's not the view's fault; he keeps the blinds drawn to avoid glare in his downstairs office. He writes on a computer with a special display, one that resembles an actual page. It's amazing to Gerry how many writers fail to grasp the visual context of their books. Then again, with people reading novels one paragraph at a time on their phones, maybe he is the one who's out of step. He has a perfect chair and a perfect desk and he keeps his assistant out of the apartment as much as possible, having learned that he cannot stand to have a breathing human in his space when he's writing.

Still, the words aren't coming.

When Thiru leaves, Gerry goes dutifully to his office, taking the two bundles of mail with him and sorting it—one pile for recycling, one pile for bills, one pile for personal and professional correspondence—but he can't find the energy to open any of it. Should he entrust Victoria with doing that as well? She's an eager beaver, approaching thirty, but with no defined ambition. She won the job when she told him that she loved to read yet had no desire to write. The worst assistants are the little vampires who try to turn an essentially menial job into a mentorship. They'll suck you dry, literally and figuratively, those young women.

Now that he thinks about it, maybe Victoria was the one who told him that Baltimore was popular with millennials, although she arrived here as a college student and seems to have stayed out of sheer inertia. They eventually figured out that she had been at Goucher the year he was the visiting professor in creative writing, in 2012, but she had switched her major to biology by then, so their paths never crossed. She has no idea why she studied biology, no idea what she really wants to do. This is baffling to Gerry, who has known since he was thirteen that he wanted to be a writer, fought with an indifferent world to make it so, and was past forty when it was finally acknowledged that he wasn't a one-trick pony but someone built for the long term. He's not one for millennial-bashing—as a tail-end boomer, he resents the stereotypes heaped on his generation, which have almost nothing to do with him. But he is suspicious of this current mania for happiness. To paraphrase *Citizen Kane,* it's not hard to be happy, if all you want to be is happy.

He forces himself to turn on his computer and a few words trickle out. He is trying to write a novel about Berlin in the early 1980s. *A memoir!* How could Thiru suggest that yet again? It isn't out of respect for his mother that Gerry has avoided writing about his father; it's out of respect for his own imagination. He has nothing to say about his father, a stultifyingly ordinary man who did one extraordinarily despicable thing. Gerry wouldn't give him the satisfaction of taking up that much mental real estate. Not that his father would know; he's been dead for almost two decades.

Gerry gives up on his own writing and reads for the rest of the afternoon until he hears Victoria entering the apartment above, dropping off his dinner. Gerry does not cook and has no patience with all the attention heaped on food nowadays. Food is fuel. Part of Victoria's job is to bring him something ready-made, from Whole Foods or Harris Teeter, for dinner every evening. He can handle breakfast on his own—oatmeal warmed in the microwave, fruit and yogurt. Lunch is a turkey sandwich, maybe with some carrots. As a result, Gerry remains quite lean and fit, requiring no exercise beyond walking and a rowing machine. He wouldn't even have the rowing machine, but it was part of the apartment's staging and the Realtor assumed he wanted it when he asked if the furniture could be included. So sometimes he puts on gym shorts and a T-shirt and he rows, twenty-five floors above the water, feeling like he's in some goddamn ad, although an ad for a rowing machine would feature a younger man, he supposes.

He eats his dinner at the kitchen counter watching the sunset. The city is beautiful at night. Flaws disappear, buildings glow. He finds himself wondering if he is obligated to get in touch with his father's heirs about his mother's death. Her lawyer was adamant that his father's second family cannot make any claims on his mother's estate. Everything goes to Gerry.

The problem is that "everything" is the house, which has three mortgages and an overwhelming amount of stuff. He's going to put Victoria in charge of emptying it, but he can't completely hand off the responsibility. His mother, it turns out, saved *everything*, including his juvenilia. Princeton, which has won his papers despite not being the highest bidder, wants a complete accounting. He'll have to go through every carton and crate, just to be sure. He supposes he should set up a system for the mail, too, archiving emails and filing the regular mail—

The mail. Fait Avenue. How could he have forgotten who lived on Fait Avenue? Well, "lived," given that she exists only in a book, his book. Fait Avenue was Aubrey's address in *Dream Girl*. An inside joke, a little homage to Nabokov and his Aubrey McFate in *Lolita*, a bit of cleverness that went unnoticed by virtually everyone given that Fait Avenue is a very real place in Baltimore. He had placed Aubrey in the heart of Greektown, within hearing distance of the expressway, walking distance to Samos. Fait and Ponca, to be precise. But the address was contrived: there is no 4999½ Fait Avenue, no basement apartment where an enchanting young woman, following her own mysterious agenda, seduced a slightly older man in despair over his life. Had that been the address on the letter, 4999? That should have jumped out at him, but he's so distracted these days. No, he thinks there was no number, only the street name. He would have noticed the number. Fait Avenue, Baltimore, MD.

He has to know. He jumps up, bumping his knee hard on the underside of the table, then stumbles, tripping over the rowing machine, staggering and sliding across the slick floors. His foot strikes unsteadily on the first step of the floating staircase and he loses his balance, his arms windmilling, finding nothing because there is nothing to find, tumbling ass over teakettle, as his mother used to say—*why did his mother say that, what does it even mean, a teakettle doesn't have an ass*—until he lands, a crooked broken thing, in a heap at the bottom. He tries to get up, but his right leg isn't having it and there is nothing within reach that will allow him to pull himself up and hop. He tries to drag himself across the floor, but his leg hurts so much and is such an odd shape, it seems ill advised. What if he aggravates the injury by moving? He tries to find a comfortable resting position—fuck, distressed concrete, what a concept for a floor—and has no choice but to wait until morning, when Victoria finally arrives.

"Call 911," he says with as much authority as he can muster, positioning his arms to hide the stain from where he relieved himself at some point during the long, miserable night.

*1968*

IT WAS THE HEATING PAD, the doctors later said, that caused his appendix to burst.

His mother was always slow to call the doctor. Not for fear of bills; not even later, when money was tight, would she ever skimp on medical care on the basis of its cost. Even as a child, Gerry was aware of what caused his mother financial anxiety (extras at school, broken things, the amount of milk that a growing boy can drink) and what did not, which was pretty much doctor's bills and holiday gifts.

But doctors, in his mother's view, were for surgery and bones, maybe the occasional prescription. It was a weakness to call them. So when appendicitis began making its claim on Gerry's body, she treated each symptom as it came, never seeing them as parts of a possibly deadly whole. His father was away—his father, a traveling salesman, was usually away—so there was no adult to second-guess his mother. Vomiting? Put the boy to bed with flat ginger ale. Fever? Baby aspirin. Abdominal pain? She draped a heating pad, something Gerry normally loved, over his midsection. Olive green, with three color-coded buttons—yellow, orange, red.

Next thing he knew, he was waking up in GBMC.

His father was not there when he came out of surgery, but he made it back to Maryland the next day. Gerry woke from a nap to his parents by his bedside, hissing. He fluttered his eyelids and pretended to slumber. His parents never fought in front of him, *never*. He was curious about the words they said to each other when they thought he wasn't listening.

"It's not my fault I wasn't here," his father was saying. "It's my job."

"Your job," his mother repeated.

"Yes, my job," his father said, responding to some tone that Gerry hadn't heard. It was as if the word *job* didn't mean *job* when his mother said it. But what else could it mean?

Gerald Andersen sold school furniture. He had a suitcase that Gerry had doted on as a child, until a neighborhood boy had accused him of playing with dolls, rather ruining it for him. His father's sample case had desks (for students and teachers), chairs, cunning little chalkboards. Gerry still sometimes unpacked the case when his father was home, marveling at the miniatures, the specially designed piece of luggage where each piece fit, almost like a jigsaw puzzle. His father's territory was Ohio, Illinois, and Indiana, one of the better regions. The 1960s were a good time to sell school furniture. The population was soaring; new schools were being built, old ones upgraded. Gerry remembered the stunning headline in his *Weekly Reader* when he was in third grade, prophesizing that the United States would hit 200 million people by the time he was in fourth grade and now here they were, in the biggest and the best country in the world, even if Nixon had just been elected president, a profound disappointment to his mother.

He wasn't so sure how his father felt about the election. "A man's vote is confidential, buddy," he had said in October, patting his breast pocket, as if all his secrets resided there.

"But we're supposed to talk about current events at home," Gerry had said. "We pick one story in the news and we talk about it at dinner, then bring in articles and make a presentation at school."

"We don't have to say who we're for, though. It's enough to know their positions, right? Okay, tell me what Humphrey is going to do."

Gerry was having trouble keeping his eyes closed without scrunching them tight, so he tried to roll on his side. But he was tender from the surgery and the effort made him yelp.

"Hey, buddy," his father said.

"How are you feeling?" his mother asked.

"Better. When do I get to go home?"

"Tomorrow. They just want to make sure there's no risk of infection."

His father said: "You can tell everyone at school that you almost died—and your mother gave you baby aspirin."

His mother defended herself. "How was I to know?"

The question hung in the air, as unanswered questions sometimes do. How was she to know that this stomach pain was something more? Fair enough. How was she to know what her husband did on his endless trips to Ohio, Illinois, and Indiana? He called home late at night, when the rates went down, reversing the charges. He described his day, complained about the motels, the food. Gerry was asleep when he called, or supposed to be. His mother didn't realize how late he stayed up, listening to Johnny Carson from the top of the stairs. Surely if she knew, she would have muffled her tears after these calls.

Once, when Gerry pulled the furniture from his father's case, a strand of long blond hair came with the miniature desk, the one for children, but a seven-year-old boy had no context for such a discovery. He uncoiled the hair from the desk leg, even as the memory coiled itself inside his mind, waiting to spring back one day. *Another child has been playing with these things.* That seemed ordinary enough. If he had bothered to investigate the idea further, he would have imagined a school superintendent's child being distracted by the objects during Gerald Senior's sales pitch. Or maybe the items had been taken out during a school board meeting and a bored board member had fiddled with one.

"Can I have ice cream?" Gerry asked his parents.

"That's for tonsils, buddy," his father said.

"Yes," said his mother.

*February 12*

THE NIGHT NURSE is named Aileen and she does not read. This is almost the first thing she tells Gerry about herself, after inspecting the shelves that cover the top floor's walls. The shelves were one of the few things that Gerry had to have installed in the apartment. He brought more than thirty boxes of books from New York, and that was after a ruthless culling. He had four boxes of kitchen equipment.

"You have so many books! I hardly read at all. I suppose I should." Her complacent tone suggests she doesn't really believe this, that her admiration for his books is a social nicety.

"How will you pass the time?"

She turns and looks at him as if he's not very bright. "Time passes on its own. It doesn't need my help."

That's almost wise, he has to admit.

"I mean at night, when you're here. It must be—" He's about to say *boring,* but stops. No one wants to hear one's job described as boring. "Lonely."

"Why, I'll watch television," she says. "Maybe movies."

"The study, which is probably the best place for you to hole up, doesn't have a television. I'm afraid the only television is up here." He points to the plasma screen, mounted to the center of the wall and now surrounded by books. The wall is really a nonwall, an architectural feature that, the Realtor said, was intended to define the various living spaces of the top floor. Gerry had shelves affixed directly to it, so the television is now surrounded by books; it almost disappears within the wall of books, a visual effect of which he approves. "It looks like something one might see in a gallery," Thiru had said, adding, "A very jejune gallery."

Gerry likes it, anyway. The news, glowing softly from inside this collage of books, has less impact, more context.

"Oh, I won't need a TV," Aileen says. "I have my tablet." She brandishes an iPad in a case covered with a pattern featuring cats doing human things. Cooking, riding bicycles, knitting. *Reading.* So cats read, but she doesn't. Whenever Gerry hears the word *tablet,* he imagines Moses holding the Ten Commandments, but now a tablet is a hunk of plastic, probably assembled by tiny children's hands in China. "You have Wi-Fi, I was told." She holds up a bag with yarn and needles. "I knit, too. If you don't bother me too much, I'll finish this coverlet before you're ready to let me go."

Gerry wants to protest, to insist that it is his prerogative to "bother" her as much as he likes, given the wages he will be paying her, but he decides she's what people now label as "on the spectrum." A little dense, emotionally and mentally, artless as a child, garrulous as a senior citizen. Perhaps that's a good quality for someone whose job involves wiping another person's ass.

Gerry's injuries are severe, but his hope for a fullish recovery is reasonable. He is in good health, although he was shocked to discover that X-rays revealed his bone density had already been compromised. He thought that was a female thing. But his primary injury is a bilateral quad tear in his right leg. He needs to remain flat on his back for eight to twelve weeks in this hulking beast of a hospital bed. His injured leg is braced to keep it immobilized and a "trapeze" hangs over him—he has to grab that if he wants to change his position in his bed or use what Aileen calls the "commode"—the correct word, yet one that irritates him to no end.

He has been told repeatedly how lucky he is—lucky that he didn't hit his head, lucky that he was on the floor for "only" twelve hours, lucky that he can pay for a nursing aide at home, otherwise he would have to be in a rehab facility. Aileen arrives at seven o'clock every evening, in time to lead Gerry through a round of exercises, serve him dinner, and then sit through the night as he succumbs to the jumbled slumber of medicated sleep. She departs at seven in the morning, leaving him alone for only two hours before Victoria arrives for her shift, which spans nine to five. And what is "alone" really? The front desk is a mere twenty-five floors and one phone call away, although it is unmanned—unwomanned—until Phylloh arrives at eight Monday through Friday.

Because the apartment's top floor has a full bathroom with a walk-in shower, it has been decided to keep him here, although it will be weeks before he visits the bathroom on his own. The walker at his bedside is, he supposes, an aspirational object. And because of the apartment's layout, the best spot for the bed is in the center of

the great room, facing the very stairs that tried to kill him, perpendicular to the wall with the TV. The bed is a bad smell, an insult, an
indignity, a reminder of what waits for everyone. Even Victoria, as
young and incurious as she is, seems nervous around the rented bed.
The rolling tray used for meals also allows Gerry access to his laptop, but he cannot work on a laptop. He needs his full-size screen,
he needs the darkness of his office; who can write in all this light?
Gerry would have been well-suited to serve on a submarine in his
youth, not that men his age had to worry about serving anywhere.

His coccyx was badly bruised in the fall as well, another excuse
not to try to write because even if he could struggle to a sitting
position, he couldn't hold it long. The word registers in his mind—
*excuse*. He had been looking for an excuse not to write and here it
is. Those lacy spots in his bones will respond, presumably, to the
calcium supplement, which Aileen provides every other day with his
nightly dose of pain and sleep meds. His bones will be fine. It's the
lacy spots in his brain that he's worried about.

"The day I fell," he says to Victoria when she enters with his
lunch, "the day I fell—I was going for some mail I left in the office."

"Yes, you tried to talk to me about it when I, um, found you."
Victoria seemed terribly embarrassed by discovering him, probably
because he had been forced to relieve himself. And yet—she has
insisted on helping him in his recovery, saying she will learn to do
whatever is necessary so he will require only one nursing shift, not
24/7 care. Which, frankly, he does not want. The idea of other people being under his roof constantly is the worst nightmare he can
imagine. During the last year, the annus horribilis when Margot
basically squatted in his New York apartment, he learned he can no
longer bear living with anyone. Maybe he never could, which is as
good an explanation as any for three failed marriages.

But Victoria quickly learned how to be here without making her presence known. He hopes she can teach Aileen the same trick.

"Any mail?" he asks.

"Nothing real." Mail itself is barely real to Victoria, who conducts her life via her phone, even depositing her paycheck by app. But Gerry insists on paper bills, paper checks, paper records.

"The night I fell—there was one letter in particular—a local one, in a—" He almost says *woman's hand*, but quickly corrects course. "In an old-fashioned cursive handwriting. Did you find that?"

"You asked me that already," she says.

"I know," he says crossly. "I just wanted to check again. I'm quite sure there was a personal letter among the things Thiru brought me."

"No," Victoria says. "There was nothing like that."

She is a wispy girl, with big glasses and a messy updo, given to enormous sweaters, long skirts, and ankle boots. In an old-fashioned movie, she would take off her glasses, shake out her hair, cinch the sweater, and be revealed as a beauty. Even in a modern film, she might be transformed, although it would probably be in a makeover montage supervised by friendly gays, who, in movies, seem overly preoccupied with helping heterosexual women find romance.

Inappropriate. All of these thoughts are inappropriate. If he says these things aloud, even to Victoria, who knows what might happen? Words, words, words—ha, that's a lyric from the ultimate makeover musical, *My Fair Lady,* which, strangely, is one of the few concrete memories he has of enjoying time with his father and mother.

"Well, if you see it around—it had a return address on Fait Avenue, here in Baltimore. That's what I remember."

"Why would someone from Baltimore write you in care of your agent when you're right here in Baltimore?"

"I don't think it's widely known I'm here."

"They wrote about it in *Baltimore* magazine, I think. Did your agent open it?"

"*Baltimore* magazine?"

"The letter. Did he read it? Did he see what it said?"

"No, it was unopened, I'm sure of that." Less and less sure the letter existed, but absolutely sure that it was unopened. He wonders if Thiru would remember, but probably not. Thiru has an eye for details, but they are the details of contracts and money, beautiful clothing and beautiful women.

"I'll go look around your office later. Now let's do your exercises."

For now, his "exercises" involve Victoria manipulating his good leg, her gaze averted. He wears heavy pajamas and, during the day, he insists on changing to a T-shirt and sweater above the waist. He is vain of his torso, which isn't bad for his age. Through the sheer power of his mind alone—and the avoidance of certain foods—he manages never to have a bowel movement during the day. That's for the night nurse, trained to do such things.

"Are you sure, Victoria, that you're okay doing this?"

"You saw the quotes, for full-time care. I'm happy to do this on the days you don't have PT, especially as it means a little more money for me." Sadly, softly, suddenly. "Baltimore's not cheap anymore, I don't care what anyone says."

"I had an apartment in the 1990s here—I couldn't get over how much space and light we got, for so little money. But then, we had moved down from New York, so I guess everything is relative."

"Hmm." Victoria tunes him out whenever he talks about his past.

"On the north side, near Hopkins, the Ambassador. It's where I wrote *Dream Girl*."

"I like the Indian restaurant on the ground floor."

*Dream Girl,* the novel about a girl called Aubrey, who lived on Fait

Avenue. *Dream Girl*, the novel that changed his life, the novel that launched a thousand guessing games about his inspiration, endless wonderment about how a man like Gerry had uncannily channeled this woman. Then, more recently, a thousand revisionist histories about older men and younger women. (His characters were only fifteen years apart; that shouldn't be scandalous, even now. It's not as if a fifteen-year-old could really be someone's father, unless he was a most unusual fifteen-year-old, one of the boys with mustaches who loitered on the edges of the package store parking lot on Falls Road.)

*Dream Girl* was, by design, an absolute product of Gerry's imagination, written in a feverish two-month period in which he had cut himself off from all stimuli to prove that novelists didn't have to embed or research every arcane detail of some tiny plot point in order to be relevant. A novel written on a computer, but an old one, without Internet access, under a cross-stitched sampler made by his first wife and inspired by the last lines of Eudora Welty's memoir: *Serious daring starts from within. Dream Girl* was what Gerry took to describing, in interviews, as an inside job, delighted by his own wordplay, the implication of a crime, but within one's own mind. "I stole a moment and created a life." He declined, always, to describe that moment.

Yet so many people wanted to believe it was, on some level, true, that Gerry Andersen had been "saved" by a seventy-two-hour romance with a younger woman. They hated learning that Aubrey was not real. Then again, readers hated being told that anything in fiction wasn't real.

Aubrey had never existed.

So who had written him from Fait Avenue?

Assuming that letter actually existed.

It did, it did, it did, it did. The letter was real. Aubrey was not, but the letter was real. He's not confused about what's real and what's not. Not yet.

*His mother's bra in the refrigerator. He should have known then. Still, Aubrey is not real.*

"Who's Aubrey?" Victoria asks.

He is surprised to realize he has been speaking aloud. More surprised that Victoria has not read *Dream Girl*. She claimed to be familiar with his work when she interviewed for the job. Ah, but she had been clever, extolling the virtues of his earlier novels, the unloved middle children between his first and his fourth.

That was probably why he hired her.

"Any mail?" he asks, picking up his letter opener, a Bakelite dagger emblazoned with the name of the company for which his father had once worked, Acme School Furniture, a jaunty salesman for its handle.

"You just asked me that."

Shit, he did.

"Would you get my doctor on the phone? I'd like to ask about my medication."

Victoria smiles at him sorrowfully. He understands her sad smile when, an hour later, she reports back that the doctor says he will try to call Gerry next week. He feels naive. "My" doctor. No one has a doctor anymore, unless they pay for one of those fancy concierge services. Gerry's mother, who worked as a doctor's administrator, is firmly opposed to that on principle. Was. There's no present tense left in his mother's life, which is still hard to absorb. There's not a lot that Gerry hopes for in his seventh decade, but he would like to live long enough to see health care for all in the United States. Good lord, he had been allowed to stay longer in the hospital for his burst appendix than he had for his quad tear. (They had moved him to a rehab facility, but, still, when had care become so careless?)

He turns on CNN. Everything is chaos. Forget the Dow. What the world needs is a ticker showing how the status quo, as embodied by the world's leaders, rises and falls hour by hour. Today, things are plummeting. Maybe everyone has dementia, maybe that is the final joke on the world and the millennials. The inmates are running the assisted-living facility.

He falls asleep as the sun sets, enjoying the happy sliver of time when he is alone in his own apartment.

## 1983

### "HOW DID YOU FIND THIS?"

"I have my ways."

A minute ago, Gerry had been trying to mask his disappointment at the Tiffany box that emerged from the silvery gift wrapping. A pen, a fancy pen, he guessed. He was surprised that Lucy would stoop to such a cliché, that she would waste her—*their*—money on such a generic gift. True, he kept a notebook and a pen on his person at all times, jotting down observations about the world as his characters would see them. But he often lost his pens, so he never invested in nice ones. Besides, a pen such as this, one that had to be refilled—certainly that was more likely to stain the breast pocket of his shirt.

Except, it *wasn't* a pen. Lucy had tricked him, probably knowing that all these thoughts would rush through his mind before he opened the box and found the old letter opener on a little bed of cotton.

"How did you—"

"Okay, okay—" She was almost dancing around him. The kitchen in their duplex was large but plain, and he sat at the wooden table where they ate most of their meals, his mug of postdinner tea warm in his hand, the late-summer sunset shooting streaks of orange-gold across the old black-and-white linoleum.

The letter opener was bright red. His father had this letter opener. Not this letter opener, of course, but one like it. His letter opener went with him when he finally left. Or did it? For all Gerry knew, this could be his father's letter opener. After he had been gone a year, his mother had swept all his things into boxes and dropped them at Goodwill. Gerry imagined the letter opener's life—someone buying it at Goodwill, then maybe taking it to one of the antique stores on Howard Street, or putting it out on their own little lonely card table of cast-off things at a yard sale, where Lucy—

"Don't you like it?" Lucy asked, no longer dancing.

"I love it," he said. It was the truth. You can love something that makes you sad.

She knelt beside him. Lucy was petite, put together. Her style icons were Barbara Stanwyck and Myrna Loy, but she adapted their trim, sophisticated looks to the 1980s, so she didn't look like one of those campy girls who shopped in vintage stores and treated every day like a costume party. She wore her hair in a simple, smooth bob, always shining and neat. Her lipstick was dark, her brows arched and slender. Even on a summer night, in shorts and a blouse, she looked polished, *soigné*. The shorts were crisp linen, the shirt a sleeveless gingham. Add a scarf and a pair of platform heels and she could have walked straight out of one of the old movies they loved.

But, again, Lucy was too tasteful to veer into camp. He should have known she would never give him something as ordinary as a pen to celebrate his first book deal.

Lucy was a writer, too. They had met in the Writing Sems, as the MFA program at Hopkins was known, where Gerry still taught. She was the acknowledged star of their class. She was so talented and full of promise that she was capable of being without envy, which astonished Gerry. She had been publishing her stories in the best literary journals since she was an undergraduate, yet here he was, with an offer for his first novel, a good one, from one of the top houses, and there was no doubt that she felt only joy. What would it be like to have so much confidence in your ability that you could celebrate someone else's success?

"It looks brand-new," he said. "As if it's never been used."

"Well, you'll use it, right? You have to get serious about your archives, after all. Universities will be bidding for your correspondence one day."

"They'll need an entire wing for the rejection letters."

"Stop."

She jumped into his lap. He loved her size, the lightness of her shape and spirit. He loved *her*.

"Let's drink to a deeply wonderful life," he said, a toast taken from a short story they both loved. They clinked their tea mugs. They weren't much for alcohol, for anything that distorted their senses. Lucy had never even tried pot and Gerry had used it only to hang with the jocks at Gilman, the boys who let him write their English papers for them, then paid him with their precious company.

"It's so sharp," she whispered, pressing the point against her forefinger. For a second, he thought he saw a drop of blood, imagined

Sleeping Beauty at the spindle. But it was just the Bakelite's red glow reflected on her skin.

She was straddling him now. The best thing about Lucy was that she was, beneath her ladylike looks, a wild woman when it came to sex. It was so easy to rise, propping her on the table to remove those crisp shorts, then stand. She was the only woman he had ever done this with, have sex standing up. She weighed 101 pounds.

The blinds were open on the south side of the house. Old Mrs. Pemberton sat in her folding chair, staring at them. Like that scene in *Peyton Place*, Gerry thought. He liked to teach that novel in his course on the pulps. Lucy was too far gone to notice, and even if she had seen Mrs. Pemberton, she probably wouldn't have cared. Gerry made sure to stay in the frame, give the old woman the show she clearly wanted.

He felt Lucy's nails rake his back, or maybe it was the letter opener. *Get a good view, Mrs. Pemberton.*

*February 14*

THE PHONE TRILLS, the double ring that signals a call from downstairs. Gerry used to ignore such calls, but Victoria is out and he is bored. He never used to be bored. He lived by his mother's maxim, *Only boring people get bored*. He considered this doubly true for writers.

Yet now he is bored, despite the fact that his life hasn't really changed that much, except for the bedridden part. He spent most of his time here in the apartment anyway, leaving only for his daily walks and the occasional errand he didn't wish to entrust to Victoria. Being forced to be here changes everything. At first, he tried to see it as a blessing. He would read more, write more. He would have time for quiet contemplation.

Instead, he has ended up watching lots of television, usually CNN, which makes him jittery and unsettled. There is no discernment in the news today, no sense of scale. Everything is BREAKING, everything is URGENT.

"Mr. Andersen?" Phylloh from the front desk. *Oh, my little pie crust,* he thinks, *I miss seeing you.*

"Yes, Phylloh?"

"There's a lady here. To see you."

"A lady?" He racks his brain. "Is she from the hospital?"

"No, she says"—Phylloh lowers her voice—"she says she's your wife."

"Which one?" An embarrassing but essential question.

A muttered exchange between two female voices. Phylloh sounds polite but firm. The other voice sounds imperious.

*Margot,* Gerry thinks, a split second before Phylloh comes back on the line and says, "Margot?"

Margot is not one of Gerry's ex-wives, although it wasn't for lack of trying. That is, she had tried very hard to persuade Gerry to marry her, but he felt that three wives was all one was entitled to in a lifetime; a fourth wife made one ridiculous. For God's sake, he wasn't Mickey Rooney. And there was no doubt in Gerry's mind that Margot would have become his fourth ex-wife and that being married to her would have been especially ridiculous.

"Let her up, the front door is unlocked," he says wearily. He is that bored.

Margot looks at once better and worse than remembered. Her body is almost terrifyingly lean, her face uncannily—uncanny valley-ily—smooth. She always insisted that she had not had "work" done, a turn of phrase that amuses Gerry, as it implies that tightening and plumping the body is a job in a way that other surgery is not. No one speaks of heart *work.* She cultivates a style that he recognizes as high fashion, although he's never really liked it. Her fine-featured face has a symmetrical perfection that can survive the strangest embellishments. Overlarge, overthick eyeglasses, a severe Louise Brooks bob, an all-black outfit with a "statement" necklace, only what is the statement? *"Hello, I am confident enough to wear this very large, ugly necklace."*

Even when he was besotted with her, she reminded him a little of a praying mantis, and everyone knows what they do to their mates.

"Gerry!" she says. She's standing at the foot of his bed, yet declaiming as if she's trying to reach the back row of a vast theater. "I have to admit, I wasn't sure I believed your assistant when she said you'd had an accident."

"Victoria shouldn't be telling anyone such personal information." *And she should be telling me when people call,* Gerry thinks.

"Not anyone, I agree, but I'm not just anyone. We lived together. We were engaged to be married for a time."

They had not been, not officially, they were not, never, but it didn't matter now that he was free of her. He could be gracious enough to allow her to tell whatever story made her feel better about herself.

"What brings you to Baltimore?"

"You, of course. Happy Valentine's Day, lover. I had to come after I heard. Do you know the statistics on broken hips?"

"It's not really my hip—"

"The thing is," she said, flinging her coat over the sofa, a habit of hers that had always irked him, "there's a problem at the apartment."

"I sold the apartment. The transaction closed almost four months ago and you were given plenty of notice. How can there be a problem now?"

"I left some of my things in your storage unit and they're gone!" She says this with great drama and flair, the way the CNN announcers every day share some new snippet of information about the unending drama in Washington.

"The storage unit conveyed with the apartment. Surely you understood that."

"Of course, but I thought I would be given the courtesy of a call."

He tries to remember the hectic weeks of last fall. Had he been told there were still things in the storage unit? Had he cared? He feels guilty, then anger at the guilt. He definitely told Margot to get her things out of the apartment; even she had to understand that applied to the storage unit as well.

"I don't know what to say," he says, and he cannot be more sincere, more literal.

"There were some very valuable things there," she says. "Jewelry. Clothes from my modeling days, things that are impossible to replace. Priceless things."

And yet he suspects there will be a dollar amount placed on these items, eventually, and he will be asked to pay it. Margot is a shakedown queen, a good one. She is the kind of woman—the kind of *person*—who has a genius for getting others to take care of her. She has no visible means of support, yet she is always in expensive places—New York City, Nantucket, Paris, St. Barts—and, although she never eats, she does her not-eating in the very best restaurants, wearing beautiful clothes. When they met, she was living in the Carlyle and Gerry had assumed she must have her own money. What she had was a married boyfriend who was resigned to paying her hotel bill until she found her next mark. Cheaper to keep her, as the song said, but it is not cheap to keep Margot, and it can be even more expensive to rid oneself of her. She has to be foisted off on another. Gerry's mother had given him an out, and then the co-op board, fearsome in its own right, had accused her of being an illegal subletter and made Margot vacate the premises. Gerry saw daylight and bolted.

"I don't know anything about this, Margot. Sorry. A waste of a trip for you, I'm afraid."

"Oh, it's such an easy trip," she says. "I took the Acela, not even three hours, although the cab ride here—well, the cab was *very* dingy. Besides, I thought you could use some hel—"

"*No,*" he says. Then, in a gentler tone: "I have Victoria during the day, a nurse at night. There's no need—and no space."

"But the place is huge," she says, twirling around, then heading for the floating staircase that was his undoing.

"No," he says again, his voice stern enough to arrest her stride. "There are only two rooms, my office, and a study, and the night nurse uses that. As for my bedroom—" His mind casts about for something, anything, that will keep Margot out of the master bedroom suite. "It's being treated for bedbugs."

It is the perfect thing to say. Margot not only retreats from the stairs, she grabs her coat from the sofa and puts it on, as if it will protect her.

"That's why I'm up here," he says, pleased by his own inventiveness. It's the closest thing to writing fiction he has done in months. "Eventually they'll have to fumigate. But for now, they've managed to contain the damage to my room. They took out the old stuff, of course, but they're in there, just waiting. The nurse went in the other evening to get my favorite pair of reading glasses from the nightstand and when she came out, her ankles and wrists were circled with bites."

Margot buttons her coat to the top. Has she had work done on her neck? It's impossibly smooth.

"Maybe I should stay nearby," she begins.

"There is no nearby," he says, hoping she can't see the Four Seasons on the other side of the harbor.

"That thing people do now, the Air thingy."

"They don't have that in Baltimore," he says. "At least not around here."

"I have to have somewhere to spend the night."

"There's an Acela every hour until nine," he says. "Buses go later still."

"You won't believe the meal I had," she says. "Or the wine. Worse than an airplane. But the meal—it was the stingiest little cheese plate, I couldn't believe it."

"Well, it's really just a snack bar," he says.

"No, I mean the meal they serve at your seat."

So she had booked a first-class ticket, which meant she paid $150 extra for a mediocre meal and an assigned seat. How very Margot. He wonders who paid for her ticket. For all he knows, she has written his credit card information down somewhere and still uses it for purchases. He will have to check the statement.

Victoria returns, her arms laden with groceries and mail. She is clearly puzzled by Margot's presence and her quizzical look reminds Gerry that Margot seems out of place in any remotely normal setting. At black-tie parties, art galleries, in first-class airline lounges, Margot fits in. But not in Baltimore, not in Gerry's apartment.

"This is—" He pauses, not wanting to describe Margot as a friend, which she isn't, and it seems rude to describe someone as a former anything.

"Margot Chasseur," she says, reaching for Victoria's hand with her long, bony arm. But Victoria's hands are not available. She hugs the grocery bag more tightly to her chest. Victoria is quite slender, but Margot, despite her fashion-model height, has a way of making everyone else seem large and awkward. Gerry used to like that. He had felt very heroic next to her, a man capable of caring for a sought-after woman, and not just financially. Only the best men could afford a Margot.

"'Lo," Victoria says, a sullen teen meeting her father's new girl-friend.

"Victoria, can you run Margot up to Penn Station when you leave tonight? She's taking the train back to New York."

"I don't have to go tonight—" Margot tries to interject.

"She was kind enough to come and check on me," Gerry says, knowing that the only thing to do with Margot is to keep talking, insistent on one's version of things. It's what she does, after all. "But, obviously, she can't stay here—the bedbug problem in the bedroom—and there's no place in Baltimore that's really appropriate."

Victoria nods. She's a quick one.

"I just need a corner," Margot says. "I barely take up any room. The sofa looks marvelously comfortable—"

"If you leave now, she can make the four thirty," Gerry continues. "Put the ticket on my American Express, then head home, as your day will be nearly done."

"I don't want to be a bother—"

"Not a bother at all."

"Perhaps we could have dinner first, and I could take a later—"

"Dinner's sorted and I'm afraid I have Victoria buy things in very small portions, as I hate to be wasteful."

Margot gives up. For now. She will be back if she doesn't find a man soon. Gerry's going to ask Thiru to take her to lunch. He will tell Thiru that it's a favor to him, that Margot has spoken often of writing a memoir. (She has, but all she has are the usual party-girl memories of the 1990s, already done, and done better than she ever could. Also, Gerry would inevitably figure large in anything Margot might write, and Gerry does not need *that*.)

His hope is that she will become fixated on Thiru, with his lovely suits and even lovelier manners. He appears to be quite rich and maybe he is. Gerry has a hard time figuring out how much money others have because he has always lived quite modestly, relative to the money he earned after *Dream Girl*. Gerry's very bad at being wealthy, a tightwad, still scarred by the money problems of his youth. If Thiru has six Gerrys, he basically has Gerry's income, no? And of the clients Thiru represents, there are at least three potential Gerrys, although Gerry believes he is the number-one earner, the biggest jewel in the agency's crown.

"Thank you, Victoria," he says. And although it takes great effort, pain even, he rises to a true ninety-degree sitting position. Victoria's eyes widen with shock; she knows how painful it is for him to sit. But she says nothing.

"I'll be in touch," Margot says. Alas, he believes she is telling the truth.

So when the phone rings in the middle of the night, that very night, and Aileen, who tends to doze, does not answer it within three rings, Gerry fumbles for the landline next to the bed, a mid-century Swedish design with a button on the bottom. His head feels cloudy, yet he is alert enough to assume the call will be from Margot, full of recriminations for being booked in business class, which means she has to fetch her own cheese plate from the snack bar.

"Hello?"

"Gerry? I'm coming to see you soon."

"Who is this?" Because the one thing he's sure of is that it's not Margot. The voice is too sweet, too high, with a hint of a Southern accent. Also too *nice*.

"Oh, Gerry, you're so funny. It's Aubrey, Gerry. We need to talk. About my story, about what really happened between us, that mess with your wife. I think it's time the world knows I'm a real person."

"The mess—who is this?"

"It's Aubrey, Gerry. Don't be silly."

"There is no Aubrey."

"Well, not by that name. But I exist, Gerry. I always knew that I was Aubrey. And I was proud, so proud that I could inspire you."

"WHO IS THIS?"

She hangs up.

Impossible to star-69 the call from this phone, assuming that one can still star-69 on any phone. He shouts for Aileen, who trundles sleepily up the stairs, taking her time.

"I just closed my eyes for a bit," she says defensively, as if he has summoned her to his bedside to chide her.

"Please grab the phone from the kitchen, check the caller ID, and tell me what it says."

She does. "No one's called since this afternoon," she announces.

"But the phone just rang. You heard it."

"No, it didn't. And it shows you right here"—she walks toward him with the receiver—"the last call was from the front desk at three oh eight. No one's called all evening. That's why I didn't wake up. There was nothing to wake me up until you yelled for me."

He fumbles for his reading glasses. Yes, the phone's screen is adamant: the last call was from downstairs, the one announcing Margot's arrival.

Was it a dream? A delusion? The drugs? Some combination of the three?

The drugs, he decides. It has to be the drugs.

Please let it be the drugs?

## 2012

GERRY WATCHED the early returns with his mother, feel-ing silly for all the effort he had put into the day. He had been worrying about this election for weeks, running all the scenarios at fivethirtyeight.com. He voted early in New York, then drove to York, Pennsylvania, on election eve to help with get-out-the-vote efforts, then headed to Maryland, where he drove his mother to the polls, despite her reasonable protests that it wasn't that vital for her to vote. Maryland was bluer than blue.

"How did blue become associated with Democrats, red with Republicans?" he asked his mother, just to be saying something.

"Well, Nancy Reagan favored red."

"But that was a response, not a cause, surely? At any rate, it has a way of reducing the whole thing to a summer camp color war."

He couldn't believe how many terrible men he had voted against—

and for—in his lifetime. His first presidential election was 1976. He chose Carter, yippee. He had supported Udall in the primary, but he no longer remembered why. In 1980, he voted for John Anderson. Mondale in 1984, Dukakis in 1988, Clinton '92 and '96, Gore, then John Kerry. What a remarkably bland slate from the Democrats, Clinton excepted. Gerry never understood the "Clinton as the first Black president" thing; surely that was offensive to everyone? Was it about his class roots? The wastrel father?

*Wastrel father.* He glanced at his mother. Her eyes were bright and focused on the television, but her dinner was untouched. She was not eating enough, nor was she moving enough. She was at once frail and plump. Fair enough, for a woman approaching eighty, but the house seemed increasingly ill-advised for her. Those steps, that bathroom. He wanted to remodel at least the upstairs bath, but she refused his aid. The only thing she would take from him was his company, the thing he was least capable of providing, living in New York. Was he selfish? She had sacrificed so much for him, worked so hard. He would do anything for her—except move back to Baltimore. He tried to make it home at least once a month, but it was more like every six to eight weeks, and then he was plunged into a miasma of errands. Doctors' visits, home repairs. He still did many of those himself, as he had in his teenage years. He was handy, something that surprised people. He'd had to be, once his father decamped.

*Decamped.* That was a nice word for what his father had done.

Gerry did call his mother every Sunday night. After five P.M., at her insistence. "That's when the rates go down," she said, inured to this habit by his father's days on the road, the collect calls coming from God knows where. Useless to try to explain to her that he could call on his cell for free.

"Mom—please eat."

"It doesn't taste right," she said. "I think the shrimp is off."

"We bought the shrimp salad today." A treat. His mother would never buy Graul's shrimp salad for herself. In fact, she wouldn't shop at Graul's at all, although it was literally walking distance from the house, could be seen from her front porch. She drove to the Giant on York Road and shopped with coupons. Graul's was for emergencies and cakes.

"Nothing tastes right anymore. I told your father as much the other day, and he agreed."

"Dad's dead, Mom," he said, not unkindly.

"Oh, I know we thought that. But can you believe it? He faked his death and skipped out on his second family."

"Uh-huh."

"Turns out he was in New York on Nine Eleven. Can you believe it? Or maybe he just said he was. Who would know, right? A colleague of his called his wife, said your father had an appointment at the brokerage there. The one named for a horse's gate."

This took a while to break down. Horse's gate, horse's gate—oh, horse's *gait*. "Cantor Fitzgerald?"

"Yes."

"I think that was a big hedge firm, Mom. Why would Dad have an appointment there?"

"Everybody needs office furniture," she said placidly. "Besides, he *wasn't* there. That's the point. He saw an opportunity and he took it. He never loved her."

"I'm not sure Dad ever loved anybody. That was his curse."

"He loves me."

The tense alarmed him. It was one thing to imagine his father alive, to entertain some cockamamie story about him faking his death (which, Gerry had to admit, would be absolutely in character).

But for his mother to insist on his father's love, something that Gerry was sure neither one of them ever really had—no, that was too much.

His first novel, *Courting Disaster,* had centered on their ill-fated romance, although his mother had died in that version, the victim of an illegal abortion. *Why does Gerry Andersen's art depend upon women's death?* was becoming a running theme in revisionist pieces on his work. But the novel had won a lucrative if unsung prize and it still sold robustly, so there.

"When did you see Dad?" he asked his mother.

"Oh, time is so vague to me. It was warm, but it might have been Indian summer, that spell of hot days we had in October? Yes, it was early October. We made love outside."

"Mom!"

"It was dark," she said. "And you know no one can see our back-yard. All those trees. I felt as if I were fifteen again, Gerry."

CNN had just called the election for Obama. Gerry remembered 2008, the one pure shining night of hope in his entire adult life as a voter. Schooled as he was in imagining the inner lives of others, he could not understand how people his age, people in his income bracket, people with his education, had considered the same thing a disaster. Could race alone explain these visceral reactions to Obama?

And was he thinking about Obama because he couldn't bear to ponder the ramifications of his mother believing that his father still visited her, made love to her, when he had been dead for at least ten years? He had died on September 11, 2001. Not in the towers, of course.

"Mom," he said, "what year is it?"

"2012."

"And who's the president?"

"Barack Obama." She practically beamed, saying his name. She loved Obama. Even when Hillary Clinton had been running in 2008, she had supported Obama. His mother despised Hillary Clinton, something he always assumed had to do with the Clinton marriage.

"Mom—will you draw a clock for me?"

She gave him a withering look, but she did it, and her clock was fine, more than fine. His mother drew beautifully.

"I'm not losing my mind, Gerald."

"It's just that—"

"Do we have dessert?"

"You haven't touched your dinner."

"Gerry, I'm seventy-six years old. If I want to eat some ice cream, I'm going to eat some darn ice cream."

He laughed. She had a point. And her joke dispelled most of his worries. His mother wasn't losing her mind. She was just making up a story that made her feel better, that restored the self-respect taken from her long ago.

His first novel, meant to be a tribute to her, an explanation of how a beautiful, intelligent woman could end up with such an inferior, unworthy man, had hurt her terribly. "It wasn't like that, Gerry," she had said. It was the worst fight of their relationship, the only quarrel they had after his teen years. He tried to remind her it was fiction, and it was, but he always thought the problem was that he had gotten too much right. He wanted to say, *I can do math, Mother.* He had been born six months after his parents' marriage. He had killed her, in the book, killed himself, to spare her the pain that followed. It was the inverse of the Sharon Olds poem. He was willing not to exist if that was what it took to spare his mother.

*Would your mother have been better off dead?* An interviewer had tried to shock him with that question at a literary festival in 2010.

"It's fiction," Gerry had said. "It's not autobiography. I can't help

it if people conflate the two, but it's not a line of inquiry that interests me."

He went to the kitchen and fixed his mother her favorite, Baskin-
Robbins Jamoca Almond Fudge. The 31 Flavors they frequented
had been in the little strip center that housed Morgan Millard, but
now you could buy it at the grocery store anytime you wanted it.
Why did that make him sad?

Maybe he was just at an age where everything made him sad,
even the reelection of the best president of his adult life. Of his
*entire* life: he had little affection for Kennedy. He didn't agree with
Obama on everything, of course. And Carter, go figure, was clearly
the best *person* to hold the office. Too good. When a saint becomes
president, it's discomfiting. One expects a president to make a few
more deals with the devil, spend less time on the White House ten-
nis court schedule.

He opened the fridge, thinking to add Reddi-wip to the ice
cream, and was surprised to see one of his mother's bras lying on a
shelf, carefully folded. It appeared to be a newer bra, brighter and
bolder than the lingerie he remembered trying to avoid in the laundry room when he was a boy.

His mother was watching the returns dreamily when he brought
her the dish of ice cream.

"Mom, you left your"—the word *bra* was impossible for him—
"your, um, undergarments in the fridge."

"They're calling Illinois," she said. "Your father lives there."

"Ohio, Mom," he said. "He lived in Ohio."

"Yes, years ago. He lives in Illinois now. Lake Forest. He's a
sexton."

He was impressed, in spite of himself, with his mother's talent
for detail in her fantasies. A sexton—one could imagine a novel with

such a character. Not a Gerry Andersen novel, but maybe one by Anne Tyler. But then, that's how his mother had survived her life, by telling stories. She conjured up fictions to comfort herself. Meanwhile, his father was a pathological liar. What choice did Gerry have but to become a novelist?

He risked the word. "The bra, Mom?"

"Oh. I read somewhere they last longer that way. If you keep them in a cold place."

*February 15*

GERRY ANGLES HIMSELF so he is more on his side than his back and taps on his laptop, using only his left hand. It's awkward, but it's less painful than trying to sit on his bruised coccyx. There is almost no position in which he doesn't feel pain or discomfort. It's an alien sensation to him, this chronic throbbing. He had never considered his pride in his health hubristic. He took care of himself. He walked, he didn't overeat, he seldom drank. Everything else was a genetic lottery—or so he had been modest enough to say when complimented on his youthful appearance, his full head of hair. Like most lottery winners, he secretly credited himself with his luck.

*Genetic lottery.* He taps only four letters into the Google maw—*deme*—and is instantly rewarded with a slew of dementia subjects, including "Dementia versus Alzheimer's," which sounds like the worst action movie franchise ever. He changes the search to *demen-*

*tia delusions* and ends up on the website of the Canadian Alzheimer's Society, where he quickly learns a distinction he should have already known, fussy as he is about words. Whatever happened last night was not a delusion, but a hallucination. Oh boy, sweet victory.

Feeling very much like the Scotland Yard inspector in Josephine Tey's *The Daughter of Time,* he rolls onto his back and reviews last night's events as logically as possible. He heard the phone ring. (Or did he?) He answered it. Assuming it had, in fact, rung. A woman spoke to him and insisted she was Aubrey. What sort of person would do such a thing?

What does he *know*?

One: It is someone who has his number, which is unlisted, although Gerry knows the Internet is lousy with services that can fetch such information, for a fee. So, basically, anyone with a little money to throw at their mischief.

Two: The voice was female, he is sure of that. So now the pool of suspects has been halved.

Three: It's someone who is familiar with his book. Hmmm. It has sold three million copies in English alone and who knows how many used or library copies have been perused. But, okay, let's say it's a woman, a woman who knows the book but, more importantly, knows *him.* The very use of *Gerry* indicates intimacy—those who have not met him always lead with *Gerald,* a name he despises because he shares it with his father. If he had it to do over again, he would publish under *Gerry,* but when he was young, his nickname felt callow. Gerry always wanted to be old, serious, imbued with gravitas.

Mission accomplished. Alas.

The woman did not sound like Margot and, frankly, this kind of mind-fuckery is not Margot's style. And although the voice is tantalizingly familiar, he can't imagine any of his ex-wives pulling such a stunt, either. He has had no contact with any of them, not really, for years, although Lucy and Sarah wrote notes after his mother died. His mother had liked both of them quite a bit; she had no use for Gretchen whatsoever. On the eve of his wedding to Sarah, a suitably low-key affair for a third-timer but a wedding nonetheless, his mother had two glasses of wine at the so-called rehearsal dinner and blurted out: "I like all of Gerry's odd-numbered wives." Everyone had laughed uproariously at his mother's wit, but Gerry recognized the confession as a moment of alcohol-fueled candor.

Then there was his colleague at Hopkins, Shannon Little, who at one point tried to claim she had inspired Aubrey—he wonders if she is newly emboldened by #MeToo to assert this nonsense again. It's true that it was very, very bad form for Gerry to have sex with a colleague, but Lucy had practically thrown him into Shannon's arms. Being accused of faithlessness when one is faithful quickly becomes tiresome; it's only natural to feel that one might as well commit the crime of which one is constantly being accused. And Lucy's paranoia about Gerry and other women was particularly wounding to him, which she knew. He had set out to be as different from his father as possible. When the day came that he succumbed to another woman—a woman who was actively pursuing him—he practically wept as he bent her over his desk and sodomized her.

Shannon Little. He tries Googling her, but the name is too common. More than one hundred profiles on LinkedIn alone and so many personae—a doctor, a salon owner, a vet.

A common name and an apt one, too—not because she was small in physical stature, but because the thing between them had been inconsequential, or should have been. She seemed determined to seduce him, if only to have something to write about. He gave in and had sex with her because he was tired of being berated by Lucy for the affairs he *wasn't* having. Funny, how Lucy's jealousy metastasized, mutated. She was so determined not to be envious of Gerry's professional success—publishing his first novel to respectful reviews, winning an obscure but cash-laden prize— that she became crazed with jealousy of other women. Talk about delusions, or would they be hallucinations? At any rate, Lucy saw evidence of Gerry's philandering everywhere. Except in the place where it was happening.

Shannon Little would be in her late fifties now. They had screwed—really, that was the best word for it; the sex was mechanical and emotionless—only once. Shannon, ironically, was the one woman Lucy never suspected, probably because she didn't hold her in high esteem. Lucy's paranoia centered on better writers. She was terrified that Gerry would outpace her professionally, but she was too proud to allow that conscious thought into her mind. So she created these phantom affairs, disrupted his writing time to hurl accusations at him. And that, more than anything, was the reason they broke up. That and the prize money that made it possible.

To be fair, the success of his first book changed him. Success always changes people, just not in the way others think. When someone enjoys success—although it's Gerry's belief that no one truly *enjoys* it—the fear among friends and family and lovers is that they will be left behind, that success is a luxury ocean liner and they are put off with a brisk "All ashore who's going ashore." Gerry, having achieved a modest success at a relatively young age, simply wanted to make sure that he kept moving forward. His second and third books were slight misfires, unfavorably compared to his first, but that bothered him not at all. The important thing was, they were *different,* they showed he wasn't going to be mining his own slender life for material. Gerry planned to be a literary distance runner. The first thing he had to distance himself from was that first book, so popular and pleasant.

He never admitted to the stupid dalliance with Shannon Little, but he recognized it as the proof that he had checked out of his marriage. Whatever Gerry was, he was not a cheater. That was Gerald Andersen Sr.'s territory. He just became a bad enough husband that Lucy didn't fight him when he asked for a divorce, and then he moved to New York, where he was generally treated like shit by the cooler, hipper writers of the moment. Best thing he could have possibly done. Best thing they could have possibly done. Fifteen years later, when *Dream Girl* ticked all the boxes and achieved that rare literary grand slam of prestige, sales, film rights, and zeitgeist, Shannon Little came out of nowhere to publish—self-publish, in truth, although she managed to disguise that fact for a while—her "rebuttal." But it was so crass, so poorly written, that nothing came of it. Not even Lucy seemed to notice. If she did, she didn't bother to contact Gerry.

Plus, Shannon's publication date was September 11, 2001, which didn't help.

Victoria comes in with his lunch, the mail, and his letter opener, the Acme School Furniture Bakelite dagger that Lucy gave him. *I'm an orphan,* Gerry thinks for the first time. He has lived without his father for so long that his status did not occur to him when his mother died. *He is an orphan.* He has no siblings, no heirs. No enemies, not really. Shouldn't he have a longer list of potential enemies; can you have lived a life of consequence if you don't have people who really, really hate you?

If the call happened—*OF COURSE THE CALL HAPPENED*—it was some sad person's idea of a joke, a variation on asking if one's refrigerator was running or if a store had Prince Albert in a can.

Gerry spends as little time as possible on social media, but even he has heard there was an Italian man who specialized in death hoaxes and fake accounts targeting literary figures; he went so far as to manufacture an interview with Gerry at one point. It's plausible to believe that there's someone who lives to make prank phone calls to well-known authors, pretending to be their main characters.

Still, as he slices through his mail, he wishes that his Fait Avenue correspondent would write again, if only to confirm that the letter had existed. No letter, no entry on the caller ID log—there must be a logical explanation, one that doesn't go to his own state of mind.

Or lack thereof.

*1986*

"MY FATHER DRANK VANILLA when he was desperate. It was awful."

Gerry had heard this story before. So had Luke. Tara had shared tales about her father's alcoholism their freshman year at Princeton, in that fit of hyperconfiding that happens in college dorms, when one finally realizes that everyone has secrets. Even then, Gerry had been careful with his. But they were the three amigos, the ones who joked that their eating club should be called Descendants of Shitty Fathers.

But why was Tara telling this story again, here at this new club, Dante's? They were only twenty-eight, after all. Weren't they too young to be repeating themselves?

Weren't they too old to be in this bar? Gerry hadn't left his marriage and moved to New York to sit in clubs and shout over the music. He was a serious writer and nothing felt more serious than living off his savings in an illegal sublet on the Upper West Side. Thiru had gotten him a modest advance for his second novel, but the jackpot of the Hartwell Prize, even halved by his divorce from Lucy, made it possible for him to live without teaching for the first time. Tara and Luke were living similar lives, although their parents subsidized their ambitions.

It was nice, spending time with Tara and Luke again, but Gerry wasn't sure they brought out the best in one another. Tara was drinking too much and dating an abusive jerk. Luke, always on the prowl, seemed determined to make the worst choices. And Gerry—well, Gerry had no criticism for himself other than his loyalty, which led him to meet his college friends in these loud, frenetic places and then sourly contemplate their lives.

"Do you worry," he asked Tara now, "that you might share your father's legacy?"

"What an offensive question," she said. "How would you feel if I asked you the same thing?"

"There's a genetic factor to alcoholism," he said. "Surely you know that."

"There is *not*," Tara said. "You're full of shit."

Luke laughed.

"I'm sorry, Tara, but that's just a fact. I'm not trying to be provocative or cruel."

"Oh no, Gerry is never provocative. Or cruel." She threw her arms out, her drink sloshing. Tara had taken to drinking vodka martinis. It was a calculated choice. Everything Tara did was calculated, a conscious decision to create an image. She was wearing a teeny-tiny hat with a veil tonight and a 1950s vintage dress. She would look so much better in those ski pants and oversize shirts other women were wearing now.

"Tara, I don't want to fight with you."

"Gerry never wants to fight," Luke said, his eyes searching the club for tonight's entertainment.

Gerry got up to go to the bathroom. In this particular club, the bathrooms were designated as "devils" and "she-devils." There was a long line of she-devils waiting. He noticed one woman in particular when he went in. She was still waiting when he came out. She looked out of place, a preppy girl, in pearls and a sweater. He was charmed by her, although her calves were quite thick.

"If you want to use the men's room," he said, "I'll spot you."

The gym nomenclature meant nothing to her and she stared at him as if he had said something rude.

"I'll guard the door, I mean. There's a stall. And it's, um, relatively hygienic."

"That's okay," she said. "I'll wait my turn."

"I'm Gerry," he said.

"I'm Gretchen."

"Okay if I wait with you?"

"It's a free country."

Charmed by the cliché, which she did not appear to know was a cliché, he waited with her. And he waited when she went in and used the bathroom. Then he proposed they go to a diner. She ordered french fries, nothing more, and ate them daintily, dipping them in mayonnaise instead of ketchup. She was the most earnest person he had ever met. He walked her home, to her apartment in Gramercy Park, the first sign that this apple-cheeked girl had a real life, a real job, at a brokerage. He kissed her on one of her apple cheeks, but that was all. "May I have your number?" he asked. She wrote it on his wrist, with an ink pen.

He called her the moment he got home.

*February 20*

THE PHYSICAL THERAPIST, a man named Claude, comes
twice a week. By all appearances, he is constantly, chronically high,
but it's a low-grade buzz that doesn't interfere with his job or, Gerry
has to hope, his driving. He is a quiet man, which normally would
be a relief, but Gerry is desperate for masculine company, cooped
up with only Victoria and Aileen. Funny, he never thought of himself as much of a man's man. He rather dislikes men. Of course
this goes back to his father; Gerry has never bothered to pay an
analyst to delve into that matter. Writing is better than therapy—
same results, but *he* gets paid for it. His wastrel father, then the
Gilman jocks, who were nice to him yet still kind of awful, direct-
ing so much energy into destruction. He noticed, even then, that
they were especially dangerous when they had too much time to
spare, given to cow-tipping and other stupid pranks. And, although

he never thought about it before, probably date rape and trains and other horrible things.

"What's going on with you, Claude?"

"Not much."

As an adult, Gerry has had basically two male friends: Thiru and his college roommate Luke, who didn't survive his thirties. The other men he knows are acquaintances, peers, rivals. Gerry likes to think himself above the fray, a true novitiate, dedicated only to the higher cause of literature, but who is he kidding? He keeps score like all the writers of his generation. Like every writer of every generation. Who got there first, who has had the most staying power, who's going up, who's going down, who has a Pulitzer, who has a National Book Award, who's on the long list for the Nobel. Over the past few years, many of these men have taken to grumbling privately about political correctness, or what they prefer to call the "overcorrection" of the literary world. "If I weren't a white man," Gerry has heard more than one white man say. In their view, every prize given to a non–white man is an act of tokenism. Gerry's not one of those judgy begrudgers.

Or is he? In the firm, racially indistinct grasp of Claude, he feels he should apologize. First and foremost for wondering about Claude's ethnic origins, which he knows is wrong, but he can't help pondering if there's a story there. Isn't that a good thing, having this kind of curiosity about someone who's obviously not like you? Claude is built like the Indian in *One Flew Over the Cuckoo's Nest*. You wouldn't call him an Indian now, of course, but that was what he called himself; okay, it was what Ken Kesey had him call himself. Did that text now need to be changed? Did Nurse Ratched deserve a sympathetic portrayal similar to the one Jean Rhys provided for Rochester's first wife? Actually, that's not a bad idea; Gerry has no reverence for Kesey, nor for the Beats. Someone should retell the events of *Cuckoo's Nest* from the POV of the nurse, surrounded by insane, subversive men, probably fearful every moment of the day. When he saw the film adaptation of *One Flew Over the Cuckoo's Nest* as a teenager, there was a rumor that many of the institution's patients were played by men who were, in fact, patients in a mental hospital, and it became a guessing game of sorts. Then it turned out that, no, they were all actors.

"What's new with you, Claude?" he asks. Even if he weren't in this fragile state, Claude would make him feel very old, very weak, and very pale.

"They say a storm's coming."

"Ah, Baltimore in the grip of a winter storm. It's a kind of lunacy. Did you grow up here, Claude?"

"No."

"Where, then?"

"Eastern Shore. Down near Salisbury. Try again."

Gerry does not want to say *It hurts,* but—it hurts. It hurts and feels ridiculous, doing exercises with these small dumbbells, which happen to be pink. It's important, however, that his upper body not lose muscle tone while he's lying here, that his good leg be worked. He has avoided bedsores so far, but he lives in dread of them, having Googled the images.

"Do you live far from here? Are you worried about getting home if the storm actually comes?"

Claude doesn't answer and Gerry feels ridiculous. Nothing worries Claude.

"Are you married, Claude?"

"Not anymore."

"Dating, living with someone?"

"I'm okay."

Gerry is about to introduce the topic of Phylloh, then stops himself just in time. What could be more racist than suggesting that his racially mysterious physical therapist ask out the racially mysterious front-desk receptionist? It's exhausting, meaning well in a world that assumes you're a pig because of the body you're born into, but then—it's so much worse for people born into other bodies, he has to concede that. If only the culture weren't moving so fast. Jokes that were fine five years ago are offensive now. Words are being outlawed and weaponized. Is it so wrong to think that overweight people could take better care of themselves? What's objectionable about words like *blind* and *deaf*? *Disabled,* sure, he gets why that's offensive, but some terms are simply factual descriptions.

Claude never asks him questions beyond "Can you do this?" or "Did you exercise on your own this week?" But it makes sense to be impersonal when one's job is so very personal. If he had to choose, Gerry would vote for Claude's stoic silence over Aileen's inane chatter, which seems designed to push his buttons. She chats, chats, chats about famous people as if they were known to her, repeatedly asks him about television shows he does not follow. And, oh God, her interest in the weather is exhausting. Or, more correctly, she never exhausts the topic of the weather and that exhausts him. He should get ready for an especially tedious day today.

Sure enough, Aileen arrives at seven, complaining of the roads, her commute, the slippery sidewalks of Locust Point. (She has to park on the street, as does Victoria, but only Aileen complains repeatedly about the lack of a space in the building's garage for her.) She serves him his dinner, a can of low-sodium chicken soup, a salad, tea. Aileen's salads are a thing of wonder, by which Gerry means they are so awful he can only wonder at the effort it requires. He has encouraged Victoria to buy those salad "kits," yet somehow iceberg lettuce keeps showing up on his plate at night, soggy and sad, loaded down with bottled dressings. Even Gerry can make a simple vinaigrette. He has tried to dissuade Aileen from serving him these salads, but she makes a big deal of "sharing" her food with him, as if she is conveying a favor. Her nightly meal is usually this salad alongside a Dinty Moore stew or a microwaved entree. Food may not be important to Gerry, but he does prefer it to be edible.

He finishes his dinner, texts for Aileen to take his tray away. Strangely, she would prefer for him to shout for her, but he doesn't like screaming. He grew up in a household where there was almost never any screaming, not even during the most vicious fights. His parents were hissers. Maybe it would have been healthier to scream every now and then, but he never got the knack of it, although if he had stayed with Margot much longer he might have been forced to master the art. His three wives were essentially passive women, as conflict-averse as he is. Margot, however, loves drama. She likes big fights followed by sex that feels like an extension of the fight, which can be at once exhilarating and a little frightening. On more than one occasion, she had dropped to her knees almost midsentence and begun clawing at his fly, yanking at him, as if to prove how much power she had over him. And she did have that particular power; when Margot got going, she was hard to beat on that score. She was, after all, a professional courtesan, a woman who had put in her ten thousand hours. It was the only reason, he supposed, so many men had put up with her, although none had ever married her. Margot told him she had never wanted to marry before she met him and maybe that was true, or maybe it was what she said to each man, hoping to make him feel special. Thank God he had gotten away from her.

He drifts off. Sleepiness is a side effect of oxycodone, but it could be boredom as well. He should be writing. Then again, what better reason not to write than recovery from a major accident? No one, not even Thiru, can blame him for not being productive right now. As a young man, he disliked sleep, tried to get by on five hours. There was so much to do, so much to write, to read. Maybe it's all the television he's watching now. As jumpy and jittery as the news is, it also seems designed to be soporific, the way it repeats itself over and over. The text running along the bottom of the screen, the anchors' voices. *The president today. The president today.* It's like a nursery rhyme. Which, come to think of it, was the source for the title of *One Flew Over the Cuckoo's Nest.* Do people still read Kesey? Probably, because the book is sentimental. Will people read *Dream Girl* fifty years after its publication date? A good movie version could ensure its legacy, but, oh, how Gerry dislikes the irony of *that.*

The snowstorm, which has been gentle and pretty, begins to pick up steam. The winds are howling around the building. He remembers his mother screaming in the night. The only time she ever screamed, as far as he knows. But she moaned, during snowstorms such as this, knowing it would be on her, and later Gerry, to shovel the driveway and sidewalks, to try to get to work. Their street had a downhill slope and she learned how to park so she could roll carefully down to Bellona Avenue, which had a shot of being plowed early, whereas their side street was never cleared. It was a good sledding hill, too, he remembers—

The phone is ringing. Where is Aileen, why won't she answer it? He picks up, assuming he will hear a warning from Baltimore Gas and Electric.

"Hi, Gerry. It's Aubrey. I wanted to check on you, make sure you're okay in this storm."

"Who is this?"

"Aubrey, Gerry. Are you okay in the storm? Do you need anything?"

"I have your number on caller ID and I am going to report you. This is harassment. This is—"

She laughs and, damn, if the laugh doesn't sound like Aubrey's as he described it in the book, a laugh that was never laughed in ridicule or unkindness.

"Anyway, I'll be coming to see you soon. So if you do need anything, let me know."

"How could I—" But she has hung up.

He bellows for Aileen. She lumbers up the stairs, full of apologies. "I don't know what happened, but my dinner hit me hard, I had to—"

"The caller ID," he says. "*Check the caller ID.*"

She has yet to reach the kitchen phone when the power goes out.

*1966*

"Don't be a scaredy-cat. Everyone else has done it."

*But everyone else has a sled.* And sleds, even in this deep, hard-packed snow, didn't go as quickly as Gerry's toboggan. He wasn't quite eight, one of the smallest kids out here, and his toboggan was taller than he was. Why did he have a toboggan anyway? Why were his parents so bad at even the smallest normal things?

It was the third day of a historic blizzard, the second day that school had been canceled. The children in Gerry's neighborhood had set up sentries so they could sled down Berwick, which meant crossing what would normally be an unthinkably busy Bellona Avenue. But the world was still, quiet except for their shouts. No one was driving anywhere and if they were, they crept along so slowly that

there was time to bail should a car approach. The adults, dull creatures, were inside, their enthusiasm for snow used up by the second
day. Yesterday, a Monday, the fathers and even some of the mothers
had joined the children. Not Gerry's mother, because she was not
that kind of a mother. And not Gerry's father, because he was out of
town for business. But he would have been out here if he hadn't been
stranded in Iowa. Gerry was sure of that. Pretty sure. His father was
the one who had given him the toboggan, after all.

Resigned, Gerry dragged his toboggan about midway up Berwick. Some sidewalks had been cleared, but not his own, not with
his father gone. A neighbor had offered, but his mother had refused.
"Gerald will do it when he returns." She had managed to shovel out
a small path to the back door, so Gerry could come and go without
tracking snow into the front rooms. Even in the early part of the
storm, when the falling flakes had been so pretty and no one had a
sense of how severe it would be, Gerry's mother had wanted no part
of it. She had shut herself up in her room, blinds drawn, as if her
refusal to acknowledge the snow would cow it. But the silent treat-
ment worked no better on the storm than it did on his father.

Gerry had to go to the bathroom, but no one would believe him.
Even if they did, he would have to come back or suffer the con-
sequences at school, assuming there was ever school again. Wallace
Wright, on the noon news today, had suggested there would be no
school at all this week. His mother had turned off the set and started
to cry. But they had everything they needed as far as Gerry could tell.
Food, toilet paper, coffee, the amber liquid his mother poured into
her coffee at night. He didn't give his mother any trouble. That was
the phrase instilled in him by his father, who traveled so much.
"Don't give your mother any trouble." When he was younger, a

nursery school baby, he had imagined a box with a bow. But what, exactly, would be inside a box of trouble? He didn't know and he didn't want to find out. Gerry didn't give his mother any trouble.

She missed his dad, he guessed. He had been supposed to fly home Sunday and now he kept calling and saying his flight was canceled. Every day so far.

The trick to riding a toboggan was getting it to stay still long enough to get on it. Gerry had learned to lay it perpendicular to the path, but one still had to move quickly. He liked the fact that one rode sitting up, wind in the face. It slowed one down. He tucked his booted feet beneath its curve. There was a steering mechanism of sorts, but how one used one's weight was more important. His father had taught him that last winter.

The toboggan almost got away from him, so eager was it to head down the hill. So Gerry jumped on, even as the sentry began to yell the word no one had yelled all day.

"Car. CAR."

Then: "No."

*Oh thank God,* Gerry thought, not that he would ever say such a thing out loud.

"TRUCK!"

It was a postal truck. A red, white, and blue mail truck, although the white part was almost invisible against the backdrop of snow. And while it was not going that fast, it was going fast enough. In fact, it seemed, from where Gerry was on his flight down Berwick, as if the truck, should it fail to stop, was moving at the exact right speed to crush him. Neither snow nor rain nor heat nor gloom of night— THANKS U.S. POSTAL SERVICE.

All the boys were screaming now and Gerry realized there must be some girls, too, for there were shrill, high-pitched squeals among the screams and shouts. Some of the boys seemed merely excited at the prospect of carnage, but all the girls were genuinely terrified. Girls were nicer than boys, except when they weren't, like when that big girl from the third grade, bigger than anyone in the second grade, asked Gerry what his father really did. The girls did not want Gerry to die, or maybe they just didn't want to see his blood and guts.

He was approaching Bellona now, the postal truck bearing down on him, and he understood that the truck could try to put on its brakes, but it would only become more unreliable and there were kids everywhere. The truck had no choice but to keep going. So he leaned hard, as hard as he could to the left, and the toboggan mirac-ulously took the tight turn without spilling him, perhaps because his boots were, in fact, stuck under its curved hood. It felt almost as if the toboggan rode along on one side, in a ninety-degree angle to the street, but surely that wasn't possible.

At any rate, the truck didn't hit him and everyone cheered and it was the best moment of his life. He had wet himself inside his snowsuit, but no one could see that. Not even his mother seemed to notice when he came home an hour later and peeled out of his clothes, reveling in that strange sensation of feeling, with that first exposure to heat, as if he were colder than ever. He tried to figure out a way to tell his mother the story without upsetting her—*Don't give your mother any trouble*—but he couldn't find the words.

*February 21*

GERRY STARES into the swirling snow outside his window. While his corner of Baltimore is dark, he can see that other sections still have power. Maybe that means his power will be restored sooner. But it also could mean there is less urgency about responding to an outage confined to Locust Point. For as long as Gerry can remember, Baltimore has had complicated conspiracy theories about city services—whose streets get plowed first, whose 911 calls receive priority. Despite the few glamorous high-rises that nestle here, the new town houses clustered around them like little chicks, Locust Point is not a place with clout. Would it matter if the Olympic swimmer actually occupied his expensive apartment?

Aileen sits nearby, in a low-slung easy chair, her plain face big and bright as a full moon thanks to the light from her tablet, where she appears to be playing some game that involves stabbing the screen with her index finger over and over again. The lower floor of the apartment made her uneasy in the dark, so she asked if she could stay up here with him after she groped her way downstairs to retrieve the tablet. Actually, she didn't even ask, come to think of it, just asserted that she would sit up here and keep him company. Gerry didn't want the "company" she offered, but now that she's here, he's miffed that she's making no effort to engage him. Normally he would be asleep by now, but it's almost too quiet to sleep. He feels more alert than he has in weeks. Did he miss his medication in the aftermath of the power going out? His pain doesn't seem to be affected, which is to say it's not good, but it's no worse than usual.

"It's getting cold," Aileen says, looking up at last. "Without electricity, the heat doesn't work. We'll have to leave if this goes on much longer."

"Leave how?" It would require a gurney to get him out of the apartment, a sobering thought. What would happen to him if there were a fire or some other catastrophic event? "Go where?"

"A hotel?" She sounds almost hopeful, as if a hotel is something she would like to experience. Must Gerry end up caring for all the women in his life, even the ones paid to care for him?

"Do the elevators work? It's hard to imagine me walking down twenty-four flights of stairs."

"I think the big things in the building are on some kind of backup system," she says.

But what if they're not? What if he is stuck here and something happens? What then?

The phone rings, but only the Swedish one by his bed. Unlike the fancy extensions in the kitchen and his office and his bedroom proper, this one can still operate without electricity.

"Would you get that?" he says to Aileen.

"You can reach it."

"It's not a question of reach. I want you to hear—I want to know—just answer it."

Watching Aileen get out of the chair is almost like watching a Buster Keaton film, except it's anything but silent. The comedy of her movements is accompanied by a startling symphony of grunts, groans, coughs. The phone continues to peal. It must be on the ninth or tenth ring when she finally picks it up.

"'lo?" she asks, breathing hard. A pause as she listens. "Hello? Hello?" She hangs up. "Nobody there."

He finds this encouraging. Assuming it wasn't a wrong number, his mystery caller wishes to speak to no one but him. The fake Aubrey is trying to make him crazy, which proves he isn't actually crazy. Or delusional.

Of course, this means someone has targeted *him* for harassment, which is—not good? And it's not random, it's not as if there is some common scam in which someone, such as a Nigerian prince, calls novelists and claims to be their characters. Could there be a woman out there who sincerely believes she is Aubrey?

Or is there a woman in his past who wants to stir him up? Who has he harmed, really?

No longer content to keep a running tally in his head, he reaches for one of the little Moleskine notebooks he keeps nearby and writes down his list of the usual suspects. A name tantalizes him, a memory or something even more ephemeral—a whisper, a scent, a bit of gossip, a suggestion of a person wronged—no, a person who *believes* herself wronged, an important distinction. Not someone who was really in his life, but maybe someone who wanted to be, who mistook something casual for something more profound—

The lights pop back on, creating that weird overreaction of relief and gratitude when something taken for granted has been lost and then restored. His thoughts scatter. At least he won't be springing for a suite of rooms at a local hotel.

"I guess I'll make myself some tea," Aileen says, clomping to the kitchen.

She doesn't even think to offer him any. Apparently Aileen is not aware that *nurse* and *nurture* derive from the same root. She makes herself a cup of tea and is about to go back downstairs when Gerry says: "My medicine?"

At least she has the decency to look abashed for neglecting the central part of her duty. She goes to the kitchen and gets him a glass of water, brings two oxycodone.

"Two?"

"You missed one, I'm guessing."

"I don't think medicine works that way."

"It's cumulative. If you don't take both now, you'll feel it by morning."

He wants to argue. But he also doesn't want to wake to acute pain. He feels like a child, staring up into his mother's face, but—no, that's unfair. His mother was beautiful. His mother loved him. Aileen performs a mother's duties, a spouse's duties, but for pay. Three ex-wives and no children. Is that natural? Has he unwittingly subverted a system in which he would have received affectionate care for free? Everything is contracted out now and the world is poorer for it.

"I'll take two pills," he says, "and call you in the morning."

A small joke, but all jokes are too small to receive any acknowledgment from stolid Aileen.

BY MORNING, it seems ridiculous that the power was ever out; the storm was truly a case of sound and fury, all wind, almost no snow, at least not on the ground. Gerry enjoys watching the local weathermen and -women try to make it seem more than it was, storytellers aware that they have overpromised and underdelivered. They move their hands over what he knows to be blank screens; Gerry has done his share of local television talk shows, especially in Baltimore. Favorite son and all that. He knows—*knew,* he hasn't done local television for years, hasn't had to—the drabness of the studios, the indignity of sitting in some corner on a Saturday morning, hoping the regular adopt-a-stray segment didn't run over, stealing the five minutes he had to try to explain his latest novel to a cheerful woman who wasn't even chagrined not to have read it ahead of time.

This was all before the expansion of the idea of *content,* but that's what he was in those situations, content. A static, wallpaper kind of content, determined to be inoffensive at all costs. Local television shows traded in the known. The stories changed, but the format never did. Crime story, traffic story, and now something to make you feel better about human nature. Weather. Sports scores. Local news was like a familiar hymn playing in the background, intended to soothe and pacify.

But national news now—wowza. It's become an insane, coked-up party girl (or boy) who simply will not leave your apartment, yakking and yakking and yakking, moving from one topic to another without transition. Last year, the *New York Times* received a lot of criticism for an article about a man who had chosen to live without news. *The ultimate in white privilege! Talk about a bubble!*

Gerry, whose news "diet" used to consist primarily of the *Times,* on paper, and the *New York Review of Books,* thinks people were simply envious of the man. They did not realize it was in their power to turn down the volume, literally and figuratively.

Which is not to say that Gerry has no interaction with social media at all. There is a Twitter account, verified, run by Victoria, which sends out one or two items a week, almost always links to favorite but obscure poems, short stories, sometimes articles about the neglected writers of other countries. His avatar (ugh, stupid word, corrupted word, but at least it hasn't been as wronged as *icon*) is a circular snapshot of his own shelves, taken at such close range that it appears to be a beautiful abstract painting, all those lovely worn spines, muted jewels. (The paper covers are stored because they're dust catchers.)

It is also Victoria's job to maintain a Google alert on Gerry—and to keep him wholly ignorant of it. Piracy issues are to be directed to Thiru, anything that smacks of libel goes straight to his lawyer, etc., etc. Oh, there was a time when Gerry Googled himself, checked his Amazon ratings, but that was in the early days of the Internet, which happened to be around the time his third book was published. He was young—well, youngish—and there was enormous novelty in obtaining any sort of data about one's books.

Then one morning, as he typed his latest title into Amazon's search box, he found himself *quivering*, there was no other word for it, and he recognized the feeling, even though it was not his: he was like a gambler in the moment before the roulette wheel came to rest. Gerry had never gambled in his life, not in any meaningful way, but his friend Luke had a chronic gambling problem and had described the emotions vividly.

So when Gerry felt that rush, he recognized it for what it was, and knew to avoid it at all costs. Long before other people began using programs to block their Internet access, he had set up his work life so he would not be disturbed. He doesn't know the password to the apartment's wireless service, so he didn't use it on his laptop until his accident. He can get email on his phone, theoretically, but he almost never does, not real ones. Again, Victoria culls it every day and handles the account through his website, a website so basic that it was kind of a punch line, or had been for a day or two last month. "You're trending," Victoria had said. "That is, #GeraldAndersensWebsite is trending. Some big literary blogger went viral when she made fun of it."

"Speak English," Gerry said, and he wasn't joking.

So today, when Victoria appears with her sheaves of paper and phone, ready to talk business and errands, he is not initially alarmed when she says: "Um, before we talk about anything, I guess I have to tell you there's something on Twitter."

"There's always something on Twitter," he says, meaning to be jovial, but she winces as if he's been cruel. "Something about me?"

"Not directly. Someone tweeting *at* you."

"You know how to handle it. Queries about work or public speaking can be directed to the proper avenues. Everything else is to be ignored." The Gerald Andersen Twitter account follows exactly three other accounts: Barack Obama, God, and Marina Hyde, a UK columnist he admires. Yet he is followed by almost three thousand people, although Victoria says at least half of them are probably robots, or bots, as she calls them.

"It's just that this one—it's a woman named Aubrey. I mean, her handle is DreamGirl@Aubrey. The avatar is, um, your book."

"There is no Aubrey. How can Twitter allow this?"

"I checked, but it doesn't violate the terms of service? It's pretty common, I think?"

He can't help himself: "Victoria, are you asking me questions or telling me these facts?"

"Telling you? I mean, telling you. This isn't a violation. Because Aubrey's not real, she—he—isn't really trying to deceive anyone."

Gerry gets that. He follows God, after all. Although only on Twitter.

"So I care about this because—"

"I thought you should know about the content?"

Is it so wrong that he wants to hold her head under water every time she ends a sentence on a rising note?

"What is the 'content'?"

"Yes, well, I think I should probably show it to you, or paraphrase it, or just—"

"Victoria, please tell me what this 'Aubrey' is doing that has you all bollixed up."

*"She was tweeting about your penis."*

At least she finally managed a declarative sentence.

*1975*

THE TOWSON PRECINCT of the Baltimore County Police Department was relatively quiet on the Fourth of July. The not-quite-arresting officer did not bother to put Gerry and his friends in a holding cell, but left them on a bench where, one by one, the other boys were picked up. Alex, Sean, Steve, Roderick. Still Gerry's mother didn't come and she didn't come and she didn't come. It was almost dark when she arrived and she offered no explanation for the delay.

He had never seen his mother's face so white and tight with fury, not with him. Not even with his father.

"What happened?" she asked once he was in her car, a second-hand AMC Pacer.

"There was this mass of wet leaves on the road and Alex was going a little too fast and he lost control—"

"The police said there was beer in the car."

"It wasn't our beer."

She gave him a look.

"Alex picks up his father's booze for him at the package store on Falls Road. Call him and ask. That's how cool Alex's dad is. Also, Alex turned eighteen two days ago." A lie, except for the part about Alex's age—his parents had held him back a year to allow him to excel at lacrosse—but he knew his mother would never call the home of Alexander Simpson III.

"I have told you before and I will tell you again—I do not approve of this fast crowd you have fallen in with, Gerry."

"They're not fast," he protested. "They're *fun*." He wasn't sure this was even true, but they were more fun than any other options he had. He helped them with their school papers and they, in turn, let him hang out with them with only a modicum of teasing. They spent their summer evenings scouting for beer, then used the liquid courage to approach girls. But they didn't really know what to do with girls. All four were star lacrosse players and they could do marvelous things with a stick and a ball, but face-to-face with a girl, they were hopeless. That's what they had been doing at the Elkridge Club all afternoon, splashing girls and tormenting them, then wondering why the girls didn't want to go see fireworks with them. Gerry secretly thought he would do better with girls without Alex and his gang, but how would he ever get into any place as rarefied as Elkridge without Alex?

They had been in Alex's green Mercedes sedan when he lost control on a bed of wet leaves on Falls Road. That part was true, too.

Alex had been driving much too fast for the curvy country road. The car spun in circles, making what felt like five rotations before it came to rest on the opposite side. No one was hurt, but the car hit a retaining wall, popping the battery cable. They had the presence of mind to hide the empties, so the only beer in the car was an intact six-pack. Still, the Baltimore County cop who came to their aid decided it was time they learn an important lesson about drunk driving, so he had taken them to the precinct and made them watch a film they had already seen in school, *Mechanized Death*, then called their parents to pick them up.

"You cannot afford to screw up," his mother said. "Do you understand that? Those other boys have parents, *fathers,* who can get them out of trouble. They have money. All you have is a mother who works as the office manager for a pediatrician."

"Jeez, Mom, I didn't even do anything."

"You drank beer! You got into a car with other boys who had been drinking beer. You could have been killed."

"Maybe if Alex drove a piece of shit car like this we would have been hurt. He has a Mercedes; you could T-bone that thing and walk away without a scratch. If the battery cable hadn't popped, we wouldn't have ended up at the police station."

His mother carefully checked her blind spots, pulled over to the shoulder, and slapped Gerry hard enough that he saw strange lights around his eyes. *So that's what was meant by seeing stars. They weren't stars, not exactly, but—*

"Apply yourself and maybe one day you can buy yourself a Mercedes. If you care about such silly, empty things. But you'll have to work, and work hard, for any money you get. That's how life is going to be for you. It's not fair and it's not right. But it's not fair to me, either, and you don't hear me complaining."

Gerry started to cry.

"I'll be good, Mama, I promise I'll be good. And I'll buy you a Mercedes. I swear I will."

"Just be a good man, Gerry. That's all I'm asking. Be a good man."

"I will. I will."

*February 22*

IT TURNS OUT that "scrubbing" one's penis from the Internet is a thing. Of course it is. There is an entire industry designed to help people manage how they appear in online searches. But trying to delete a *mention* of one's penis from Twitter is something else entirely—and more complicated.

"You're not understanding me. I did not send anyone a 'dick pic,'" Gerry tells Thiru. "I have never even taken a selfie, or allowed anyone to make a video, a sex tape, of me. I don't know what this 'woman' is talking about. And let me remind you, no photograph has been posted. She's just, um, claiming to know something about my personal anatomy."

He can't believe he even has to say these words—*dick pic, selfie, sex tape*. To utter them is an affront to his dignity. He has been assiduous about not cluttering his mind, his work, his life with this silly digital world, and here it is, dragging him in, like some whirl-pool or abyss. Then again, it wasn't that long ago that a porn star told the world a sitting president has a penis shaped like a mushroom. The claim about Gerry is not only preposterous, it's derivative.

"But you are not, in fact, circumcised?"

"*Thiru.*"

"I'm sorry, it's just that's what she—"

"If it is, in fact, a she. I have my doubts."

"Why?"

"Because I don't think young women are that vulgar." Gerry may have doubts about the gender, but he assumes everyone on Twitter is young.

"Gerry, do you *know* any young women? Our firm signed a mem-oir by a twenty-seven-year-old the other day who could make Nor-man Mailer's testicles retract in a casual conversation. You would not believe what these young women are willing to—"

"Thiru, let's not get sidetracked. What can be done about this?"

"Not much. She didn't violate the TOS."

"The what?"

"Terms of service. She didn't threaten you, she didn't post a photo, she didn't defame you. I mean, I don't think it's defamation to say that a man has an unattractive penis. Rude, subjective, but not defamatory."

Gerry wants to weep, literally. He has lived too long—and he's only sixty-one! Did the world feel this way to his mother, his father, like some science fiction film in which everything jumps to warp speed? He had wondered, frequently, if the affair that led to his father's second marriage was a reaction to the changing mores of the early 1960s, to the sense that the world was moving rapidly and Gerald Andersen Sr. had just missed the party.

But that was part of his father's myth-making, that he had met wife number two in an airport bar the week after Kennedy was shot, or maybe it was during the Cuban Missile Crisis. Something Kennedy-adjacent. Gerald Andersen Sr. wasn't a run-of-the-mill horndog cheater, he was a man who believed himself on the brink of annihilation. They had been married by some local yokel justice of the peace who had asked for no proof of anything. And what proof would Gerald Senior have been forced to provide? As Gerry came to learn, to his great sorrow, proof is required if one remarries after a divorce. Much less paperwork is needed if one has not shed one's current spouse. Of course, he married her a second time, once he was divorced from Gerry's mother. He sent a postcard from their honeymoon.

Auntie Mame had declared, *Life is a banquet and most poor sons of bitches are starving to death.* Gerald Andersen Sr. lived by a similar motto: *Life is a buffet; take what you want, skip what you don't, stick your head under the sneeze guard if necessary.*

But Gerry was skeptical from a very young age of what he called buffet culture, a problem that became more pronounced with each technical innovation. Watch what you want when you want to watch it! And music, don't get him started on music. Like most men of his generation, he had a lovingly gathered collection of albums and he respected the fact that the album was a whole, not a series of singles; that the artist had dictated the order. The occasional duds on, say, Pete Townshend's first solo album were part of the experience. The CD had seemed ominous enough, with its ability to skip songs. Then came shuffle and now people had their own "stations" on streaming services. Everyone's so worried about political bubbles, but what about art bubbles? Was it only a matter of time before museums created virtual reality versions of themselves, in which visitors were allowed to *curate*—hideous word, but at least correct in this instance—the experience they desired? *No, no Motherwell for me, show me only the Rothkos.*

Then they would come for the books, allowing readers to reorganize the chapters, the sentences. The crime novelist Elmore Leonard, whom Gerry respected about as much as he could respect any genre writer, had famously said to cut out the parts that readers skip. Gerry *hated* that glib aphorism. If anything, writers should be committed to putting in more passages that readers were likely to skip. More details about the whaling industry in *Moby-Dick*, please! In a world that was speeding up, novelists were *obligated* to make people slow down.

But the only thing people today want to slow down for is food. Artisanal this and artisanal that. It's *fuel*. Who cares where your potato came from?

"Gerry, the woman has fourteen followers," Thiru said. "Ignore her for now."

"She's using an image from the cover of my book as her avatar. Isn't that an infringement of the artist's copyright?"

"Possibly. But attention to a troll is like, like—well, it's what they want. They blossom, they get bigger with attention. Your account is verified. When fake Gerald Andersens sprout, we do go after them, sometimes. But usually the best course of action is to ignore. This is an unknown person pretending to be a fictional person."

*A fictional person who has been writing me and calling me, claiming to be a real person who inspired the fictional person when no such person exists. A person who says I have an unsightly penis. It is not an unsightly penis. It is simply uncircumcised, something that would be known by almost forty women.*

Who is Gerry kidding? He knows the exact number, which is

thirty-seven. He was a late bloomer, a truly late bloomer, in part because of his early marriage. He had more partners in his forties than he did in his twenties and thirties combined. But not a single woman—not a wife, not a girlfriend, not even Margot—had ever commented unfavorably on his penis, even in passing, even if it was their first of that variety. Circumcision was a false aesthetic, like fake breasts, that had somehow become the norm. He gave his parents credit for very few things, but Gerry was proud of them for resisting circumcision at a time when almost all U.S. boys went through the procedure. That said, he never doubted it was his father's usual narcissism at work: *My son has to look like me.*

*Joke's on you, Dad.* While Gerry has his father's coloring and blond hair, his father was a small, narrow-shouldered man. When things were at the very worst between him and Gerry's mother, in the years when he refused to make child support payments, Gerald Senior had once suggested that Gerry wasn't even his son. "How I wish that were so," Gerry Junior said to his father, hoping they would be the last words he ever spoke to him. And they almost were.

Done with Thiru, Gerry summons his assistant back. "How did you find this Twitter account?"

"She tagged you."

"What?"

"She used your handle in her tweet, so it was in your mentions. You don't get tagged a lot. When you—I—post poems or the sentences from books you love, there are retweets and a lot of replies. But it's unusual for someone to tag you in an original tweet."

"Did anyone notice?"

"She received"—Victoria checks her phone—"seven likes and no replies. Whoa!"

"What?"

"Just like that, it's unavailable. It disappeared while I was looking at it. I should have grabbed a screenshot."

She showed him the phone.

"What do you mean? She—'she'—is still there."

"The account is there, but the tweet is gone. I wonder what happened? Did your agent complain after all, do you think?"

"No, he was adamant that we should ignore her. Victoria—is
there any way we can find out who this is?"

"I don't know. Maybe some kind of IT person knows how to do
it. But I wouldn't worry about it. You gotta remember—you're seeing
this, but most people aren't. And now it's gone."

"But if there's a Twitter account, that could be connected to the
letter and the phone calls."

Victoria nods politely. Has Aileen briefed her? Does she also believe the calls are a figment of his drug-assisted imagination? It's
true, the caller ID once again showed no evidence of a call. And the
next call, the one in which no one spoke, turned out to be a wrong
number. He had asked Aileen to call back and the person, an elderly
woman, had been quite huffy.

Finally, finally, the day ends with no more penis drama. Gerry
has begun to think of the two hours between Victoria's departure
and Aileen's arrival as his best hours. Even when the girls (women,
sorry) are quiet, he feels their presence. To be alone is at once
a luxury and a poverty. He craves it, he needs it, but he cannot
afford it for more than a few hours right now. Victoria still comes
and goes during her shift, but she feels more present these days,
hovering.

And while Aileen appears to be avoiding him as much as
possible—her work as a night nurse seems to have been chosen because it allows for quite a bit of napping time—he can feel her in

the apartment, imagines he can hear her, wheezing like an old dog in her sleep.

The days are getting slightly longer, the sun setting at about six. An orange light suffuses the apartment, the kind of sunset that tempts a writer to do his worst work. Sunsets are for painters or photographers; writers should leave them be. Elmore Leonard also told writers never to begin with the weather, yet *Dream Girl* begins with the weather—

The phone.

He lets it ring three times before he picks up.

"Gerry? I'm so sorry."

"You have to stop this stupid prank—"

"I never should have said that. About—you know. I got a little drunk last night. I miss you so."

"I have your number on caller ID." He doesn't, but it will be on the other phones; he will tell Aileen to look for it the second she arrives.

"I can't wait to see you, Gerry. It's been far too long. I have such a wonderful idea. I shouldn't say anything, but—well, I've figured out how you can repay me."

"*Repay* you?"

"For my story. My lawyer said I could sue you for half of everything you've made since *Dream Girl* was published, but I don't want to do anything that contentious. Also it sounded so tedious—forensic accounting, blah, blah, blah, and it's really hard to separate *Dream Girl* from your net worth because it's the foundation of your net worth, you know? I mean, if you're worth ten million dollars, one could argue that I deserve five—"

"YOU DON'T EXIST. Even if you did—"

"Oh, I exist, Gerry. I exist. And I'll see you very soon." With that, she's gone.

When Aileen comes to work, he asks her to check the caller ID.

"Someone did call," she reports from the kitchen. "At six thirty-seven."

"Is there a name?"

"Wipper."

"What?"

"Wipper."

"WHAT?"

"WIPPER." She writes it down for him. *W-Y-P-R.*

"That's the local NPR station."

"Is it?"

"Bring me the number."

"Would it kill you to say please?"

She walks back to the kitchen, returns with the phone, fumbling it in her meaty hands. "I think you just have to press redial—"

The phone rings three times and goes to voicemail. "Thank you for calling WYPR. Our offices are closed now."

Technically, WYPR is part of Johns Hopkins, or used to be. There was definitely some sort of affiliation. Gerry thinks of the moment that *Dream Girl* came to him, the young woman who—

But he had not written about that young woman, he did not know that young woman, and he had never told the story to anyone.

Or had he? Had he told someone and forgotten? Was tonight's conversation even real?

*2015*

"OUR NEXT QUESTION is from Gretchen in Baltimore," the interviewer said.

*But my Gretchen is in New York,* Gerry thought, then laughed at his own solipsism. The world was full of Gretchens. And this voice—a young, lilting voice—was nothing like his second wife's, not even when she was in her twenties.

"I know you've always been obscure about the actual inspiration for *Dream Girl*—" the caller began.

"Not obscure," Gerry said. "I just don't think it's important. The book was a feat of imagination. The book and the character. The story. I made it all up. That's what novelists do and I felt that concept had become lost in a world where people spoke of 'creative nonfiction.' I had no patience with these reported stories, all these writers bragging about their copious research. Per Eudora Welty, I wanted to show that a quiet life can be a daring life—"

"Yes, yes, because all serious daring starts from within." There was a familiarity in the way the woman finished his sentence, a good-natured impatience, as if she were a former student. Or a former wife. "The thing is, the Aubrey sections, when we see her view of things—they are outstandingly nuanced. In your other novels, you've never managed to write a female character as credibly as you did with Aubrey."

"I have to take exception to that." He tried to say this with good humor and thought he pulled it off.

"Of course you do." The caller laughed. It was a warm laugh, seemingly without malice. "But I have to ask—did you actually have a collaborator on the novel? Did a woman write or extensively revise the Aubrey sections?"

This was a new one. "That's a new one," Gerry said dryly. "All these years, no one's ever thought to question whether I had a secret collaborator."

"Or maybe there was something you read, a student paper, when you were teaching—"

"*Dream Girl* came out in 2001. I taught at Goucher in 2012."

"And at Hopkins in the 1980s and 1990s, no?"

"Believe me, I did not—" He stopped himself from saying, *I did not have a student whose work was worth stealing.* "I'm sorry, these are inflammatory charges."

He looked to the host for help, but she seemed to be enjoying the discussion. Served him right for being gracious, doing this nonsyndicated radio show because it was easy to stop in Baltimore after last night's event for PEN America down in DC.

"But even you would have to concede that Aubrey is an outlier in your work? You had never before written a female character as complex as she is, nor did you do it again. Although you did kill her. Even Aubrey had to die. It's reminiscent of the Mary Gordon essay, 'Good Boys and Dead Girls' in which she posits—"

"I am familiar with the essay, which applies that critique to Faulkner, Dreiser, and Updike," he said. "I understand your *point*. But just because you say something doesn't make it true."

"Which part isn't true? The part about Aubrey being your best female character or my speculation about how that came to be?"

"I reject your thesis, which means that your speculation is specious to me."

The host interrupted. "I'm afraid we're out of time. Our guest today was Gerry Andersen, a prizewinning novelist and a Baltimore native. His latest novel, *Isolation,* is now out in paperback."

Gerry left the radio station. It was less than ten blocks to the train station and he decided to walk, despite the typical April weather— blustery, cutting back and forth between clouds and brilliant blue skies, a very Jekyll-and-Hyde day. He could not quiet his thoughts. The woman knew him, he was sure of it, but it was not Gretchen, not his Gretchen, with whom he had not spoken for years. She had sounded so pleasant, yet the conversation had felt aggressively nasty. It was true, when *Dream Girl* was published, there had been a lot of praise lavished on Gerry for his depiction of Aubrey, for giving a voice and an inner life to what the novel's main character, Daniel, saw merely as an object of his desire. Daniel's inability to see Aubrey as a person was the tragedy of the novel. Somewhere, in the notebook he had kept while working on *Dream Girl,* Gerry had jotted in the margin: "*The Sterile Cuckoo,* but good."

As he walked to the train station, he thought about his youthful discovery of John Nichols, a writer he now disdained. Thesis and antithesis, leading to synthesis. Was that not the path of a creative life? Embrace, reject, combine the two, move on. Was that not the path of his life? He was fifty-seven years old, thrice married, thrice divorced. But—but!—he was admired, an acknowledged leader in his field, and quite wealthy to boot. And the work (his true drug, his true obsession) was getting better, despite what anyone thought.

Baltimore's Penn Station seemed absurdly small to him now, but pretty in a way that New York's Penn Station could never be. He sat on one of the wooden benches that lined the high-ceilinged space, waiting for his train to be called. He was rising to his feet to go down to the track when his phone rang. A Baltimore area code. Had he left something at the radio station?

"I hope I didn't upset you," said a woman's voice. It was the woman from the radio show. "I really am sincerely curious about how you created Aubrey."

"Do I know you? Who are you?"

She laughed. It wasn't a cruel laugh, but it wasn't friendly, either. "Do you know *anyone*, Gerry? Even yourself?"

The woman hung up. He called back, but no one answered, even as the phone rang and rang, never going to voicemail.

*February 26*

AS A TEENAGER, Gerry had read Chandler, Hammett, John D. MacDonald, although his favorite was Ross Macdonald. By college he was mildly embarrassed by his affection for the private detective genre, and he no longer reads it, although he recognizes there are a few outstanding practitioners working within crime fiction, albeit almost accidentally. Still, the affection remains.

So when he decides to hire a private detective to investigate the Case of the Vanishing Tweet, among other things, he is vaguely disappointed that his condition will not allow him to visit some seedy little office with a frosted pane, the agency's name stenciled in chipping black paint. A silly fantasy, and even if such detectives existed, why would he want one? He wants someone honest and reputable, up to date, but it's hard to find online reviews for private detectives. He can ask Victoria, of course—it's her job. He Goo-gles, but the information that comes back is daunting in its volume.

He takes it as a nudge from fate when he picks up a *Baltimore* magazine from the pile by his bed—it has come to this, Gerry has read all his *New Yorkers*, cover to cover—and sees a feature on the back page, Five Questions With. The subject in January was Tess Monaghan, private detective.

She is a handsome woman. Not his type, but broad-shouldered and capable looking. Somewhere in her thirties, with a sardonic way of speaking, at least on the page. She has a partner, male, but he is not pictured. Is it silly to call a PI because she happened to be on the back page of a magazine? Well, so be it. He calls and is happily surprised to hear a human voice, more surprised still to realize it is the woman herself.

"I'd prefer to meet face-to-face," she says when he starts to ex-plain why he is calling. "You won't be billed for it. Even if I end up taking the job, the first consultation is complimentary."

*Even if*—funny, it had not occurred to him that she could turn him down.

"That can be arranged," he says. "Although—I'm confined to bed, for now, as I've had a bad injury. Can you get to Locust Point?"

"Sure. Last I heard, they weren't checking passports to get onto the peninsula."

"Can you come between five and seven? Those are the only hours I am alone, and I want this to be confidential." He isn't sure why he feels that way. He just knows that he could not bear to have Victoria or Aileen nearby, eavesdropping, rolling her eyes when he describes the letter that can't be found, the calls that leave no trace.

"Tonight?"

"If possible."

"I'll have to work out child care."

"Oh, you have a child?" That didn't fit with his image of a PI at all.

"Allegedly, although she's more like a cranky divorcée in the body of a fourth grader. If this is urgent—"

"I think it is."

"Then I'll be there."

She is, at five thirty sharp. She is even taller than he had imagined, her reddish-brown hair tousled by the February wind, which has been howling formidably again, but maybe it sounds worse on the twenty-fifth floor. She is of a type he knows well from growing up in North Baltimore—a female jock, possibly lacrosse, attractive despite her disdain for makeup and clothes.

She is remarkably free of judgment, even kind, when he begins to describe what has been happening to him. She listens intently, interrupting only to clarify facts.

"So first there was a letter? With a return address that matched the address you gave—a made-up address—to a fictional character? Only the letter disappeared?"

"Yes. Things were hectic after I fell. I assume it was thrown away by accident."

"Then a couple of calls and this one tweet? Alleging, um, intimate knowledge of your anatomy."

"Yes."

"But the tweet disappeared within twenty-four hours, followed quickly by the account itself."

"Yes, but my assistant saw it, she can vouch for its existence."

"The calls—the first two weren't on the call log at all and the third time the listed number took you to the main switchboard at WYPR?"

"Yes."

She nods and smiles, still without judgment. "What do you think is going on, Mr. Andersen?"

He couldn't feel more ridiculous.

"Someone's trying to—I don't want to say *gaslight,* that word is everywhere now, no one even remembers what it means."

"It's from the film, of course. The husband manipulates the lights."

Oh, he *likes* her. "Yes. The things this person is saying, they're just not true. I made the character up. People want to think it's a true story—people always want to think there's a true story—and I made it a policy not to be drawn into that conversation about my work and my silence has become a void that people fill with their own crackpot ideas. But now I'm beginning to think—well, what if she says she expects money from me, to be repaid? What if this is leading to some kind of attempted extortion? Even a frivolous claim could burn up quite a bit of money. And time."

Not that time is a precious commodity for him now, stuck in bed, not writing.

"That's a legal issue. The attorney I work for—he's not really much on intellectual property, but he could find someone—"

"I don't think someone is actually going to come after me for money."

"Then I'm sorry, Mr. Andersen, I don't understand. What do you think is happening?"

"Someone is harassing me. Someone wants to upset me. But I don't know why. I thought, maybe, my second wife—she waived all her rights to my writing income, which proved not to be the smart thing to do. Technically, *Dream Girl* was marital property."

"And where is your second wife?"

"In New York, as far as I know."

"So for her to call from the local radio station or to mail a letter with a Baltimore postmark—" The private eye was smiling, sympathetic, but he still feels foolish.

"There's another woman."

"Well, there were two more wives, based on your Wikipedia page."

He doesn't like this, although he supposes it's pro forma for an investigator to investigate. "No, we parted on good terms." Close enough to the truth. "But I had a girlfriend"—ugh, the word sounds so horribly teenage. "We were living together in New York until about a year ago, but it wasn't really a formal arrangement. She sort of showed up and never left. Then I sold my apartment and bought this place. My mother was ill and I assumed I would be here caring for her for a while. She died."

"I'm so sorry."

There is a refreshing frankness to everything she says, but maybe it's because he's been spending so much time with Victoria, whose voice is always sliding up into uncertainty, and Aileen, whose responses are always a little off, as if she's in a slightly different conversation.

"Thank you. Anyway, my ex—Margot—showed up here recently."

"And?"

"And she went back to New York on the train. With a ticket I bought. But Margot's very sticky."

"Sticky."

She repeats the word without judgment and yet he feels judged. He is judging himself. He sounds silly and paranoid. He sounds not unlike Margot, who was always convinced that people were speaking about her, plotting against her. "What was that woman saying to you?" she would demand when they got home from a party. Or: "I happen to know for a fact that someone on the committee changed my table assignment at the luncheon." Manufactured drama in a life where the only drama was who was going to pick up the tab for Margot's lifestyle. Which, it now occurs to Gerry, is a pretty big dramatic conflict, Maslow's hierarchy.

"Margot is an unusual woman. She's sort of like a virus, a cold, that moves from host to host. The only way to get rid of her, usually, is to introduce her to her next—" He doesn't want to say *victim,* because he hates thinking of himself that way. Besides, Margot isn't a conscious schemer. She is helpless, in her own way. One can't blame her for how she is. It's like faulting a flower for trying to get water.

"Do you know the Cheever story?" he asks abruptly.

"I know quite a few. I majored in English."

"Where?"

"No place as fancy as Princeton." Another reminder that she looked into him. "Washington College in Chestertown."

Why hadn't he found a woman like this, Gerry thinks. Someone who reads, but is capable and down to earth. Such broad shoulders—she's probably very strong. *She* should be his nurse.

"I'm thinking of 'Torch Song.' The woman who shows up when men are dying. I think that's why Margot is always being . . . jettisoned by her men. She's quite beautiful. She can be good company. But she always seems to be waiting—"

He did not want to finish his own thought.

"For men to die? Is she a black widow? Does she have a string of dead men in her past? Does she inveigle her way into people's wills?"

"No, no, of course not. She's harmless. Relatively."

The PI sighs, although not in a mean way. "Look, I could take your money. I like money. I always need money and you seem well fixed. But, alas, I'm too ethical to take on a job where I don't think I'm going to get any real results."

"There must be something you can do—"

"I could generate some reports on your second wife, or this Margot—get their financials, check around to see what they've been up to recently—it would be more than you'd get from a Google search, but not that much more. Or I could sign you up for the big ticket, surveillance. Maybe twenty-four/seven security, which is costlier still. But—this building is pretty secure. I don't know what kind of security system you have in here, but there's a front desk and the elevator has a camera. No one's coming and going here without being seen."

"Do you believe me? About the calls, the letter?"

"Sure," she says. "Why wouldn't I believe you?"

*Because my mother had hallucinations before she died of dementia and I could be headed down the same path.* But Gerry, having presented such a physically depleted self to this woman who radiates health and competence, does not want to reveal that his mind could be going, too.

"The missing letter, the lack of proof that the first two calls happened at all."

"Technology is imperfect. Still, I'm going to give you a technological solution: You order this piece of equipment, a very basic recorder that works on any phone. Attach it to the landline here next to your bed. Technically, it's illegal to tape people in Maryland without their consent, but it won't matter as long as you don't try to use the tape. Right now, it's my sense that you want the peace of mind that these calls are actually happening. Right?"

"Right." It's a relief to feel understood.

She takes out her phone, shows him a website called the Spy Store, points to the model that she recommends. A solution, but it feels like a letdown. He likes her company. He would be happy to be under her warm, watchful eyes. He wants to hear her laugh.

"Even if you think I don't need it—what if I did want to hire you for surveillance?"

She shakes her head. "No."

"No?"

"It's not that I don't like you"—his heart soars a little—"I've worked for lots of men I don't like. Comes with the territory." And now his heart thuds down, down, down; he could be sixteen again, listening to Mary Ellen King's earnest assurances that she liked him *as a friend*. "And it's not that I think you're paranoid or delusional. It's just that—you're sixty-one years old. You've been married three times. Dated quite a bit. I mean, the most basic Newspapers.com search unearths lots of information on your, um, social life. Yet you look back over the last twenty or so years and you can think of only two women who might want to upset you. I'm sorry, but if you think you've gotten to the age you are, lived the life you've lived, without having more potential enemies than that—you're not delusional, but you're not very self-aware. Obviously, the relationship between a PI and a client never works if the client lies to the investigator. But over the years, I've learned it also doesn't work if the client is lying to *himself.*"

"I can make a more complete list, if that's what you want." He says this stiffly, wanting her to know his feelings are hurt, but even as he does, his mind expands and he reconsiders the various candidates. Lucy became convinced he had cheated on her, she was that paranoid. He had cheated on Sarah, but only once, a one-night stand that barely mattered. There were the assistants who worked for him between Gretchen and Sarah, who always ended up in bed with him, but they had pretty much demanded his sexual attention. If anyone was the victim there, it was him. Tara? Their last conversation, so many years ago, had been a little fraught. Yes, maybe the list was longer than he knew.

"That's admirable," Tess said. "Most people can't take such bluntness."

"So you'll investigate if I give you a full list?"

"No, no. I didn't want to say this, it sounds so woo-woo, but I've learned to respect my intuition about such things. I couldn't—I couldn't spend a lot of time in this apartment. It gives me the creeps. Don't get me wrong. It's beautiful, absolutely gorgeous. I could stare out these windows all day. But—there's something wrong here. I felt it when I crossed the threshold. I don't know, maybe it's like the Spielberg movie where it turns out a grave has been desecrated. Only the thing that's buried beneath your beautiful apartment is jobs."

"Jobs?"

"There were silos here. Grain silos. There were jobs all over this peninsula. Baltimore's citizens made things, put them on ships and trains. I know I should be happy, seeing these big apartment buildings going up. It's property taxes; my kid goes to public school. But this place gives me the creeps, big time. I could never do surveillance here. My partner would probably be cool with it—"

"No, that's okay."

He doesn't want a man's company. He doesn't need a private detective. He understands that now. He needs a friend, someone bright and lively, a woman who has read Cheever and knows the origin of *gaslighting* and makes casual references to the film *Poltergeist*. And even then—does he really want such a woman or is he simply enamored with this woman because of the plain gold band on her left hand, the casual reference to her "kid"—and her utter indifference to him? There comes a moment in life when everything is the road not taken, when it's just fork after fork after fork.

VICTORIA ORDERS the tape recorder for him and it is, indeed, quite easy to set up. He can't wait for the next call. Only there are no calls. He finds himself waking in the middle of the night, thinking—hoping—if only for a moment, that the phone has rung. But the phone is quiet and his mind is still. He should be happy—and yet.

Finally, eight days after Ms. Monaghan's visit, he awakens at 2:08 A.M. He knows that something has brought him out of his dream-less sleep, but it's not a ringing phone. Was someone whispering his name? Yes, he heard his name, but how is that possible? *Gerry, Gerry, Gerry.* Aileen calls him Mr. Andersen, when she bothers to address him at all.

It takes a moment for him to realize that there is a slender silhou-ette by the window.

"Oh, Gerry," the form says, "your view is so beautiful."

"Margot?"

"Margot? Who's Margot? It's—well, you called me Aubrey in the book. But you and I know I have a different name."

He is frozen. He must be back in the dream from which he thought he woke, one of those nightmares where you can't move, can't make a sound. It takes him a moment to realize that he can turn on the light, all he has to do is turn on the light, and he will see who is torturing him, although the woman's back is still to him.

Instead, he watches in wonder as the woman turns from the win-dow and heads into the kitchen area. It turns out she is wearing a veil, sort of a black beekeeper effect, so he can't make out her face. She could be anyone. It could be *anything*. He hears the click of the back door, which leads to the stairwell.

Then, and only then, he begins screaming his head off.

*2012*

**Syllabus for Advanced Creative Writing**

*Suggested Reading*

   *The Speed Queen,* Stewart O'Nan

   *Zuckerman Unbound,* Philip Roth

   *Sister Carrie,* Theodore Dreiser

   *Bury Me Deep,* Megan Abbott

   *Red Baker,* Robert Ward

   *Ghost Story,* Peter Straub

   *The Getaway,* Jim Thompson

   *The Godfather,* Mario Puzo

*Suggested Viewing*

   *Misery* (1990)

   *The King of Comedy* (1982)

*A Place in the Sun* (1951)
*I Want to Live!* (1958)
*The Wire,* season 2
*Ghost Story* (1981)
*The Getaway* (1972)
*The Godfather* (1972)

GERRY DISTRIBUTED his syllabus among a baker's dozen of students. Although Goucher had been coed for three decades, the school was still overwhelmingly female, as were those admitted to this class. There were three boys and ten girls, two of whom were distractingly beautiful. He had not chosen the students himself, not wanting the chore of reading dozens of submissions. He had trusted the English department to vet the candidates carefully and send him the best, and they had pressured him to take thirteen instead of the twelve he had requested. So this should be the cream of the crop. Should be. He wasn't so convinced after he read the work that had gained them entrance.

"Although we will be working on short stories in this class—anyone who wants to attempt a novel must have prior approval, please see me during office hours before this week is out—the reading and viewing list is key. I will schedule viewings during a to-be-agreed-upon time that works for the majority of students. You may, of course, watch the films on your own."

A thin girl, not one of the knockouts, raised a nervous hand. "What do you mean by 'suggested'?"

"Suggested," Gerry repeated. "Encouraged. Recommended. Not compulsory, but something that will enhance your experience." Blank stares. "Not part of your grade." Happy smiles.

"Here's what *will* affect your grade. Turning your work in on time.

Providing comprehensive critiques on others' work. Finally, it is important that you show up. Attendance is literally thirty percent of the grade in this class. You can't be successful in a fiction workshop if you don't show up. You can't be successful at anything if you don't show up."

He had not taught for almost fifteen years, but it was like muscle memory. The words rolled out, familiar and yet new. He was energized in a way he had not been for a long time. Goucher might not have Hopkins's rep, but what it did have was an alum who had donated a ridiculously wonderful amount of money for a visiting professorship. He would receive $150,000 and a living stipend as the first Eileen Harriman Creative Writing Fellow. It would have been foolish to say no, even if it meant returning to Baltimore, tricky because his mother assumed he would move back into his boyhood bedroom. He did not. He took a sterile short-term lease behind the Towson mall, telling his mother he had to be within walking distance of campus. She accepted this lie readily, which made him feel guilty. Hadn't his mother endured enough lies from men? But the house on Berwick was like something out of a ghost story—only not Peter Straub, more Shirley Jackson. He worried that if he went back in, he would never get out.

Besides, he was a newlywed of sorts, married less than a year to Sarah, and he would be boarding the train to New York every Friday to return to her.

He had taught this class before, more or less. The Abbott book was new; he recognized that he needed some women in his syllabus. He expected the students to assume he would be Team Novel all the way, and he generally was, but there was some subtlety to his method. Obviously, *The Godfather* (film) trumped *The Godfather* (book). *Ghost Story* (book) defeated *Ghost Story* (film) handily. *The*

*Getaway* was the best one-on-one matchup because novel and film both had their merits, but the book was an existential nightmare whereas the film was a straight-up love story.

The *Red Baker–Wire* bracket, as he thought of it, was interesting because the novel was working on a human level, whereas *The Wire* had bigger fish to fry. Gerry preferred the former, but he understood why others argued for the latter. The idea was to shake the students up, to get them to form their own ideas. The novel had been changed forever by film and television; there was no going back. The question was how to go forward.

Their own short stories, the ones they had submitted—they were more scenarios than stories, but so it goes, that's why they needed a class—were clearly shaped by cinema. The nonlinear ones owed much to *Pulp Fiction* and maybe the TV show *Lost,* not that he had ever watched the latter. Then there were the zombies. So. Many. Zombies. What was the appeal of zombies? He really didn't get it. They weren't even a good horror device; he had hoped *Shaun of the Dead* would kill the zombie motif forever. But zombies, being zombies, kept coming back.

"Given that this is our first meeting, let's start with an exercise—I want you to take the line, 'He was vacuuming the rug when the phone rang' and proceed from there." They looked disappointed by the prosaic line, or maybe they just didn't understand a world where phones sat on tables and *rang.* He would tell them when they were done that the line was Raymond Carver's and Carver had written a short story once with nothing more than that opening line in mind. Not that Gerry was a big Carver fan, but it was a good exercise.

Or was it? When he asked who wanted to share their work, he was amazed at how their imaginations defaulted to mundane or hyperbolic. One girl had a SWAT team enter in the second paragraph.

Another simply described vacuuming. The best were two of the three boys; they were clearly the most talented, and that was going to be tricky in this environment, but what can one do? Luckily, the third boy was a moron, so that balanced the scales a bit.

One of the gorgeous girls was also surprisingly good—there was real wit in what she wrote and her comments on others' contributions were compassionate but incisive. When the class left at the end of the three hours, Gerry noticed the moron had his hand on the small of the gorgeous girl's back, piloting her, the way some men do with women. It always made Gerry think of a wind-up toy with a key in its back. Well, this girl was quite a toy. Slinky, Asian—

"Mr. Andersen?"

Another student had planted herself in front of him, blocking his view. A large girl with cat-eye glasses and blue hair.

"Yes?"

"I want to work on a novel."

"As I said, we should talk about that during office hours."

"Which are—?"

"It's on the syllabus."

"See you then."

God help him, it was the girl with the SWAT team.

*March 6*

"THERE'S NOBODY HERE," Aileen says.

"Are you sure?"

"Where would she be?" With a sweep of a thick arm, she indicates the lack of hiding spaces on Gerry's top floor. Really, the only place for an adult human to hide would be under his bed, and isn't that something to contemplate.

"I saw it—*her*—go into the kitchen."

"I opened every cupboard, every door."

"There's a back door, to the stairwell. I heard it close, I think. And you don't need a key to go down, only up."

She shrugs. "So there you have it."

Have what?

"But there should be video, right? There are cameras in the service corridor, on the elevators." There is no camera in the communal hallway he shares with the sheikh and the swimmer, but there are cameras in the elevators. He thinks. And both elevators require a key to reach the twenty-fifth floor. Phylloh, at the main desk, has to insert it for guests.

"It was probably a bad dream. Look, Mr. Andersen, I know you don't like the sleeping medication, but tonight I think it might help."

"That stuff is addictive—have you followed the news about the Sackler family?"

"Are they the meth heads who burned down that house over on Towson Street? Look, this is Ambien. It's not a big deal."

"I've heard people do strange things while using Ambien. Sleep-walk, drive—"

"Well, you're not getting far, are you?"

A stray memory, a mordant cartoon from the funny papers. *He won't get far on foot.* Gerry's mind feels like a kaleidoscope, endlessly rearranging bright bits of glass into patterns that dissolve with the next shake of his head.

"It was so real," he says. "It *was* real."

"Nightmares can feel that way. Dreams, too. Dreams can be awfully real."

"What were your dreams, Aileen?" Gerry is that desperate. He doesn't want her to leave him. He doesn't want to take the pill, sur-render to sleep, a world in which he's even less sure of what's true.

"What, you don't think I'm living them?"

He snorts, impressed by the fact that literal, humorless Aileen has made a joke. Only—she hasn't, apparently, and she is angered by his reaction.

"It's funny to you, that I think I'm happy? A life like mine, it can't be someone's dream? I'm not saying it's my first dream. I mean, when you're a kid, everybody wants to be something they're never going to be, right? A ballet dancer, a fireman?"

Gerry nods, although he doesn't remember a time when he didn't want to be a writer. That was his first vocational dream, and his last. Before that, all he wanted was to be courageous.

"But the second dream, the one you pick when you grow up —that's all about comfort. Warmth. Enough food in your belly, not worrying about your car throwing a rod or how to pay your bills or whether you can afford to buy something better than the generic box of macaroni and cheese."

Her words were bizarrely familiar, but maybe it was just that they were so very bland. Although "throw a rod" had a nice specificity—oh lord, he was workshopping his night nurse's sentences. Talk about the generic box of macaroni and cheese. His thoughts go back to the woman at the window, swathed, her face averted—that, too, is familiar.

"She spoke to me—it reminded me of a movie. A terrible movie based on a very good book. *Ghost Story!*" He trumpets the book's name so loudly that Aileen winces. But being able to come up with that title makes him all the more sure that it wasn't a dream, that his mental faculties are fine. "Did you ever read it, by chance?"

He feels foolish as soon as the words are out. Aileen has made it very clear that she does not read. "It was a movie, too, although you would have been—" He has no idea how old she would have been. "Much too young to see it, maybe not even born. I was in my twenties when it came out. It had some very famous people in it. Fred Astaire. John Houseman."

Her face is so stolidly blank at those two names that he kind of wants to throttle her. She must be younger than she looks to be stone-faced at the mention of Astaire. Fred Astaire is a name that brings only joy; one would have to be a soulless, heartless husk of a person not to smile at the very thought of Astaire, even those who (wrongly) preferred Gene Kelly. Wait, was Gene Kelly in *Ghost Story*? No, but it did have Melvyn Douglas, who indirectly spawned that insanely gorgeous, curvy granddaughter, the one who showed up in some Scorsese films.

It's interesting, Gerry thinks, the order in which the men die (or don't die) in *Ghost Story*, how it aligns with the audience's natural affections toward the actors. Take Douglas Fairbanks Jr., the first to go. No one remembers him anyway. There's a logic to Douglas's death, a culpability in the larger story, but Gerry has forgotten the details. And of course frosty Houseman has to die.

But never Astaire. Astaire survived even the *Towering Inferno*.

As did O.J.

With Aileen's help, he navigates the "SmartHub" on the television and finds a version to rent, inviting her to watch with him. She looks dubious. "Seems a bad idea, to watch a scary movie now." But Gerry assures her that the scares are mostly jump shocks. He screened it for his class at Goucher, after having them read the novel on which it was based. The exercise was intended to make his students see what the written word could do with suggestion, how flat-footed film, with its myriad tricks, could be. He could watch *Ghost Story* all night long and never feel anything deeper than annoyance. But he wouldn't *read* it tonight on a bet. The book was absolutely terrifying and surprisingly erudite. The passages about teaching—an instructor at the height of his powers, his subsequent fall from grace—are outstanding, as good as any Gerry has read. Maybe even written.

And yet, he feels as if this is the scene that has just played out, his own *Ghost Story*—a woman, face averted, with that beautiful voice.

The voice he stole.

*The voice he stole.*

Not from the real-life Aubrey, who does not, in fact, exist, not really. When he gave his creation a voice—how had he never realized this before—he had taken the beautiful vowels of the actress in this movie, the one who also had been in *Chariots of Fire*. For a moment, when he was in his twenties, she had seemed to be everywhere. Then, suddenly, she was nowhere. The culture has such an endless appetite for beautiful young women, like a volcano, requiring sacrifice after sacrifice. Only a few women have long acting careers and they are seldom the great beauties.

But the culture does it to young men, too. And not just handsome ones. Not just actors! Gerry has written better books since *Dream Girl,* even critics agree on this. But he has never *mattered* quite as much as he did in that fleeting moment; nothing can be written about him without citing that one particular novel, whereas older writers were allowed to transcend individual titles. Gerry always felt more in step with the writers of the previous generation. They were the little pigs who built their houses of brick, whereas Gerry's peers tended more to straw and wood.

And, oh, how people loved to blow them down. Everybody huffs and puffs, intent on destruction. What do they call it now? Cancel culture.

Lord, the movie is really terrible, even worse than he remembered. He hopes Straub got a lot of money for it. Yet it's so naked, so wonderfully literally naked, in a way that movies aren't anymore. Alice Krige—ah, yes, that's the actress's name—has very natural breasts that are on display quite a bit, but there's also the leading man's penis. He's falling to his death from a great height when you see it, but still, it's an example of equal opportunity nudity.

"The women in this movie have nothing to do but bicker at the men," Aileen grumbles at one point. "They're better actresses than that."

"Alma is a huge part. She's the center of it all."

"Not her. The wives. One of them is—well, that one"—she indicates Patricia Neal, on-screen with Astaire—"she's famous, right?"

"She is, and yet—I couldn't name a single film which she was in."

"*Breakfast at Tiffany's*," Aileen says promptly. "Funny because she shouldn't even be—anyway, she's in that and she was in *The Subject Was Roses*."

She doesn't know Astaire, but she has seen these films? "How old are you, Aileen?"

She stiffens. "That's not a question to ask a lady. I'm older than I look, let's just leave it at that."

Funny, he would have sworn it went the other way, that her weight and mannerisms aged her. "Did you grow up in Baltimore? Do you remember *Picture for a Sunday Afternoon*?"

Her eyes are fixed on the screen. The film's alleged shocks seem to have no effect on her. They are pretty weak and she is, after all, a nurse. But she pays strict attention. She does not answer his question, does not speak again until the end of the film, when she says, "That makes no sense. The woman's still dead. They still killed her. Why do any of them get to live?"

"In the book—"

"I"—She stops, almost as if she is trying to tamp down anger, out of respect, but she's not quite successful. "I don't care about the book. This is a *movie,* I'm watching a movie, and according to this movie, if four men put a girl in a car and roll it into the lake while she's still alive and she dies a horrible death, one of them gets to take his wife to France!"

"He is the least culpable," Gerry offers, thinking, *And it's Fred Astaire*. You don't kill Fred Astaire. In *The Towering Inferno,* Jennifer Jones died, but Astaire lived. Gerry saw that film in the old Rotunda Cinemas, where he saw so many movies. *Monty Python and the Holy Grail,* most of Woody Allen's work. Was that the Baltimore theater that had shown *The Rocky Horror Picture Show? Antici—SAY IT— pation!* No, that had played in another, larger venue. The Rotunda had been a dark, smelly dump of a place, off a narrow hallway in a large brick building that was sort of a mini-mall. Gerry felt up a couple of girls in that movie theater. He misses it. The last time he drove past the Rotunda, the old enclosed shopping center was surrounded by new apartments, and the movie theater was now a detached structure, something called a CinéBistro. What the fuck is a CinéBistro? What is happening to words?

Aileen marches downstairs, grumbling to herself. Gerry sleeps better than he has in days, paradoxically relaxed by the movie's insipid, special-effects horrors. Maybe he should watch more movies, less news.

When he wakes, he can barely wait for Phylloh's shift to start so he can ask her to review the security camera's video. She hems and haws, says she's not supposed to do this for residents, but he cajoles and bullies until he gets his way.

She calls back at about eleven A.M.

"I looked at the hours between midnight and three," she says.

"And?"

"There's nothing on your floor, Mr. Andersen. Nobody coming and going. Nobody. No one in the elevator."

"How can that be?"

"I guess nobody came to see you then, after all?"

"HOW CAN THAT BE?"

A rhetorical question, but dutiful Phylloh tries to answer. "It is an unusual time to pay a call."

That night, he stays awake like a child waiting for Santa Claus. Like a child, he can't go the distance. Like a child, he sees nothing.

Like a child, he still believes.

*1970*

AT THE AGE OF TWELVE, Gerry was much too old to believe in Santa Claus. But this, the first Christmas since his father had moved out, he decided to give his mother whatever pleasure he could by pretending to keep the faith. He even wrote a letter to put out with the cookies and milk, promised not to wake her up too early.

Only this year, he had no problem falling asleep and he knew he would have no problem staying in bed until a reasonable hour.

Christmas Eve had been a flat, gray day, with no chance of snow. The next day was expected to be quite cold, in the teens. He would be cooped up in the house with his mother, with no place to go, even if he did get the new bike he coveted, the one with the banana seat.

He was pretty sure he wasn't getting a new bike and the cost was only part of the problem. A week ago, his mother had struggled for hours to secure the tree in the holder, at one point going into the kitchen to weep. But she had come back out, eyes defiantly dry, and managed to get the tree up.

Still, he couldn't imagine his mother assembling a bike. What would he get tomorrow? He had, of course, taken a careful census of the presents beneath the tree. There had been one or two gifts large enough to be promising. And his stocking was always filled with interesting things.

When Gerry woke up and saw that it was four A.M., he was determined to go back to sleep, let his mother sleep in until at least eight. He wondered why he had awakened. Oh no. She was crying again. Or maybe talking in her sleep. More than once, he had heard her call out his father's name at night, angry and bitter. At least, he assumed that was the Gerry whose name she called, given the tone.

Yes, there it was again. His name. But also *his* name, the man who had left them. She was saying it over and over and over. "Oh, Gerry. Gerry, Gerry, Gerry. Please, Gerry."

He hated hearing this, but it usually ended after a minute or two. He never tried to interrupt because waking up a sleep talker had to be as bad as waking up a sleepwalker.

Only it didn't end tonight. She sounded as if she was in pain. He got up and tiptoed to the hall. His mother's door, usually closed tight at night, was cracked. Gerry put his eye to the gap.

His mother was sitting upright in bed, moving up and down, as if she were on a merry-go-round, but going very fast.

She was on top of a man.

She was on top of his father.

Her back to him, her dark hair loose and wild, she couldn't see him. But his father seemed to look right at him. It was all Gerry could do not to scream or run. But he backed away slowly and went to his room, marveling that they were still going. He had learned about sex in school that fall, but he had assumed it happened quickly, requiring no more than a few seconds. And he thought that the man had to be on top. But maybe that was for making babies. Clearly, his mother and his departed father wouldn't be trying to make a baby.

His mother's voice notched up a bit. "Do you love me, Gerry? Am I the one you really love?" He couldn't make out his father's answer, a low rumble.

He put his pillow over his head and, somehow, went back to sleep. When he woke to the cold house—their old oil burner was no match for temperatures in the teens—his mother was already up and dressed, her bed made.

She was in the kitchen. Alone, thank God. It was a dream. It had to be a dream. What a strange, awful dream to have about one's mother.

"Look at you, slugabed. I guess you want to get right to the presents before breakfast. Just let me get my coffee."

When there had been three of them, they had each taken a turn opening a gift. This year, the first with just two, Gerry started by giving his mother his present for her, a boxed set of perfume and moisturizer from Hutzler's.

"Now you pick."

He knew which of the two big boxes he wanted to open first and was about to grab it when he noticed a third box, even bigger than the other two.

"Where did this come from?"

"Read the card," his mother said.

*To Gerry, from Dad.*

"When did this get here?"

"Oh, your father had it sent weeks ago."

"When, though? I get home from school before you come home from work. I'm the one who signs for packages."

His mother paused and he saw, in the pause, that she was deciding which lie to tell.

"He sent it to Dr. Papadakis's office, knowing what a nosy parker you are. It's been hidden in the basement for weeks. I put it out last night," she said. "After you went to bed. Your old mother still has a few tricks up her sleeve."

*Oh, don't you just.* Could it have been someone else in his mother's bed? Another man, not his father? Maybe another woman, too. There had been two strangers in his mother's bed while she was readying the house for the morning. That made more sense than what he thought he had seen.

His father's gift to him was a tool kit, but a babyish one, insulting. Gerry was already using real tools, the tools his father had left behind, learning to make small repairs as the house needed them. Sitting there with this toy in his lap, knowing he was long past toys, Gerry decided his next project would be going to the hardware store in Towson and buying a chain lock for the front door, which would keep him and his mother safe at night, while making it impossible for anyone to come and go.

*March 8*

AND SO, at the age of sixty-one, Gerry enjoys—no, that's the wrong verb—Gerry *receives* his first actual house call from a doctor. It has not been easy to arrange. In order to find a specialist who is willing to see him in his home, he first had to join a so-called concierge medical practice, talk to the doctor, and then ask for that doctor's help in procuring a neurogerontologist, one who is willing to travel to him. The head of the practice asks him a lot of questions about his pain medications, seems far more interested in those than his mother's Alzheimer's. But, ultimately, she finds him a specialist.

The specialist has a name, Andre Bevington, that could be lifted from the pages of a romance novel—and a face to match. He is beautiful, there is no other word for it. Devastatingly beautiful, there is no other adverb for it. Gerry has never been attracted to men, was never comfortable with the way Luke joked about corrupting him.

Complimented, but not comfortable. But this man is like a work of art. No—in portrait form, his beauty would be crass, not unlike that portrait of Donald Trump that Trump bought for his own country club, using his foundation's fund. In art, this kind of perfection is tacky. But as a work of nature, it is something at which one can only marvel. Gerry finds himself thinking, *Of course you work with geriatric neurological issues. If you worked with age peers, everyone would fall in love with you. Good lord, if you had been a gynecologist, women would be begging to climb into those stirrups three times a year.* A connoisseur of beautiful women—isn't every straight man?—Gerry has never really spent much time thinking about beautiful men. But this! What's it like to walk around inside such a body? Does the doctor know? How could he not? Is he grateful? He'd better be.

"Andre," he says, holding out his hand. "Pleased to meet you."

They talk through Gerry's history—the fall. *Had he been experiencing any tremors or instability before the fall? No? Excellent.* His pain meds. The doctor is curious to pinpoint the time of day of what he calls the "instances."

"You're very thorough," Gerry says at one point. "Patient." A thought strikes him. "Why are we called patients? Do you know the etymology?"

"It's the same Latin root for the noun and the adjective. It comes from *pati,* the word for 'suffering.' I like how your mind works, Gerry. And your mind seems to work well. But we have, by my count"—he looks at the small notebook in which he has been jotting—"six instances, and they seem to be escalating. A letter, three phone calls, a tweet, a visit. If we put aside the tweet, which was seen by your assistant before it was taken down, I do detect a pattern. These things happen when you're close to sleep. In fact, they happen when you *are* asleep. And they're remarkably consistent. They all center on a person, a woman, claiming to be the model for a character in your novel, but you say there is no such person."

"The letter doesn't fit, though. I saw that during the day."

"True. And it was before the accident. But there's an Occam's razor explanation for the letter—you probably did get something with a familiar address, but it was the mass mailer you initially took it for. That's why you didn't open it right away. I think you would have recognized the precise address used in your novel. You strike me as quite sharp, detail-oriented. But it was junk mail and it got tossed. One of those extended car warranties or something like that. That's all there is to it."

He should yearn to believe this doctor, but he finds himself wondering if anyone this good-looking can really excel at his job.

"Are you sure it's not my meds? Or something worse? I have to be mindful that the disease that killed my mother does have a genetic component."

"Look, the good news is that delusional disorder is exceedingly rare. *Exceedingly.* And these are not the sort of delusions a person normally experiences. They're almost too logical, too consistent. My hunch is that they really are dreams. You're experiencing a kind of déjà vu. Do you know what déjà vu really is? It's a sequencing error. Epileptics often have a déjà vu experience right before a seizure. It also can be related to small strokes."

"Strokes!"

The doctor holds up his hands. Even his palms are beautiful. "Your blood pressure is good, you've taken excellent care of yourself. When you're in better shape, I'd like to get you in for an MRI, just to be sure. But I'd also like to ask—how are you feeling, Gerry?"

"What do you mean, exactly?"

"Are you unhappy?"

"Well, of course, I'm not happy with the situation. The injury and these—unexplained phenomena."

"Were you happy before you fell?"

It takes him a long time to answer. Who wants to answer such a question? It's why he has avoided therapy all these years. Everyone's unhappy if they have even a sliver of intelligence. Who can be happy in this world?

"My mother had died and the last months of her life were awful. I moved to Baltimore, thinking I would be tending to her for quite some time, and she died almost immediately after I closed on this apartment. I don't like Baltimore. Well, that's not quite right. Baltimore's okay. But I prefer New York. I had a life there. I don't know anyone here, not anymore; my work hasn't been going well—I'm not sure I want to write anymore, even if I'm not on the verge of becoming a gibbering fool. I broke up with my longtime companion, which was all for the best, believe me, but I'm lonely. Who wouldn't be unhappy?"

His words surprise him, in their specificity and volume. *Unhappy* is such a big word. Once said aloud, it can never be taken back. He has tried so hard never to say it out loud over the past twenty years. He is too aware of the good things in his life—the career, the money, the freedom. How could he possibly be unhappy?

Because he is.

"How do you feel about trying an antidepressant?"

Whoa. One thing to admit to unhappiness. He's not ready to make the full leap to *depressed.*

"I don't know—I've never used anything of the sort. I'm sorry, I don't like medication, I just don't. I'm practically a Christian Scientist that way."

"It's something to think about. If I had to make a bet, my hunch is that an MRI won't find anything. I don't think there's a thing wrong with your head, Gerry. Your brain is fine. Again—Occam's razor. What's the likely explanation? You're having bad dreams."

"What about the phone calls?"

The doctor's beautiful face clouds. "Maybe someone *is* punking you by phone. But the woman at the window—there's no other explanation. For now, take notes. Don't worry. Establish a good sleep system—less TV time, and don't fall asleep while watching it. No screens for at least an hour before bed. But I am confident that you don't have dementia."

Gerry knows he should be cheered by this assessment. He is not crazy. He is not declining. He's depressed, and who wouldn't be? The delusions are bad dreams. The phone calls are—

*Phylloh,* he thinks. Phylloh knows he's here, knows when he's alone. Phylloh has the power to let people upstairs. Phylloh is the one who checked the security video. Or so she said. He will make a discreet inquiry about Phylloh. He has no idea why she would do such a thing, but clearly his tormentor is crazy and crazy requires no logic, no rhyme or reason.

*1978*

## "LET'S GO TO ATLANTIC CITY."

"Why?"

"To enter the Miss America pageant. To gamble, Gerry. Let's gamble."

Gerry had no interest in gambling and he wasn't sure it was a good idea to go on a road trip with Luke. "We don't have a car."

"We can borrow Tara's."

"Won't we have to ask her to come with us, then?"

"Would that be a problem?"

"We don't have to do everything as a threesome," he said.

"You dumb fucker. You did it with her, didn't you?"

"She's my best friend. It was—inevitable."

"*I'm* your best friend. Hey, does that mean you're going to sleep with me now?"

Luke had come out to Gerry at the end of their freshman year. Matched up by the housing lottery, they had been happy to discover that they genuinely liked each other, and they pledged to continue living together. But it was important to Luke, once they made their compulsory arrangement a voluntary one, that Gerry know he was gay. At the time, the relatively few gay students on campus tended to be flamboyant. Luke was promiscuous but discreet. He and Gerry had never worked out a code for what to do when one of them wanted the room alone because Gerry's girlfriend during sophomore year had a single and Luke preferred to go to New York. He would take the train up on Friday night and return late Sunday. Gerry had no idea where Luke went or what he did, if he had a steady man or if he preferred having sex with lots and lots of strangers. And he had no vocabulary with which to inquire.

Luke's schtick about being attracted to Gerry was a running gag, which made him uncomfortable. The fact that it made him uncomfortable made him even more uncomfortable. And then Luke would go for a while without making the joke and Gerry would wonder why he stopped.

"Based on what happened with Tara—no. It was a stupid thing to do and it loused up our friendship."

"Women can't do just-sex."

"*I* can't do just-sex. That's why I screwed up the friendship. We have so much in common; we make each other laugh. I just had to know what the sex would be like."

"And?"

"Not that great. For either of us." Gerry was still puzzling over that fact. He was even more puzzled by Tara's assessment: "Our damage doesn't mesh." What damage? He didn't consider himself damaged and, frankly, Tara's alcoholic father seemed small potatoes to him.

"Maybe your luck will change in Atlantic City."

Luke managed to get Tara's car without Tara attached and they headed to the beach. It was amazing to Gerry that one state could contain both Princeton and Atlantic City. It was delightful, at first, to smell the ocean air and see the street names he remembered from his Monopoly set. He called out the names and Luke responded with the colors, then the costs and even the rents.

"Kentucky Avenue. Three houses, seven hundred dollars. Four houses, eight-seventy-five."

Gerry wanted to play blackjack, because it was the closest thing to a game of skill, but he was not prepared for the speed at which it was played and he quickly lost the forty dollars he had staked himself. Luke left the table up fifty dollars. He wanted to shoot craps, a game Gerry could not follow at all. Luke started a run and people gathered, enjoying the vicarious thrill, or perhaps rooting for his lucky streak to end. A woman in a bareback leotard and filmy skirt tried to flirt with him, but Luke ignored her, ignored the drinks that started coming his way. Gerry realized that Luke was in his own private world, just him and the dice and the chips. He won another hundred dollars, tipped the croupier, and moved on to roulette. Gerry decided to go in search of a beer. When he left the roulette table, Luke was up two hundred dollars.

By the time he got back, it was all gone.

"I bet on the black," Luke said. "Fifty-fifty shot and I lost. Do you have any cash?"

"No."

"I wonder if I could get a line of credit—"

"Luke, don't be crazy."

"But that was the point of coming here, to be crazy. Do you know the single best moment in gambling, Gerry?"

"Winning, of course."

"No, it's the moment *before*. Before the ball lands, before the card is shown, before the dice settle, one of those rare moments when you don't know what's going to happen next. Think about all the books we read, the movies we love—how often are you truly surprised by a story? Or your life? We always sort of know where we're going, what's going to happen. But not in a casino."

Gerry opened his mouth to object, but he could not think of a story that truly contradicted Luke's point. Only last week, they had gone to see this new movie, *Halloween*, which was full of surprises, but—was it? It was clear which girl would live, that the children would not be harmed.

"Sounds unsettling to me," he said. "Like staring into the abyss."

"Oh, no, it's the greatest feeling in the world. I would live in that moment every waking second if I could. It's like *Rocky Horror Picture Show*. 'I see you quiver with antici—'" He held the pause even longer than Tim Curry. "'—*pation*.'"

"Okay, do you know what I'm going to say next?"

"Something sensible, no doubt."

Somehow, Gerry got Luke to take a walk on the boardwalk, where the fresh air was a shock to their lungs after the casino. Despite the autumnal chill, they took off their shoes and walked on the beach.

"If I can't gamble, I need to find someone to fuck," Luke said. "Don't worry, it won't be you. Not tonight, at least."

"Let's just drive back, Luke."

"I'll meet you at the car in an hour."

"Luke, that's crazy—"

"What?" Mock outrage. "You don't think I can get laid in an hour? Gerry, I could probably be done in fifteen minutes."

In the end, it took him ninety. He showed up at the car, brandishing a twenty. "He thought I was trade and who am I to disabuse someone of that notion? I would have paid him, not that I had any money. I like older men. They're experienced."

Gerry drove, although Luke had promised Tara that no one else would touch the wheel of her precious Tercel. It was evening now, but still not late. They would be back on campus before midnight. They could order pizza, drink beer.

Gerry had no words, no context for his friend's behavior. Luke, exhausted by whatever he had been doing, fell asleep in the car and Gerry kept stealing glances at his profile, so smooth and perfect and pretty. What was it like to be that pretty? What was it like to be a homosexual? Would anyone choose to be one? Gerry had been with only three women, but the first time he entered one, he couldn't believe how amazing it was, how literature, which he held in such high esteem, had failed to inform him fully of the wonders of sex. According to Luke, it was the moment before winning—so therefore the moment before ejaculation, or maybe contact—that thrilled him. That made no sense to Gerry. When he came inside a woman, it was about as happy as he had ever been. And he knew, because of his father, that he had to guard himself against becoming obsessive about this particular joy, that he must never hurt another person in his pursuit of that pleasure.

Was Luke happy? He could not ask the question without immediately jumping to the Auden line: *The question was absurd.* Of course Luke wasn't happy. The things he had done in Atlantic City—that was not what a happy person did. That kind of compulsive behavior was the opposite of happy.

"I don't know, Gerry," Luke said, his eyes still closed. "Are you happy? Is anyone happy?"

Gerry had not spoken aloud. He was pretty sure he had not spoken aloud. Was Luke sitting there wondering at Gerry's behavior, judging his choices?

"I certainly think happiness is possible," he said.

"Even for people like us? I don't know. If we were happy, we wouldn't want to be writers, right?"

"There have been happy writers. Good ones. It's possible. I have to believe it's possible."

"Which is it, Gerry? Is it possible or do you have to believe it's possible?"

When Gerry failed to answer, Luke sighed and rolled to his side. "I can remove the cause," he said, "but not the symptoms."

It took Gerry a beat to realize that Luke was simply finishing the *Rocky Horror* song "Sweet Transvestite."

*March 12*

"**WHAT DID YOU DO TO PHYLLOH?**" Victoria asks him.

"Nothing!" Gerry says, offended by the very suggestion that he's in the position to do anything to anyone.

"She's gotten terribly frosty."

*Phylloh is phrosty,* he thinks. Then he remembers. He had called Phylloh's supervisor, to make sure she wasn't lying to him about the tapes. He had decided the girl meant no overt harm, but it had occurred to him that maybe she'd simply fibbed about watching the security tapes from the elevator. Phylloh had always struck him as a little lazy. He had forgotten that she'd told him she wasn't supposed to review the tapes for residents under any circumstances.

"Maybe it's a general mood? Or she has a specific grievance with you?" *Phylloh should be happy she wasn't phired,* Gerry thinks.

He is trying to work the *New York Times* crossword puzzle with his astronaut pen, which turns out not to be an invention of *Seinfeld* but a real thing, an essential tool given how often Gerry is flat on his back. He has splurged on three, at a cost of $150 total, and he is careful to keep them in the drawer of the table next to his bed, along with his usual cache of Moleskine notebooks. He is horrified that he is having trouble finishing the Monday puzzle. During the months of caring for his mother, he had lost the habit of completing the puzzle daily, but he has been working it again since his accident and this is troubling. He sometimes used to stall on Saturday, the hardest day, but never Monday! Mondays were for morons.

Victoria says: "I can't imagine anything *I've* done, but I don't care if she doesn't want to talk to me. She's so chatty and it's all so banal. I just want to pick up the packages and move on. If I didn't have to check for packages, I would take the elevator from the garage straight to the apartment, bypass the front desk entirely."

Sometimes he feels as if Victoria is trying on his personality, his attitudes. They do not suit her. In this world where people are quick to speak of entitlement and privilege, some nuances have been lost, it seems to Gerry. Yes, there are privileges in being white, male, and moneyed, and he supposes one should be alert to those birthright perks. He certainly tries to be. But there are privileges that one *earns* through accomplishment and sheer longevity. Victoria has no right to be haughty about another person being "chatty" and "banal." Has she ever listened to herself? Besides, Gerry's six decades of life trump Victoria's two and change.

But if he said those exact words out loud, she would take great offense. She might even complain that the use of the forty-fifth president's name as a verb *triggered* her. *Triggered*. A sloppy term, to Gerry's way of thinking. A trigger is something someone deliberately pulls and it leads to a very specific sequence of events. If one is triggered, then one is the weapon or the snare, no? The recurrence of painful memories is simply day-to-day life. It's nothing at all like firing a gun.

He does his upper-body exercises. At least his body seems to respond to stimulation, even if his mind does not. He is getting stronger above the waist, but sitting is still terribly painful and there is nothing to be done for that. Maybe he should cut back on his medication, although Aileen is phlegmatically determined that he take the full dosage.

The phone rings with the staccato double-buzz that indicates the front desk is calling. He's so bored he picks it up.

"She's back," says Phylloh. She *is* frosty.

"Who?"

"Your wife."

"Wife?" Lucy? Gretchen? Sarah? He's so desperate for stimulation he'd be happy to see any of them. Even Gretchen.

"The one who was here in February."

*Keeping careful track of my visitors, are you, Phylloh?*

"Oh. She was never my wife."

"Well, she's here."

"I guess you can send her up."

"I already did. She said you were expecting her."

He isn't. Then again, Margot's talent is for the unexpected. Exciting in the early, heady days of dating, especially when applied to sex. Extremely tedious as life goes on.

"Gerry," she says, sweeping in, "you are going to have to find me a place to stay."

She is wearing a voluminous cape. No—a coat with a cape-like attachment. Dark and velvety. Not unlike what the woman in the window wore that night, but if at night all cats are gray, then all coats are black.

"Why?"

"Because you sold the apartment, silly."

"Months ago, yes. Besides, what about *your* place? Don't you still have that studio in Chelsea?"

"The tenant, the subletter, is refusing to leave. Can you believe it?"

Yes, he can. He also can believe that there is no tenant, that Margot no longer has her studio apartment in Chelsea, that she was, in fact, the subletter.

"Surely you have some legal standing?"

"Thiru thinks it will be okay when the lease is up—that's what I get for doing things according to Hoyle."

The quaint old saying, something that has no meaning in today's world, reminds Gerry of why he was charmed by Margot once upon a time. Ditzy as she can be, she is clever and well-read; he never had to explain his references. It had not been a mistake to take up with her. His only mistake was thinking that he would have any more luck than his predecessors when it came time to leave her. Clearly, foisting her off on Thiru isn't working, not yet. Thiru is much smarter about women than Gerry. Despite or maybe because of having logged one more marriage.

"Margot, I'm going to have to tell you a hard truth. I cannot provide for you and, furthermore, I am under no obligation to provide for you. What we had was lovely. But it's over. It's been over for quite some time, as we both know. I thought you understood that when I came down to Baltimore and put my apartment on the market *six months ago.*"

"I assumed you would be moving back."

"So did I." He still does, just not for a year or two. New York is a much better place to grow old than Baltimore, he is sure of that now. Oh why had he sold the apartment up there? He is never going to be able to buy anything as nice as he had. New York seems determined to shed itself of everything but billionaires and those old-timers who had the good luck to buy and hold property when it was cheap.

"What am I supposed to do? Where am I supposed to go?"

He has the strangest feeling of déjà vu or, as dreamy Dr. Bevington described it, a sequencing error. He realizes that she's basically playing the final scene of *Gone with the Wind*. She swept in here like Scarlett visiting Rhett in jail, and now she's jumped to the end of the story. He can't say he doesn't give a damn; he's not that cold.

But he doesn't give a damn.

"Margot, I'm sure there's someone who can help you. Right now, I'm not that person. Obviously, I'm not in the position to help anyone."

Her eyes narrow. "You always were a selfish bastard. Everyone thinks you're so good. *You* think you're good. But you're a terrible person, Gerry. Nothing's worse than a bad person who thinks he's good."

"I'm sorry you feel that way, but then—all the better that we cease contact."

"I know things about you. Things you wouldn't want me to tell people." Her voice is rising. There's no doubt that Victoria, at work in his office downstairs, can hear the tone, if not the actual words. "You think your secrets won't catch up with you, but some have. I could make life very difficult for you, Gerry."

This threat of exposure, the penny-ante blackmail essence of it all—hollow as it is, Gerry is enraged, which is probably what Margot is counting on. Gerry has always had a horror of being talked about. He has been lucky to have the kind of career in which his biography is of little interest, despite the three marriages. He never lied about himself, but he downplayed the more extreme aspects. *Only child of a salesman and a housewife, parents divorced when he was young, father remarried and had a second family.* No one needed to know that the two families had overlapped for almost ten years. He's lucky that no one ever tried to find Gerald Andersen Sr. when he was alive. Gerald Senior would have been happy to talk, talk, talk to anyone who expressed interest.

"If you have stories to tell, Margot, tell them. Better yet, write them down for that memoir you're always threatening to write. Oh, wait, that's the one thing you can't do, create. You've had to settle for fucking the men who can."

He knows his words are cruel, that he has used his intimate knowledge of Margot to locate her single greatest insecurity and press hard on it. Still, he is not prepared when she slaps him and then, for good measure, scrapes her fingernails across his cheek, drawing blood.

He yelps, more in shock than pain. No one has ever touched him in this way, *no one*. And he has never longed to put his hands on a woman, but he does now. He pushes her, hard, and when she comes back at him, he instinctively reaches for the heretofore useless walker by his bed and deploys it as a combination shield–jousting pole. Some ludicrous part of his mind triumphantly dredges up a fact: *Jousting is the official sport of Maryland! Not lacrosse, as many people assume, but jousting.*

On his third thrust, he connects and sends Margot flying. She lands hard on the floor; her purse flies open, the contents scatter. She still carries a healthy supply of condoms, Gerry sees. It's a paradox worth noting that the spontaneous courtesan has to be prepared.

Victoria comes running up the steps, only to freeze at the tableau before her. Margot rises to her knees, makes a great show of rubbing her backside, but Gerry knows what a fractured tailbone feels like and he is confident she would be screaming in pain if she had injured herself seriously. She begins crawling across the cement floor, gathering her things.

"Call the police." But it's Margot who says this to Victoria, not Gerry. He has no desire at all to bring police into this ugly scene, to have it recorded officially. Victoria, her back pressed against the wall in horror, would seem to be in accord with him.

"I don't think that's what you want," he says, pointing to his face. "You drew first blood."

"I'm surprised you have blood, you amphibian."

"Just go, Margot," he says. "And don't come back. The front desk will be informed to have security escort you out if you show up here again. I'll get a restraining order, if that's what it takes. Stay away from me—"

"Or?" she says with a sneer, still daring to question his manhood despite the fact that she's just been bested by him. She takes her things to the kitchen counter, puts her purse back together, in no hurry at all.

"You'll be sorry."

"No, you'll be sorry. I know things, Gerry. Things you don't know I know, things you wouldn't want anyone to learn."

He has no idea what she's talking about.

She sees his wallet on the counter, where it has sat for weeks now, used primarily by Victoria when she orders food deliveries, but always with some cash. Gerry feels insecure without cash. Margot picks it up, rifles it, takes out several bills. "The least you can do is pay for my fucking cab," she says.

At the front door, she stops by a little mirror that hangs next to it, an organizer with hooks for keys, a shelf for mail. She checks her hair, touches up her lipstick, taking her sweet time.

"Could you just leave, Margot?"

"This isn't over," she says.

"No, I'm pretty sure it is." He feels an enormous burden lifted when she goes, slamming the door behind her. He has survived the curse of Margot Chasseur.

HE IS WORRIED, as he drifts off to sleep that night, that the delusions will return. It was after Margot's last visit that he received— or thought he received—the first call. He swallows his Ambien and calcium pill and, for the first time in a while, enjoys an almost dreamless sleep, one in which there is an overall feeling of well-being. The phone doesn't ring; no terrifying apparitions interrupt. When he opens his eyes it is past seven o'clock and light has begun seeping into the room. Daylight saving time arrived only a few days before, so the dawn's early light isn't quite as early as it was a week ago. In the gray, gauzy gloom, he looks at the ceiling and wonders at his sense of contentment. He feels warm this morning and, strangely, *loved,* although the one person who loved him reliably is gone. He doesn't remember dreaming, but he feels the way a child might after being comforted for a nightmare.

He finds the remote that raises the blinds. The sky to the east is shot through with streaks of orange-red. When he bought the apartment, he had pretended to be disdainful of this high-tech touch, but the blinds were essential, given the eastern exposure. And the remote secretly gave him a thrill. In his childhood, villains and playboys always had lairs with remotes that closed screens, turned on music, lowered desks, raised beds. *"No, Mr. Bond, I expect you to die."*

He thinks of Francis Scott Key watching Baltimore hold its own against the British in the War of 1812. His mind is lively this morning, his mind is itself again, hopscotching from cultural reference to cultural reference. When he visited St. Paul's Cathedral in London as a cheeky twentysomething, how he had delighted in reminding his tour guide that the illustrious Major General Ross, honored there with a plaque near Wellington's tomb, had not been victorious at the Battle of North Point. *The rockets' red glare! Bombs bursting in air! Gave proof through the night. Oh, say can you see?* Or, if you're at an Orioles game, *OOOOOOOOOOOOOOOOOOO, say can you see?*

Francis Scott Key was one of F. Scott Fitzgerald's ancestors, Gerry thinks, enjoying the free association. Gerry used to take women to Fitzgerald's grave site in that little cemetery smack-dab in the middle of Rockville. He had ambivalent feelings about *Gatsby,* but he almost always got laid after that maneuver. God, he misses sex.

*What is the dark heap on the floor?* It looks like a pile of clothes. Except—is that an arm?

*Wake up,* he says to himself. *Wake up, wake up, wake up.* But he is awake.

He struggles to a sitting position. The pile of clothes—or maybe it's a pile of sheets and Aileen, prone to distraction, left them here, she can be quite messy—is fairly close to his bedside and while he cannot move his bad leg, he has the core strength to lean out of the bed for a better look.

The pile of clothes is Margot, her black cape surrounding her like a velvety puddle. Did he dream the second part of their encounter? Did he push her hard enough to harm her? Didn't she leave? Wasn't Victoria here when everything happened?

Margot's face is turned away from him. He takes the walker, the one he used in his own defense, and prods the body until her head lolls toward him. A happy little salesman appears to be dancing on Margot's face.

It's the handle of his father's old letter opener, Acme School Furniture, and it's been plunged into Margot's left eye up to the hilt.

Light fills the room; the crimson sunrise has yielded quickly to a blue sky with cumulus clouds skittering by like sailboats. It's going to be a gorgeous day. *Oh, say can you see? Oh, say can you see? Oh, say can you see?*

# PART II

# GIRLS

*March 13*

THUD, THUD, THUD. Thud, thud, thud.

It's a familiar sound, but Gerry can't identify it, not with the blood pounding in his ears and his mind darting around, trying to make sense of the tableau before him.

Thud, thud, thud.

Maybe it's the telltale heart, although how would one bury a body beneath a floor of poured concrete? If only. If only there were a heart still beating inside that black puddle of cloth, if only a brain were still humming inside Margot's damaged skull.

Thud, thud, thud.

It's Aileen's heavy tread on the stairs. Shit. She always comes up to say goodbye in the mornings, although Gerry usually feigns sleep to avoid conversation with her. Maybe he should do that now, play possum. Maybe he *is* asleep. A dream would be dreamy. This is a dream, it has to be a dream, and when he awakes, the shape will be gone, in the same way the apparition disappeared that one night. Opioid-fueled delusions, dementia, who cares? All that matters is an explanation for what he thinks he sees on the floor. He closes his eyes. Maybe his eyes were always closed.

Thud, thud, thud.

Then—nothing. The moment of silence stretches out. He keeps thinking she will scream and when she doesn't, it gives him hope. Her breathing is regular, in and out, a little huffy as always after she climbs the stairs, but normal, measured.

"Oh my," she says. "What happened here?"

He opens his eyes. There stands Aileen in her puffy coat, arms akimbo, the not-so-little teapot, tall and stout. Her knitting bag dangles from the crook of her elbow.

"I don't know, I honestly don't know," Gerry says. "She showed up yesterday, but I sent her away. She attacked me, she scratched me, and I fended her off, but I didn't—I wouldn't. And that was earlier, when Victoria was here. I didn't—I couldn't—I don't know how—"

"She sneaked back in," Aileen says. Or asks. Her calmness is surreal, but she is a nurse, she has seen things that others have not.

"She must have. I don't know how. She knows I have to leave the front door unlocked, maybe she hid in the stairwell between the floors—"

He sounds ludicrous. Could he have done this? That sounds ludicrous, too, the idea of Margot spending hours in a stairwell. But Victoria was here until five and there was no body on the floor when Aileen arrived at seven. This has happened overnight. He is proud that he can pinpoint this, then appalled. Margot is dead, in his apartment, and not even she is drama queen enough to plunge a letter opener into her own eye.

"This is bad, Mr. Andersen." For once, he is grateful for Aileen's flat aspect, her gift for understatement.

"I guess we need to call the police," he says.

"Sure," Aileen says, although she doesn't move. "Obviously, it was self-defense."

"*Yes,*" he says. "I mean, I think. I don't remember anything." He wonders if sleep-murdering is another potential side effect of Ambien. "Any statement I give would be inherently false."

"You need time," she says. "The worst thing to do in an emergency is go off half-cocked without a plan."

"Yes," he agrees fervently. "Maybe call a lawyer or—"

"No, not a lawyer. Trust *me,*" she says. "I can take care of this."

"How?"

"Trust me," she repeats. She takes off her coat, drapes it over a chair. He does not remonstrate with her for this. "Put yourself into my hands."

Not the image he would have chosen, but he will do exactly that. He has to. He literally cannot imagine what it would be like to follow any other course of action. To call the police or a lawyer. To tell Thiru. No, he will trust Aileen.

She continues with appealing confidence, energized by this new task: "Cancel Claude. Then call Victoria and tell her not to come in today."

"On what grounds?"

"You're the writer. Make something up."

He does. He calls Victoria and tells her that he needs her to drive up to Princeton and inspect its special collections. "I want to find out what the experience of accessing my papers will be like for future researchers," he says. "Tell them that you are interested in seeing the collections of Toni Morrison and, say, F. Scott Fitzgerald."

"Do you think those are the best, um, comps?"

An impertinent question, but he doesn't have the luxury of challenging Victoria's assessment of his place in American literature. Although, he can't help noting to himself that his body of work is larger than Fitzgerald's.

"My thinking is that those will be two of the most in-demand, that library staff should be used to scholars asking to see their papers. If they can't handle this request, then I can't expect them to do well by those who might want to examine my papers."

"The drive alone—"

"I know. It is a lot. You could take the train, but it wouldn't save much time in the end. And it will be a long day no matter how efficient you are. Why don't you stay in a hotel—I can recommend a nice inn, near campus—and spend the night, break the work up over two days and then take Friday off to make up for all the extra hours."

Aileen, who is scrubbing the floor, gives him a rubber-gloved thumbs-up.

Aileen's efficiency today surprises him. Aileen, so slow and dull when going about her normal job of caring for him, has rallied admirably in the matter of removing a corpse and cleaning up after it. It's like a reality television show in his own living room. He had watched from his bed as she wrapped Margot's body in a fitted white sheet, presumably one of the ones he keeps for the never-used sofa bed in his study, then dragged it down the stairs like a toboggan.

"Good thing you like the skinny ones," Aileen had said, huffing and puffing.

"Where will you—"

"The fewer questions you ask," she told him, "the better. Not knowing anything, not remembering anything—that's an asset."

So the body has been removed, the floor is scrubbed. She has washed the letter opener, a cheerful Lady Macbeth, humming as she works, and placed it back on the end table he uses as a nightstand. Gerry asks the Google app on his phone a question: "How do police find blood evidence on objects?" This takes him down a rabbit hole of luminol stories. The letter opener is far from their only problem. Maybe they should just get rid of it? But they can't get rid of the poured concrete floor, which potentially could hold on to its trace memories of Margot's death forever.

"Aileen, do you think that—?"

"You have to let me do the thinking."

Terrifying, but he accedes.

She asks for his credit card and makes a series of mysterious phone calls. He catches references to cubic feet and expedited delivery. Aileen gets testy at one point. "Tomorrow is not expedited," she says. "Today is expedited. Don't you know what words mean?" She hangs up on that person, dials another number. This conversation is odder still. "Yes, I am aware that deer season is over, but I hit one with my car."

And, more often than usual, given that she is not normally here during the day, she appears by his bedside with pills. He wants to protest, but he is so grateful for the sleep, which provides the hope that this is a nightmare from which he will wake.

He picks up the letter opener, presses it to his own face, just below the eye. Skin and bone would be no match for it.

## 2016

"YOU MUST HAVE THE UNI."

Gerry looked up, skeptical. Already grumpy at being tricked into going to a fancy restaurant—he had thought he was meeting Thiru for soup dumplings, having no idea where Extra Place was, beyond being on the Lower East Side—he was in no mood to be told what he must eat, or drink. He wanted to get out of the restaurant as fast as possible.

But this Momofuku Ko was not designed for speedy dining, much to Gerry's dismay. The only option available was a "tasting menu," dreaded words to Gerry's ears. Probably Thiru's reason for choosing it. He had an agenda, one that would take time to lay out. And the service was oversolicitous, which Gerry hated. He preferred the gruff indifference of the city's diners, places that were disappearing one by one. Where was the New York of the late 1980s, or even the one at the beginning of the twenty-first century? After the second or third course, he stopped the pretense of eating, regarding his food with arms folded, like a grumpy child.

But the woman who was insisting that he must try the uni was another patron. Tall, thin, stylish. Sexy, frankly. She didn't linger or try to introduce herself, simply returned to her table, where she was dining with what Gerry assumed was a finance type, based on the pinstripes and the pocket square.

He didn't realize he was still looking at her until Thiru snapped his fingers to get his attention. "Gerry."

"What?"

"I was saying Rudin gets things made." Thiru began ticking off the names of various film and television projects, most of which meant nothing to Gerry.

"He didn't get *The Corrections* made," he said. Although Gerry disdained most gossip, even literary gossip, there were certain writers whose careers he tracked. He didn't consider Franzen the gold standard of his generation, but others did, so he kept tabs. And he was sincerely disappointed when the *Corrections* adaptation fell through. He had hoped the television series would highlight what Gerry considered the novel's myriad flaws.

"No one bats a thousand," Thiru said.

"Look, it's not even a good option. It's insultingly low."

*Dream Girl* had been optioned three times so far. The book was like a trick wallet, tied to a string. Gerry and Thiru put it on the sidewalk and people kept chasing it. But he couldn't tell Thiru that he would prefer just optioning it over and over. The film production of his first novel had been disappointing, in large part because no one seemed to care that much. Gerry had hoped for either an outstanding adaptation or a total botch that would lead to impassioned tributes to the source material. No one had anything to say about the movie, good or bad. They took his firstborn, in many ways his sweetest and most pliable child, and rendered it *dull*. Boring, polite, bloodless, with nothing really there in the end. So, no, he didn't want to see *Dream Girl* produced. He wanted people to pay him for it over and over again.

Also, he was miffed that Rudin had bought Franzen's book, not his, back in 2001. He didn't want to be anyone's second choice.

"Options have changed, Gerry. It's hard to get that big money now. But an actress is attached, someone who wants to play Aubrey." Thiru shared a name that meant nothing to Gerry, then showed him a photograph on his phone.

"Beautiful. Absolutely beautiful. Too beautiful, in fact. Aubrey isn't conventionally pretty. That's central to the book."

"Jesus Christ, Gerry, of course she's going to be beautiful. Have you been to the movies?"

"Not recently, no. I do like that one television show."

"Which one?"

"That one that people talk about."

"You're going to have to narrow it down, Gerry."

"He sells drugs?"

"*Breaking Bad*?"

"That's it."

"Gerry, it's not even on the air anymore."

"I guess I'm watching it on iTunes."

He sampled the uni. He had no idea what it was, but he had to admit, it was pretty good.

"What's next?" Thiru asked.

"I want to take something low-culture and elevate it."

"Like *Zone One* or *Station Eleven*?"

Gerry frowned. He always insisted he did not begrudge any *talented* writer his or her success, but he also considered himself an original, marching to the beat of his own drum. He was trying to be a good sport about the attention that Colson Whitehead was getting for *The Underground Railroad* right now, but it wasn't always easy.

"Yes and no," he said. "I'm not interested in zombies or pandemics. I'm interested in—don't laugh—soap operas."

Thiru's chopsticks clattered to his plate and came dangerously close to sending up a flume of sauce onto his beautiful lapels. Today's suit was plaid. Probably a precise kind of plaid, with a special name, but all Gerry knew was that it was gray with subtle crisscrosses of burgundy, gold, and green. Fashion bored Gerry even more than food did. He lived in khakis and oxford cloth shirts, cotton sweaters from the Gap.

"What?"

"My mother watched them and then, in the 1970s, when I was a teenager, inevitably I did, too. There was only one television in our house and she had one afternoon off, Thursdays. We watched the ABC shows together. *All My Children, One Life to Live, General Hospital.* And even though she could watch only once a week, she never really missed anything. It was amazing, how much happened and yet how slowly it happened."

Yes, the horrible lighting, the strange slowness, the fact that it was done *daily,* that the writers and actors were chained to this vehicle that had to keep hurtling forward. Soap operas dared to take their fucking time even as everything else in culture rushed, pushed, competed. The soap opera, in its slowness, its comfort with redundancy and exposition, had its merits—and now it was dying. If he were a younger writer, one in need of attention, he would write an essay in its defense. As it was, he wanted to take what worked—the pace, the human scale, how huge it could feel to be inside a dying marriage, or an affair—not that he had any knowledge of the latter—and place those problems against the backdrop of something large. Not 9/11 or the 2008 economic collapse, but something truly epic.

"It sounds"—Thiru took a bite and chewed, making Gerry wait a long time for his adjective—"promising."

"I hear the doubt in your voice. Trust me, Thiru. My instincts are good. You know that. I actually have a talent for the—" He did not want to say *zeitgeist,* a word he loathed. Gerry preferred to say he understood the present's subtext. He saw the currents, what was going on underneath. His parents' marriage had trained him to do that.

"How far along are you?"

"Writing every day, but I haven't felt the quickening yet, the moment I know this book is the one." Gerry had a high fail rate, starting at least three books for every one that came to fruition. It was part of the reason he no longer took advances, instead insisting on selling finished books. Not that there was ever any suspense about his longtime editor making an offer, or whether the offer would be a good one. Still, it made him feel less encumbered, not being under contract. And it gave Thiru the leverage of potential bidding wars, Gerry always being available.

"Maybe if the soap opera thing was part of a memoir—" Thiru began.

"No. Never."

"Even with your father dead?"

"With him dead, when my mother is dead, when I am dead— there will never be a memoir."

"I can see waiting until your mother is gone—"

"Wasn't I right about the uni?"

The magnificent woman was back at their table, clearly on her

way out, a striking coat of boiled red wool tossed over her arm. Gerry
was doubly grateful for her reappearance. She not only derailed the
conversation about the memoir, she was wonderful to behold, sexy
yet classy, with long, praying mantis limbs. He had dated desultorily
since he and Sarah split. He didn't like dating. And the women he
saw were disappointed in his preferences, which came down to long
walks in Central Park, carryout or delivery from his favorite neighborhood places, watching the Orioles on cable.

"You were," Gerry said. "It was quite good. I still don't know what
it is."

"Sea urchin." She laughed at the face he made. "Actually it's even
worse—they're *gonads*. Not that I mind, but you might."

Oh, wasn't she a saucy one.

"Anyway, I don't want to bore you—I'm a fan. We met briefly
at that PEN benefit last year, although I doubt you remember. You
were mobbed. And I was just another admirer."

"I'm not bored. You'd be surprised how not boring it is." He was
sincere. If only all fans simply said this: *I won't bore you, I'm a fan.*
How lovely that would be. How lovely this woman was. "Remind me
of your name?"

"Margot Chasseur," she said. "Although it sounds as if I wrote
*Canterbury Tales,* the spelling is French. *C-H-A-S-S-E-U-R.*" Her
hedge fund date had approached and she tucked her hand in the
crook of his elbow. "Enjoy."

He watched her leave, taking note of the name, which was unusual enough to track down even in what the old television show
had called the naked city, with eight million naked stories. From
behind, she was practically naked above the waist and, despite the
cold night, she kept the coat draped over her arm, so her shoulder
blades remained visible. He could see almost to her coccyx, but it

was the shoulder blades that caught his attention. They were sharp and beautiful. A man could impale himself on those shoulder blades. It would be worth it.

"Gerry?" Thiru prodded.

"No memoir. I'm still living, Thiru. I'm nowhere close to writing a memoir."

"I just wanted to know if you were going to finish your gonads."

*March 15*

"TGIF," AILEEN SAYS cheerily when she brings him lunch. "With Victoria gone, I have three more days to put everything to rights."

She has not left the apartment since Wednesday, except for errands. One of those involved fetching a small suitcase, as she says she needs to be here 24/7 to get everything done. He realizes he has no idea where she lives, or if there is anyone in her life—family, roommates, a partner.

"I'm sorry you have to, um, work this weekend."

"It's fine," Aileen says. "I'll put in for overtime. I'm going to assume no one has access to your checking accounts except you? You can just write me a check for overtime. Which is time and a half, by the way."

Part of him wants to object that she is gouging him. But a larger part of him is so relieved that Aileen has taken over that he would gladly pay her anything. Money is for solving problems. Who told him that? Surely not his mother, who had worried constantly about her lack of money. And not his father.

*Margot said that. "Money is for solving problems" was a Margot-ism.* Said whenever she wanted Gerry's money to solve her problems.

"I think I'll have to tell my accountant, though," he said. "So they can calculate the taxes. That's how it's always worked with my assistants. There's withholding so they don't end up having a big tax bill at year's end."

"You know what? Once we calculate the amount for this weekend, just write on the check 'Supplies.' So it looks as if you're reimbursing me for something I paid out of pocket."

"Ooookay," he says.

Gerry doesn't want to be a snob, but it seems to him that Aileen speaks differently since what he has decided to think of as the *accident.* Of course it was an *accident.* Gerry has never raised his hands to anyone, except in consensual, mildly kinky moments. Sarah had liked a little light spanking. It was her idea and he had to be persuaded. He had felt mildly ridiculous. He doesn't like women with daddy issues. He has his own daddy issues and he prefers to keep them out of the bedroom.

"What are we doing, Aileen?" he asks.

"Buying time," Aileen says. "Trying to figure out exactly what happened. Maybe in a day or two you'll remember and we can take it from there."

*Wouldn't it be pretty to think so.* Gerry wants to do the right thing and he can't help believing, childlike, that there is a way out of this dilemma that he just hasn't been able to envision yet. He simply cannot believe he killed Margot, not even if she attacked him while he was in an Ambien haze. Buying time—yes, that's all they're doing. Affording themselves the time to figure out the best way to proceed.

"I wonder if I will ever remember," he says.

"It must have been a horrible shock, something that didn't even register as a dream," Aileen says. "That woman sneaking back in here and doing God knows what as you slept. It was only natural to protect yourself. The letter opener was right next to you, as it usually is. What else could you do?"

"If only I had the presence of mind to call for you." Had he been terrified of making a scene even while in a fugue state? Luke had always said that decorum was Gerry's fatal flaw, that it would be his failure to ask for what he wanted that would kill him, in the end. *You wouldn't ask for a glass of water in the desert.* Yet it was Luke, who never had any problem demanding what he wanted, who had been dead by the age of thirty-one.

"I can't believe you didn't hear anything," he says, then feels guilty for implicitly reprimanding the woman who is now trying to save him.

"I am a sound sleeper," she says, frowning, as if angry at herself, which makes Gerry feel even worse. This isn't Aileen's fault. Margot was crazy. That threat she made—he doesn't even know what she was talking about. Gerry has an exceptionally clear conscience for a man in his seventh decade. He has hurt some people, yes, who hasn't? But he did right by his wives; his fortune would be threefold what it is if he had not. Some of the things he has done would not pass muster today, but in the times that he did them they were socially acceptable.

*Had* a clear conscience. He had a clear conscience. Now he has a hole in the center of his memory, a lost sequence of events in which he did something horrible, yet he has not even a whisper of recollection. Must he feel guilty for that?

And what did Margot think she knew about him? Had her threats not been so empty, after all? What if she had told someone else whatever she thinks she knows?

Thought.

The service bell, the one on the lower level, rings. "Delivery!" Aileen says. He has never seen her so animated. She goes downstairs and there is the sound of something large-ish being moved around. "Try here," she instructs someone, who mumbles back in a low, masculine voice. "I know it's an odd place for a freezer," Aileen replies. "It's temporary. My father decided to buy an entire cow on the Internet, lord help him. He read something about climate change and thought ordering a side of beef from a small farmer would reduce his carbon footprint. He thought a side was like, I don't know, four steaks and some ribs."

*What is going on?* Better not to know.

He dozes, only to wake later to another ring of the bell. Aileen comes up and gives him an afternoon dose of Ambien, which he takes without protest. He drifts in and out of sleep, aware of a loud buzzing sound, which reminds him of something. *And now the leg.* Aileen comes in with his dinner, more pills. She seems so much more energetic, flush with purpose. Perhaps babysitting a sixty-one-year-old man has not been the most stimulating of activities. She needed actual problems to solve.

"Isn't it amazing," she says, "what you can find on YouTube. They have a how-to video for *everything.*"

## 2017

HIS MOTHER ASKED to go to Al Pacino Pizza after the meeting
with the neurologist and how could he say no? He certainly didn't
want to remind her that the Al Pacino's they had loved had been over
at Belvedere Square and that they had stopped going there years
ago because the quality declined, and then it closed. For now, when
possible, he was trying to avoid reminding his mother at any lapse
of her memory.

It was a dull November day. Would Gerry write it that way, in a
novel? Or was the weather too on the nose? What kind of weather
would work for a scene in which a mother and son eat pizza together
after receiving her death sentence?

"I'll have the Monzase," she said. "That was always my favorite."

She was right about that, at least, but her syntax made him want
to cry. Last week, she'd had a brief moment of confusion in which

she thought he was his father, which had fucked with his head on so many levels. For one thing, he never wanted to be confused with Gerald Andersen Sr. Worse still, he did not want his mother, in her confusion, to say urgently: "I still love you, Gerald, and I'm so glad you realized you love me, too. But what will Gerry do when he finds out?" His father had been dead for sixteen years and his mother hadn't seen him for almost forty years.

But today had been a good day. It would not be the last good day, the doctor had said. Soon, however, the bad days would outnumber the good. They needed to act quickly, have a plan in place for when she could no longer care for herself. They did not have the luxury of a "normal" meal. There was no more normal.

He plunged in.

"Mom—money is no object, not for me. I can afford to give you the best, not one of those grim, overlit places. More like a hotel than—well, like a five-star hotel."

"I want to stay in my house, Gerry, until it's time for hospice. You heard the doctors. It's not as if it's going to be a long time."

"But the *quality* of your life—they said in a relatively short time—"

"I know, I'll need care. But, Gerry, all I want is to stay in our house for as long as possible. Can't you move down here? As you said, it's a relatively short time."

Probably shorter than his mother realized. Gerry had to give her credit. Eleanor Andersen didn't settle for ordinary Alzheimer's, oh no, she had to go Creutzfeldt-Jakob.

He supposed he should feel lucky, having only her to care for. Other people his age complained of being the sandwich generation, pressed on either side, scorched paninis crushed by such differing demands. But, although he had been looking after his mother in his own way since he was barely a teenager, he felt he would be more prepared to step up here if he had been a parent at some point. He was missing a basic skill set. He could not imagine caring for his mother's physical needs, which meant a nurse, 24/7. Nurses. The house on Berwick Road would feel suffocatingly small with even one more person there.

"You know the doctor who received a Nobel for some of the initial research into this, the proteins—he had a Maryland connection, I think. But then he was arrested for child sexual abuse. He died in Norway."

His mother looked at him strangely. He deserved that look. But what was there to say? Only—yes. He had to say yes. He could put it off for a while, but he would have to move to Baltimore and help care for her. And once she was in hospice, he would have to stay to the truly bitter end.

He had no desire to do this and he hated himself for his reluctance. Baltimore was a kind of death for him now. It didn't matter that he had conceived and written the book that had changed his life here. Whenever he returned, he felt as if he were touring the history of his failures. Baltimore had tried to make Gerry small.

"Whatever you need, Mom." He owed her.

"Thank you, Gerry."

"Do you know why this place is called Al Pacino's?" he asked. "All the years we've been coming here, I never thought to ask. And there used to be, what—three or four in the city and now there's only the one."

"Now there's only the one," his mother echoed.

Their food arrived. Gerry realized his pizza, which had red onions and mushrooms, was named the Golden Arm, in honor of Johnny Unitas's Baltimore restaurant, which had closed more than twenty years ago.

*March 18*

**BY THE TIME** Victoria returns on Monday, it feels as if the world has righted itself. The buzzing noise has stopped, everything in the apartment is back in order, although the new freezer remains outside the laundry room. Victoria is an incurious person, but even she has to wonder at the sudden appearance of a small freezer.

"I hear you did a little Ambien shopping?" Victoria says, after giving him a dutiful report on her visit to Princeton's special collections, perhaps one of the most tedious accounts he has ever heard. She may be a reader, but she has no idea how to tell the simplest story, what details to include, which to jettison. So she tells everything in straight chronological order.

"What?"

"Aileen left me a note, explaining that you, um, got a little weird

and ordered an entire cow on the Internet, that she had to scramble
to get a freezer when it arrived."

"Oh, yes. I had a . . . bad night last week. I probably took a little
more Ambien than I should."

A bad night. That's true, at least.

"But no more, uh, calls or incidents?"

The question jolts him. He realizes he has stopped thinking
about the mysteries that were torturing him—the calls, the apparition. Was Margot his lady in black? It would have been wildly out of
character for her. Margot, for all her faults, is not passive-aggressive.
She always fought with a direct and terrifying viciousness. Margot is
the type of person who figures out what will hurt a person the most
and then uses that information to her advantage. She plunges the
knife in face-to-face, straight to the heart.

*Plunges.*

*Was,* he reminds himself. *Used.* She had mocked him for being
a "mama's boy," dismissed him as bourgeoise, unworthy of his own
money. *You don't know how to live, Gerry,* she had said more than
once. They were an ant-and-grasshopper couple. A time for work
and a time for play had been the moral of that Aesop fable. And
while some modern educators had tried to gentle the story, with the
ant taking pity on the grasshopper, in the original the ant had turned
his back and allowed the grasshopper to die.

"No," he says. "Life has been, if anything, too real." Victoria gives
him an odd look and he amends: "I mean tedious and boring. What's
more real than a life of tedium and boredom?"

"You're not going to be immobilized much longer," she says.
"That's something to look forward to."

"Yippee." He has tried for a light tone, something funny and self-deprecating, but he sounds self-pitying to his own ears. He watches Victoria gather her things to head downstairs to the study where she works, desperate to give her some Bluebeardesque order about the freezer, but, of course, the order is Bluebeard's undoing. Well, it's the undoing of his wives, except the last one. Gerry will have to assume that Victoria, a vegetarian, has no interest in a freezer full of what she believes to be beef. Wasn't it a deer in Aileen's original story? Didn't she tell at least one freezer company that she had hit a deer with her car? Or maybe that was whoever sold her the cordless saw. Does it matter if she told different stories to different vendors?

Oh God—his life is completely dependent on the ingenuity and attention to detail of someone whose most beloved narratives are so-called reality television. But what other choice does he have?

"It is nice," Victoria says, "that you're going to donate the food to a local soup kitchen. I mean, there's no way you could eat it all. You seldom eat beef, except for Chinese carryout and that flank steak salad."

"Someone should benefit from my, um, temporary insanity."

"And to give them the freezer, too—but, then, I guess you won't need it once the meat is gone." A tiny pause. "I should show you this chart, about how various meats affect the environment. I don't expect everyone to follow a vegetarian diet, but different proteins have different impacts on the planet. Some of us are playing for larger stakes than others."

He does not appreciate Victoria's tone, or her dig at his age. He considers chiding her for her cheekiness, but he is suddenly anxious to go online via his phone and check his credit card bill. This is one area of his life where Gerry has embraced technology. He does not pay his bills online, but he likes being able to monitor his credit card accounts and his various balances.

He had given Aileen his Amex, the "business" card, and the trans-actions from last week have already posted. A cordless reciprocating saw from Home Depot. Multiple items from a kitchen supply shop. The inn in Princeton—right, Victoria has her own card linked to the account. *How did a vegetarian spend that much on room service? She must have ordered an entire bottle of wine.* Here is the invoice for a side of beef from a farm in New Windsor, Maryland, delivered to—he doesn't recognize the street. Is it Aileen's home? He's not sure he approves of this. Why would Gerry enter Aileen's address in an Ambien haze, when he doesn't even know it?

Ah well. It's her story. Let her sweat the details.

Aileen arrives that evening with a large insulated bag from Whole Foods, which appears to be empty, given the way it dangles from her wrist. When she says goodbye in the morning, it is slung over her shoulder, bulging with whatever has been stored inside.

Gerry takes his Ambien and asks no questions.

*1986*

"GERRY, THERE'S BEEN A COMPLAINT."

The head of the Writing Sems looked sheepish, yet jolly. Still, his words hit Gerry hard. He was not used to being in trouble. He never got in trouble. He led an exemplary life. Just this week, he bought a case of wine at Eddie's, for a party he and Lucy were planning, and when he got home, he realized he had been charged for one bottle, not twelve. He had called the store and made sure they charged his credit card for what was owed. It wasn't expensive wine, not even eight dollars a bottle, but it was the *principle* of the thing.

"Gerry?"

"I don't know what to say. From a student?" He had flunked a student last semester, which was rare. But the student had failed to do her work and received multiple warnings, even an extension into this semester. After assuring him she would submit her outstanding assignments, she called and said the registrar had said it was fine to grant her another extension. He had refused and given her an F, a rarity at Hopkins these days.

"Your colleague, Shannon Little."

"Oh."

"She says you, um, approached her and that you commenced a relationship."

God, there are so many things wrong with that sentence. She "approached" him. It was not a relationship, which was the true source of her complaint, Gerry was sure. Also, how disappointing that Harry would use the word *commenced* in this context. Embarrassment must have rendered him less articulate than usual.

He took a deep breath. "Shannon made it quite clear that she wanted to have sex with me. It was not something that interested me, not really. But she was adamant. Determined. One night we were alone, going over applicants for next year's Writing Sems. We had sex. Once. I was disappointed in myself, but it's not a mistake I wish to repeat. And, no, I haven't told my wife. Lucy has always been very clear that if I am unfaithful, our marriage is over."

Lucy's attitudes about sexual fidelity were more nuanced than this, but his boss didn't need to know that. She would, in fact, divorce him if she learned about Shannon.

"Shannon's version of the story is somewhat different."

"I'm sure it is. I'm trying to be a gentleman here, Harry, but, I'm sorry, she's a woman scorned. Well, not scorned—I like to think I've been cordial—but she didn't get what she wanted. I'm not excusing my own behavior. I have regretted what I did every day since then. I've been waiting for the shoe to drop. I guess this is it. Humiliating as it is, I'm almost relieved that she decided to make it a professional issue, rather than call Lucy and make it a personal vendetta.

Although I suppose she thought filing a complaint against me here might have a ripple effect."

"'Heav'n has no rage, like love to hatred turn'd, / Nor Hell a fury, like a woman scorn'd.'" Coleman used his reciting voice, plummy and pompous. "Do you know the source?"

"One of the Restoration writers, I think?"

"Congreve, *The Mourning Bride*. His only tragedy. I was briefly enamored with Restoration comedy, as an undergrad. In 1969, it felt *radical* to care about Restoration writers. I was quite the pedant."

Harry Coleman was still enamored of pedantic corrections of famous quotes, but that wasn't something Gerry was inclined to point out.

"What happens now?" Gerry asked.

"It was a consensual, um, encounter, by your account, and you haven't pursued it in any way. No calls? No trying to get her alone here in Gilman Hall, no repeat, uh, performances?"

"*No.* Is that what she's saying?"

"More or less. More or less."

Gerry felt a cold fury quite unlike anything he had ever known. Yes, he had done something wrong. *But it wasn't his fault.* She had initiated it, after weeks, months, of insinuation and pressure. She put her hand on his leg, just above the knee, and began working it up. He had said no. He had said it was wrong. That was the problem. It was wrong and that excited him. Lucy had only one rule, a rule that most men would have been happy to live by. *I know you will be tempted, Gerry, and that's okay. I have only one rule.* But who was Lucy to make rules for him? He was the one who had published a novel. It was successful. He had won a prize. No one got to tell him what to do. Especially not Lucy, who refused to own her envy. If Lucy were honest, he would be honest. But she wasn't, she wasn't, she wasn't—

And that was all he had been thinking about as he plunged into Shannon Little. The next day, he called her and said it was a terrible mistake and it must not be repeated. He said she was a lovely woman, but he was married. She didn't take no for an answer, Shannon Little. She had cajoled, she had threatened, she had cried, she had even claimed she would kill herself. He had gone to her apartment that night, taken pity on her, held her and—okay, so there had been a second time. Maybe a third. But he had never wanted those subsequent episodes. Now she was trying to destroy him.

"She's a liar, Harry. I made a horrible mistake. But this is outright slander. And you know what? I won't have it. I will not stand for these false accusations. How can I continue to work alongside such a woman? I recognize that this situation is my fault and therefore my responsibility. I will look at other programs—I know people at Columbia, Stanford—"

Coleman was rattled now. "Gerry, please don't overreact. We'll work something out. You can see why I had to have this discussion. I have no reason to doubt your version of things—it's not as if you denied everything. It's not as if there's anything wrong with two colleagues having sex. Please don't do anything rash."

"I won't."

Was it rash to go home that very night and tell Lucy that he was going to leave the Writing Sems and use the Hartwell Prize to allow himself the gift of being a full-time writer, for at least a year or two?

Was it cruel to say that he wanted this adventure alone, that he no longer wished to be married to her? He had broken her only rule, a generous rule, a rule that most men would kill for in a marriage. If he told her the truth, she would kick him out anyway. So why not just go, without hurting her feelings? Wasn't that the kindest thing to do? Make the break in a way that would hurt her the least—and deprive Shannon Little of whatever power she thought she had over him. By leaving now, he was offering everyone a clean slate.

He was so tired of women thinking they could control him. *Be regular and orderly in your life, so you can be violent and original in your work*, Flaubert had recommended.

Fuck Flaubert. There was no reason Gerry couldn't do both.

*March 21*

MARGOT WAS DEAD, *to begin with.*

That riff on *A Christmas Carol's* opening line plays in Gerry's head. He keeps expecting Margot to haunt him, although in Chanel instead of chains. He waits for all his ghosts—past, present, future.

Yet since Margot's death—since the *accident*—everything has stopped. No more phone calls, no more "visits." The obvious answer is the obvious answer. Margot had been taunting him, Margot thought she had something on him. But what?

Life goes on. For everyone but Margot. Aileen no longer arrives with her insulated sack; the freezer has been donated to a local homeless shelter, along with a side of beef from New Windsor, Maryland. Clever Aileen—the shipping address was for the shelter, not her home. It's a fine little story, as clever and compact as the ones he used to read in those *Alfred Hitchcock Presents* anthologies. Kill your husband with a leg of lamb, serve the leg of lamb to the detectives. And maybe this is a dream from which he will finally wake.

As if on cue, the phone rings, the short staccato tone signaling a call from the front desk. So, no, he's awake.

"Mr. Andersen?" Phylloh from downstairs, still phrosty. *Were you Margot's collaborator?* He knows that someone had to be helping Margot. Why not Phylloh? It would explain how Margot got back into the apartment that night.

"Yes?"

"There is a man here to see you."

"A gentleman?"

"A police officer."

The first *o* is long, the tone skeptical. Phylloh probably has many reasons, life experiences, not to think that Officer Friendly is friendly, whereas Gerry is a white man who has spent six decades driving, walking, running, *existing* without fear of police officers. Oh, sure, he has known the frisson of nervousness when glimpsing a patrol car in his rearview mirror, but the fear is of a ticket, not death.

Now his heart feels as if it's throwing itself against his rib cage, a bird stuck in a soffit, trying to escape. (This happened in his mother's house when he was away at college. She listened for days to the terrible scratching and did nothing until Gerry came home from Princeton and found an infestation of flies in the linen closet, as the bird had finally starved to death.)

Terror has feathers, too, Emily Dickinson. A woman has died in his apartment. He may be responsible. (He is definitely responsible.) The body is gone. Another person has made that possible, which gives that person significant power over him. Gerry is in bed, taking far more Ambien than he should. He could use his condition, his pain, his fog, to send the officer away.

Yet when an inspector calls, the suspects always open the door to him. The only way the guilty can pretend to innocence is by acting as if they have nothing to hide.

"Send him up, by all means."

The detective who arrives a few minutes later, admitted by a clearly curious Victoria, does not fit any archetype that Gerry knows, but then every detective archetype Gerry knows is from television or literature. He is not a slow-talking good ol' boy with a shrewd intelligence under his coarse, buffoonish manners. He is not a Black Dapper Dan with an ornate vocabulary. He does not wear a rumpled raincoat. He is a man of indeterminate race named John Jones, who looks as if he were made in a factory. His one distinctive feature is his glacial blue eyes, but those only make him seem more android-like.

"I'm with the NYPD. A woman—Margot Chasseur—has gone missing. We believe you may be one of the last people to see her."

Dates are fuzzy for Gerry, but that's to his advantage. There was nothing momentous about his final meeting with Margot. Okay, his *penultimate* meeting, and she attacked him, forcing him to push her hard enough that it might have left bruises, not that there's any skin left to inspect. Still, he honestly can't remember the date.

"I've seen her twice since my accident. Both were unexpected visits."

"When was the last time?"

"I couldn't say. Maybe a week or two ago?" *Because it's not an important date to me because I didn't kill her, I really don't think I killed her, does it count if you're on Ambien, if you can't remember anything?*

"According to Amtrak, she bought a round-trip ticket here on March 12. Was that the last time you saw her?"

"That sounds right. Dates, days—they mean less to me now. When you're in my condition, the days run together."

"But she was here?"

He is aware of Victoria, bustling around in the kitchen, taking an inordinate amount of time to make tea. A nosy parker, his mother would have called her. Gerry realizes he has no idea what a nosy parker is. His mother's speech had been full of mysterious anachronisms, a by-product of her voracious, indiscriminate reading.

"Yes, she was. My assistant was there that day. Victoria, do you remember the date?"

"It was the day before you sent me to Princeton—yes, the twelfth." Victoria takes her tea and goes downstairs. Eavesdropping is one thing, but she apparently has no desire to be pulled into the conversation. Good. Gerry wouldn't want her to share what she saw that afternoon. But if the detective asks to talk to her, he supposes he will probably have to let him.

"That train ticket is the last thing we can tie to her. She hasn't answered her phone or used her credit cards."

"Oh my God, are you suggesting—" Gerry catches himself. *Because he does not know she's dead, he would be distraught, this news is unexpected.* He is a character in a novel. He knows how to do this, how to inhabit a character's POV without authorial omniscience.

"She never returned to New York."

"Oh." He feigns relief. Because a normal person, an innocent person, would default to optimism, right? "Margot is a . . . an impulsive woman. She could be in St. Barts. Or anywhere warm. She hates New York in the winter."

"Winter's pretty much over, though."

"You live there, Detective. You know how the cold weather creeps along into April, and then it goes straight to summer by late May."

"Her mother is worried."

Margot has a *mother?* The news is not only surprising, it is infuriating. How dare Margot have a mother when Gerry has none? She never mentioned having a mother. Margot does not deserve a mother.

"I don't know what to tell you." True enough.

"The thing is—she bought a round-trip ticket. Amtrak confirmed her ticket was scanned for the trip down. But her ticket for the trip back was never used."

Gerry thought about *Columbo,* another show he and his mother had watched together. The hubristic rich villains always fell into the trap of trying to explain inconsistencies. But if you're not the killer and you're not the detective, why would you bother?

He said: "How do they know?"

"Everything's computerized now. She bought the ticket online. There's a, whatchamacallit. A little square that the conductor scans. Anyway, she was in the reservation system, scheduled to travel back the next day."

Gerry yearns to tell the detective that it's possible to be overlooked on Amtrak, that he has made the trip between New York and Baltimore more than once without anyone asking for his ticket. Or he could say Margot, dismayed by the quality of the food on the trip down, might have chosen another way to return to New York, which, come to think of it, would be pure Margot. But, no, that's what the big-name guest stars always made the mistake of doing, trying to help Columbo with his case. Again, it's not on him to figure out why Margot didn't use her return ticket.

"Interesting that she booked her return for the next day. The first time she visited me, she expected to spend the night here. I made it clear that she was not welcome and had Victoria put her on the next train."

"What did you talk about?"

"Which time?"

"The last time."

The truth, or at least a portion of it, seems the best gambit. "She had no place to live. She was distraught. She could not accept that I had sold my place in New York, that she had to find her own apartment."

"Why did she expect you to help her out when you had already told her you wouldn't?"

Gerry sighs. Strangely, he has almost forgotten the body on his floor, the blood, the disturbing noises in the night, the buzz of the cordless handsaw, the freezer that has come and gone. He feels fatherly toward this younger man and wants to warn him about women, what the worst ones can do.

"Margot was—is, I hope, I hope she's alive, I wish her well— Margot is a woman who makes a habit of taking things for granted. Last year, I moved down here to care for my mother, having been told that she had a very short time to live. I expected to be here a month or two, but it stretched out for much of 2018 and it became apparent that I needed to sell my apartment, where Margot was ensconced. My mother's decline, her death—it exposed the—I wouldn't call it superficiality, but the lack of seriousness in our relationship. It's easy to fall into *arrangements* as one ages. To re-create patterns that look like things we call 'relationships' or 'marriages.' But it was, for want of a better phrase, a passing fancy. When I relocated to Baltimore, I assumed Margot would move on to another man. She never went long without the company of a man. I'd bet almost anything she's found someone else to support her."

"If that's so, it's news to her mother."

"Well, the fact that she even has a living mother is news to me."

"She lives on Long Island. Gertrude Chessler. Appears Ms. Chasseur changed her name legally when she was in her twenties."

Gerry tries to remember what Margot had told him of her past. Very little, he realizes. She had always presented herself as an Aphrodite, rising on her clamshell in New York circa 1995, young and lovely and feral. He had not known her then—he was back in Baltimore, living with Gretchen, teaching at Hopkins—but Margot had shown him the photographs taken of her in her heyday, the little society squibs in which she made appearances. He had pretended to care.

He repeats, stuck on the fact: "I never even knew she had a mother."

"Why would Ms. Chasseur come see you if she knew she couldn't stay here?"

"Because she wanted money." He allows himself another sigh. "It's all she ever wanted from me."

It's depressing, this accidental truth. He was a meal ticket; she was a gold digger. He never saw it this way before now. Their relationship was completely transactional. All Margot's relationships were transactional.

"Did you give it to her?"

"No. She's an adult woman in her fifties. I feel no obligation to support her. Truthfully, I never officially asked her to live with me. She just moved in, bit by bit. If I hadn't sold my New York apartment, I'm not sure how I would have gotten her out of it."

"Her mother says that her daughter was saying she knew something about you."

There it was again, the vague threat. To what could she possibly be alluding? Gerry's conscience was clear. Except for the part about Margot dying.

"She knew a lot about me. We were together for several years."

"Her mother said she said she had a secret about you. That she was going to confront you."

"Yes, and she did, but it was nothing more than an empty threat." His gaze is level and cool. He is a man immobilized by injury. He cannot be a suspect in anything. "The sad truth is that Margot was— is—a hysteric. She'd say anything to get what she wants. She was very angry at me. She attacked me in my bed. Victoria, my assistant—she was here, she'll tell you what happened. Margot hit me, she scratched my face, I managed to push her off with this walker I can't yet use." He indicates his walker, his trusty sentry. "I could have filed a police complaint. I let it be, because—well, she was a delightful companion once. I preferred to remember the good times. My scratches are no longer visible, but the night nurse saw them. She bought me some Mederma to help them heal."

Detective Jones smiles ruefully. "Women." Then: "I'd like to talk to your assistant. And maybe your nurse?"

*Shit, shit, shit.* As competent as Aileen has proven herself to be, Gerry does not think this is a good idea. Why had they not anticipated this, agreed on a mutual version?

"She wasn't here when it happened. Only Victoria. It was the afternoon and my nurse is here at night. You can check that with the front desk."

"Yes, I asked the young woman if she remembered Ms. Chasseur. She did. She says she arrived here that afternoon, then ran out about fifteen minutes later."

*Then how did she get back in, in the middle of the night, without being heard or observed by anyone?* Gerry has to stop himself from asking the detective that question.

"It is baffling," he says instead. "Did she get a cab, take an Uber?"

"No one knows. She vanished into thin air."

Gerry turns the cliché over in his mind, wondering why it's always *thin* air. It's not as if people disappear only at high altitudes.

He also wonders where Margot spent the hours before she returned, how she got into the building. The front desk was unmanned— unwomanned? unPEOPLED?—after nine P.M. Another resident could buzz one in, but otherwise, someone would have to have a key card to enter the lobby, and a key for the twenty-fifth floor. It was also possible to take the elevator from the garage straight to the apartment. But, even then, one would need the elevator key.

*Oh my God*—he *knows*. He knows, he knows, he knows. He sees Margot, picking herself up from the floor, then taking his wallet and eliciting several bills, saying the least he could do was pay her cab fare. His security card for the building was in his wallet. Obviously he had no use for it, wouldn't notice it missing. And his keys, they hung by a hook next to the front door, under the mirror where she had stopped and fussed with her hair. Margot would have been able to identify his key ring, a sterling silver loop from Tiffany's. She had given it to him. He would bet anything it's not there now.

"It's a dangerous city," Gerry says. "That's all I can tell you."

"But not a city where a fifty-one-year-old white woman disappears without a trace."

"I guess you've never heard about Susan Harrison." Gerry decides to distract the detective with his knowledge of the 1994 case, which he had researched for a novel he ended up abandoning. A woman and a man in a folie à deux, although that term was considered politically incorrect now, he supposed, given that the man had almost certainly killed the woman, and where was the "folie" in that? Gerry had been drawn to the fact that a drunk, an unsubtle man with little intellect, seemed to have committed the perfect crime almost by accident. But as he burrowed into the material, he could find nothing more to say about it. The story almost begged to be written as a dark comedy, a nasty *Candide* or another riff on *Being There,* and even Gerry realized that was not going to fly in the twenty-first century.

The detective listens politely, but he is clearly bored. Good, that's what Gerry intends. He plays the part of the garrulous old man shut-in, rambling and desperate for company. It is discomfiting how easily this persona comes to him, how readily this younger man accepts this version of him. He is sixty-one, not eighty-one! Two months ago he was in vigorous health, a person who required no medications beyond a daily vitamin.

He wonders if the detective is indulging Gerry's wandering narrative, in part, because he hopes Gerry is going to offer up some inconsistency on which he can pounce. But one of Gerry's great strengths as a writer is POV. The man in his bed is not him. The man in his bed is "Gerry Andersen," an injured writer who has no idea what has happened to his former lover, Margot. Where *did* Margot go, he wonders. How did Aileen dispose of her?

He thinks about the incinerator where he and his mother used to drive their crab feast refuse. She was particular about this; they must never allow the shells and cartilage to stay on their property overnight. She believed they would lead to terrible odors that could never be eradicated if left inside the house. But in a trash can outside, they would attract raccoons, who would scatter them across the backyard. So they would wrap up the newspapers littered with crab carcasses and put them inside garbage bags and drive them all the way into town, to that terrible hulking furnace.

It was one of the favorite moments of his youth. His father had done this task before he disappeared, but always with reluctance and complaint, and refusing to let Gerry accompany him. Once he was gone, Gerry joined his mother in the front seat—remember when kids could ride in the front seat?—and he had felt powerful, grown-up. There was a sense of mission about the journey.

If it wasn't too late, they stopped at Windy Valley for soft-serve and he patted the ponies that were penned there.

He is aware of his brain working on all these levels—Gerry the writer, telling the story that will bore/beguile the detective; Gerry the twelve-year-old riding in that old Ford station wagon with his mother. He sees himself as Duncan in *The World According to Garp,* reaching for his brother's hand as they descend into the hellmouth of their driveway, toward the literal and figurative collision of their parents' failings, failings that will take one child's eye and another child's life.

"Well," the detective says as Gerry finally winds down, "you've given me a lot to think about."

Of course, no one says that unless they mean the opposite, so Gerry is pleased. He has bored the detective into submission.

"Happy to help."

"Okay if I talk to your assistant?"

"Sure. She's downstairs."

The detective gone, Gerry pulls his smartphone out from under his blanket. He turned on the audio recorder when Victoria opened the door to the detective. He has fallen in love with his phone, for its capabilities and potential. It is a *smart* phone. It is smarter than anyone who works for him, that's for sure. And generally silent, bless its heart. He will listen to the recording later, commit his own words to memory.

*2012*

"SO I WON'T be able to speak in class tomorrow, but I don't think that should affect my grade."

Without his class roster in front of him, Gerry could never remember this student's name, only that she kept reminding him that it rhymed with the name of a character in a Judy Blume book, as if *that* would be helpful to him. He thought of her as Wizard Girl because she submitted fantasy stories about wizards and warlocks and vampires. Never had fantasy been less fantastic.

"Just so I understand, tomorrow is a day of solidarity for gay people—"

"LGBT."

"And by not speaking, you are somehow helping them. As an ally." That had been her word, *ally,* and she had seemed keen for

Gerry to know she was not, in fact, described by one of the letters for which she was willing to be silent.

"It's a symbolic gesture, but it's my right to participate."

Gerry wondered from where, exactly, such a "right" would be derived. He supposed the freedom of expression had a corollary, the freedom *not* to express oneself. He loathed this idea on principle, saw it as a cheap way to slack on the participation requirement, but why argue? Nothing could affect Wizard Girl's grade. She was a B-minus student at best. Bad as she was at writing, she was even worse at workshopping her classmates' stories, overly prescriptive. It would be a relief to be spared Wizard Girl's "ideas."

"It's fine," he said. "As long as you bring your copies of the other students' manuscripts, marked up and annotated. In fact, maybe put a little more work into your written comments, which will make up for your decision not to participate. But, please, don't tell the other students what to *do,* only what you think."

She glowered, then nodded. Having won what she came for, she made no move to gather her books and the enormous fountain drink she was never without, which was now sweating all over Gerry's desk.

"Professor Andersen—"

"I'm not a professor, merely a writer. MFA, no Ph.D." In his heart, he secretly believed novelists superior to professors.

"Do I have potential?"

"Everyone has potential. By definition. It would be rare to be without potential."

"But do you think I could be a novelist?"

What was the right thing to say? He warred with himself, wanting to be true to art, yet not unkind to this young woman, who seemed unusually sensitive. But, hey, Jacqueline Susann was a novelist.

Anyone could be a novelist. She hadn't asked if she could be a *good* one.

"With hard work, disciplined habits, and an ambitious reading life, yes. My hunch is that you don't have a lot of life experience. That will change. Believe me, that will change."

"But you told us the first day that life experience was overrated. You talked about Philip Roth, how relatively eventless his life had been. You quoted Eudora Welty, the thing about having led a sheltered life, but also a daring one, because all serious daring comes from within."

*Shit,* he had.

"There's a big difference between eighteen and twenty-five, which was Roth's age when he published *Goodbye, Columbus.* Also, it's *Roth.* He's only one of our greatest living writers."

"I'm twenty-two." Such a pedant, always fixating on the wrong details.

"Yes—still, I'd love to see a piece of writing from you that wasn't full of wizards."

"I showed you what I hoped could be the beginning of a novel the first week of class, but you said I had to work on short stories this semester."

Ah, yes, her "novel," that wisp of a scene about a girl who was sad, contemplated suicide, but then saw the sun come up and felt hope. If he had to choose, he'd take the wizards.

"A novel is impossible to complete in a semester, that's why I discourage them. I think finishing something is important. People can get lost in novels, wander in and not come out for years."

"Do you ever get lost in one of yours?"

The question startled him with its acuity. He thought of the abandoned books, about which he felt guilty, as if they were his children. Or, worse, wives. But he knew no other way to work. In order to find the book he was meant to write, he had to keep moving. At least he had settled down as far as women were concerned. Three was proving to be his lucky number.

"I suppose so," he said, opting for the answer that would end this meeting as quickly as possible. "See you tomorrow." Then, in an imitation of Dianne Wiest in that Woody Allen film, he threw up his hand and said in a hoarse, patrician voice. "Don't speak!"

The girl frowned and gathered her things, insulted. If he had explained the reference, she probably still would have been insulted. People aren't allowed to like Woody Allen anymore. He tried to salvage the moment.

"Good luck with your performance of *The Silent Woman*." She looked at him, confused, clearly never having heard of the Ben Jonson play. Who was Gerry kidding? She'd never heard of Ben Jonson.

The next day, she showed up for class with two lines of tape across her mouth, in the form of an X, but she had to remove the tape to suck from her enormous fountain drink. He was glad she wasn't speaking, as one of the stories up was by Mona, one of the best students in the class. Also the most beautiful, but that was sheer coincidence.

*March 22*

"WE NEED TO TALK."

"Funny," he says to Aileen. "I was about to say the same thing."

Also funny, he thinks, how those words, the worst words a person in a relationship will ever hear, can be neutral in other contexts. Yes, he and Aileen need to talk.

"I guess you may go first," she says.

She has taken to sitting next to him with her knitting in the evening, although they seldom speak. The click-clack of the needles drives him crazy; the click-clack of the needles also soothes him, helps him sleep. Along with the drugs, which he is still taking. To which he looks forward now, if he's honest, his Ambien and oxycodone chased some nights with a calcium supplement. Without the pills, there's no way he could sleep. It's temporary, he assures himself. He won't always need to dope himself up so much, not forever.

He tells her about the New York detective, shows her the recording on the phone, says she can listen to it if she likes.

"But it's better if you don't, I think, because none of this would be known to you. The key point, if he should come back to talk to you, is that you know nothing."

She seems affronted. "I know *everything*."

"Of course you do. It's like playing a part, in a play. You have to remember—you never met Margot. Never saw her, never heard me speak about her. Victoria met her, drove her to the train station the first time, overheard our argument. But you know absolutely nothing about her." He pauses, decides to air his worst fear. "Unless you and Victoria gossip."

"How could we gossip? We never see each other."

Fair point. Gerry's being paranoid.

"Meanwhile, I've figured something out. How she came back, how she got in."

"Huh." Is it "Huh" or "How"? At any rate, he decides to tell her.

"Did you find my keys or the pass in her purse? You and Victoria always come and go through the lower level—"

"The service entrance," Aileen says. *Service* or *servants*? She really has the most terrible diction. A stray memory darts around his mind. *Speak up, don't mumble so.* He sees a pen-and-ink drawing of a monstrous child. Augustus Gloop. Willy Wonka. Willy Wonka would accuse the children of mumbling when he didn't like what they said. But, no, it was Mike Teavee that Wonka pretended he couldn't hear.

"Anyway, that's how she got back in. And that means if anyone ever pulls the security footage from that night, they will see her returning in the middle of the night, but there will be no footage of her leaving a second time."

Aileen's eyes widen. "Then we have to do something about that security footage."

"No. NO. That's a fatal error. There are hours of footage and, as of now, there's no one saying she came back at all, so no one's looking at the tape. We do nothing."

"I don't know, maybe there's a way to erase the footage. I saw this TV show recently where someone used a magnet—"

"We do *nothing*," he says sternly. "Every action carries a risk. Inaction has far less. If it were to be discovered, we would both say, plausibly, that we have no memory of her returning to the apartment, that we heard nothing and saw nothing. It's not on us to explain why she's on the footage, coming back later that night. Real life is filled with things that don't make sense."

"Right," she says. Yet she still seems angry and affronted. "I was only trying to help. I'm in this up to my neck, you know."

Not an appealing image, Aileen in something up to her neck.

"I don't mean to sound bossy," he says, even as he thinks: *I am your boss.* "But I was interviewed first; my version has to be the official one. I was here, the detective visited, I've started the story. Certain things are set in stone and cannot be revised. It's like a serial novel. We can't pull anything back. Now, what was it that you wanted to tell me?"

"Oh, not tell," she says. "Ask."

He waits, but she is suddenly tongue-tied, shy.

"Yes?" he prods.

"You know, I really hate parking on the street when I come here. If you were to get a parking place in the building, I could use it."

"I have a space, the one that is deeded to the apartment. But my mother's car is in it and I can't do anything with it until her estate clears probate." His mother's car is a 2010 Mercedes-Benz that needs body work and repairs to the engine. He had it towed to the garage to get it out of the elements up in North Baltimore.

"Can't you get a second space?"

"I could, but it's expensive."

"How much?"

"I don't recall the exact figure. I know only that each unit here comes with one deeded spot, but the second one is dear—they were trying to discourage two-vehicle households, which is funny, given how unwalkable this neighborhood is."

"Hmmmm. I just thought—I'm so scared at night, when I walk those three or four blocks. Scared and cold."

"Spring is coming. And it's staying light later."

"Gerry."

She has never used his first name before. Now that she has, he realizes what is happening—the bill has come due. She cleaned up his mess, and she expects to be compensated. No such thing as a free lunch. No such thing as a free accomplice. Everyone always has an agenda. He stares at the cats frolicking on Aileen's tablet cover, which is peeking out of her knitting bag. One, a black one with round eyes, seems to be staring back at him, taunting him, stopping just short of sticking its tongue out at him. *I know you*, he thinks. *I have seen you before.*

"Is the parking space all you require, Aileen?"

"For now," she says.

*2014*

## "YOU'RE NOT FROM HERE, ARE YOU?"

Gerry was in the hotel bar. He didn't really want a drink—if it were alcohol he had required, he could have remained at the reception held in his honor after his talk that night at the university. But Gerry's standing joke was that his fee for speaking doubled if he was expected to make small talk.

Still, he had dutifully made the rounds, put in a respectable forty-five minutes at the reception and then retreated to his hotel, driven by a student. He asked the student if he knew the story of David Halberstam's death in a car accident, while being driven by a student. The student did and they had made the twenty-minute trip in silence, which was what Gerry wanted.

He had been to Columbus several times before, visiting the Thurber House, once even staying in the no-frills apartment on the top floor, the very place where the bed had fallen. He had loved Thurber when he was young. He even liked the television show that used Thurber's drawings, *My World and Welcome to It*. He would have preferred to be in the Thurber House right now. It was quiet at night, near downtown yet removed. Hotels made him feel lonely. So he sat at the bar and drank Bushmills, which he had taken up years ago because his father disdained it. "Protestant whiskey," said his father, a Jameson man. Gerry didn't even like it that much.

The woman who had spoken to him had come in after he did, chosen a stool three seats down, ordered a white wine, and taken out a book. She looked familiar at first, then he decided she just had one of those faces. Pretty, but not shockingly so. Light eyes, blond hair worn in a ragged bob. But the brows and lashes were dark. Eyes put in with a dirty finger, his mother would have said. An Irish expression, more meaningful before all women, everywhere, began darkening their eyelashes, outlining their eyes as if they were Cleopatra, wearing false eyelashes. Women were increasingly fake these days. Gerry liked *real* women—slender, small-breasted, with their natural hair color.

Like this woman, although she was young, much too young for him, in her twenties.

Still, she had spoken to him. It was only polite to answer.

"Safe question to ask in a hotel bar," he said. "People in hotels generally are from somewhere else."

"I'm from here."

"Ah." She was flirting, he was sure of it. He liked it, and what was the harm in a little banter? "Is this one of your hangouts?"

"Hardly. A bit on the expensive side to be a regular hang. But I needed a treat tonight, after I got off work. I just wanted to sit with a glass of wine and my book."

The book was *The Master and Margarita,* one of his cherished favorites, although he did not recognize this particular cover featuring a black cat with a forked tongue. Gerry told the bartender to upgrade the woman's chardonnay from the house brand to the most expensive one on the list, then moved down one stool. Good taste in literature deserved to be rewarded.

"I'm Gerry Andersen," he says. His name evinces no recognition. Good.

"Kim Barton."

TWO HOURS LATER, the woman was in his room, but suddenly much shyer than she had been in the bar, where she had touched his arm. Her leg had even brushed against his once, he was sure of it.

"I knew who you were," she said. "All along. I was at your talk tonight and I know from my days at the university that they put the big-name speakers up here. In fact, I majored in creative writing and I used to work on this speaker series."

Her confession had the odd effect of at once amplifying and suppressing desire. Felt like a bit of a rigged game, if his reputation preceded him. But who cared? She was so pretty in that midwestern way. Technically, her features and coloring were not that different from his. But there was a milk-fed, corn-fed quality to her heart-shaped face. She looked like—America.

He was a little buzzed.

"How did you know I'd be in the bar?"

"I didn't. I really did stop in for a treat. Your talk was great, by the way. As I said, I have a degree in creative writing, but—I work in a nursing home. In administration, not in care."

The distinction seemed to matter to her, although Gerry couldn't fathom why.

"I'm married," he said.

"I know. You mentioned her during your talk. It's your second marriage?"

"Third."

His matrimonial record hung over him, like that black cloud that hung over the character in *Li'l Abner,* Joe Btfsplk. He knew in that moment that he and Sarah would divorce within a year. It would be costly to him, and not only financially. Sarah Kotula was the wife he had taken—archaic phrase, but apt—in the flush of success. She was perfect in every way, even more perfect than Lucy had been. Sarah was a gift he had chosen for himself in much the same way he had splurged on furnishings for his New York apartment. Sarah was a top-shelf prize at boardwalk Skee-Ball, suddenly, finally within reach. A little bit younger than Gerry, but not young enough to make him look ridiculous. An accomplished journalist in her own right, with family money. She was so perfect that she was a bit of a turn-off. Even their best sex had a workmanlike aspect. He was Sarah's trophy, too. This young woman wanted *him,* he could tell. Did it matter if she desired him as a man or as GERRY ANDERSEN?

He put his hand on her hair and waited. She looked down at her lap, but she didn't move away, so he leaned in to kiss her neck. Very quickly, he had her flat on the bed, her skirt pushed up, her sweater pushed up, his face pressed against her midsection.

"No," she said.

"Let me put my mouth on you." He pulled down her tights—no underwear beneath them, oh, these young girls—and tasted her. "I just want to make you happy."

"No. Please—no." But she didn't try to move from the bed and her back arched, her body responding to his touch. He was on his knees, his face buried between her legs. She could get away from him if she really wanted to. Heck, she could break his nose with her foot or her knee. She was moaning now. She was excited and her excitement was a tonic for him. She yelped when she finally came and he could tell it was a long orgasm, one that flowed and rippled. She was panting.

He went to the bathroom, swirled some mouthwash around, returned to the bed and kissed her gently, then placed her hand on his crotch. "What about me?"

She looked startled. "I—do you have a condom?"

"I don't." He wasn't a cheater. He really wasn't. But it had been months since Sarah had touched him with genuine passion and this girl had clearly wanted him.

"Maybe I do," she said, rummaging around in her purse.

"Would you prefer that to—"

"Yes, I would like that better."

She flipped over so she was on all fours. Oh, these younger women were so interesting. She seemed to come again, he couldn't be sure, but the important thing was he did. After it was over, she went to the bathroom. He hoped she wouldn't stay, and she didn't.

In the morning he found her book, a name inscribed inside. Kim Karpas. The surname was not the one she had given in the bar, he noticed that. But it was a used book, so maybe that was the name of the previous owner. He wondered if she had known it was one of his favorite novels, an easily sussed-out fact. Maybe the whole encounter had been carefully planned to seduce him.

He didn't care. He was flattered. He was going to go home and ask Sarah for a divorce. *Tell* Sarah they were getting divorced. Life was too short and he had too many opportunities, still. It was time to enjoy himself. *On with the dance, let joy be unconfined.* All his life, he had tried so hard to be good, and where had it gotten him?

*March 25*

GERRY'S PHYSICAL CONDITION is improving, day by day, and he couldn't feel worse. The longer, prettier days mock him through his huge windows, cheery postcards from a world he cannot imagine himself ever visiting again. He longs for a particular scent in Baltimore's early-spring air, but he can't smell it up here on the twenty-fifth floor. Sometimes he feels as if he can't smell anything at all.

But then there are the days when he thinks he can detect the fragrance of "real life" coming off Victoria and Claude—although not Aileen, never Aileen, Aileen smells like Lysol and iron ore. He wants to smell fresh-cut grass, sun, mulch. Then he remembers that is a detail in a short story he loved as a boy, about the people who live in a department store, pretending to be mannequins by day, coming to life when the store is closed. A writer, a poet, goes to live in the store, thinking it his singular brainstorm. He is delighted to find an entire colony of dropouts like himself. But the girl he loves is in love with the night watchman because he smells of the outside world. The story had been in one of those Alfred Hitchcock or Rod Serling collections that Gerry gobbled up as a child, collections that often had quite good stories. He had been astonished to realize in college that he had read a chapter from Waugh's *A Handful of Dust* in its original incarnation as a short story, "The Man Who Liked Dickens."

Waugh. Do people still read Waugh? Does Waugh matter? Do any writers matter anymore? Wah! There's Shakespeare, of course. No one argues against Shakespeare. *They will, one day,* Gerry thinks. Some information will come to light, they'll decide his wife wrote the plays or that he yearned to be a woman and cross-dressed in his spare time. Do people still speak of cross-dressing? He knows not to say *tranny* anymore and is proud of himself for that knowledge, but he's a little confused about the difference between *gender* and *sex*.

The bottom line is that Gerry is terrified of full recovery, because then what happens? As long as he stays in this bed, it seems possible to ignore the terrible thing that occurred in this room. Once he is himself again, won't he have to plumb his memory, determine his responsibility, and finally choose to act? Once he can stand on his own two feet, he will really have to stand on his own two feet.

Victoria comes in. Even if he can't actually smell the world on her, he can see it in the way her wardrobe is changing. For much of the winter, she wore a huge, fluffy yellow coat over black leggings so she resembled a tiny Big Bird. Today she is in a jaunty plaid trench coat. She just misses being his type, he thinks. His old type, the kind of woman he liked in his twenties, a Lucy. Margot, Sarah before her, even Gretchen—those had been attempts to change his type. He should have stayed true to himself. As Shakespeare would have said.

"Good morning, Vic—"

"Did you give Aileen a parking place?" She is working hard to control her emotions, whatever they are. Her cheeks are flushed, her voice trembles.

"I have arranged for her to park in the building," he says. "She was feeling vulnerable, walking here after sunset."

He wonders at his immediate impulse to fudge the information—*arranged for her to park in the building.* As if the plan is temporary—it is, he won't need Aileen forever—as if it's an act of kindness, no more. Gerry has always thought of himself as an essentially honest person, and not simply out of virtue. He lies for a living, he doesn't want to do it for free. Besides, it's wearying to lie, a waste of time and energy to track one's mistruths. Being honest is expedient and efficient.

Yet soft, tactical lies, so-called white lies—is it okay to call them *white* or is that now racist?—are the social WD-40 of day-to-day life, greasing all the tiny connections, keeping things frictionless. It's his money. Victoria has no right to inquire how he spends it. Victoria is on a need-to-know basis, whether she knows it or not. How did she even hear about Aileen's parking place? The two women never cross paths, as Aileen pointed out.

*Phylloh,* he thinks. *Phylloh is stirring the pot.*

"I'm the one who comes and goes, running your errands during the day," Victoria says. "If anyone gets a parking space, it should be me."

"I hadn't thought about it that way," Gerry says. "But given that your schedules don't overlap, why can't you share it?"

She opens her mouth, as if to object to this reasonable offer, then closes it, nods stiffly. She's gotten what she wants, yet she's still un-happy. Gerry has spent a lifetime trying to please women like this, women who cannot allow themselves to let go of their grudges and principles.

"Anyway, remember that registered letter they tried to deliver to your mother's house? The one I had you sign for? It was a wrangle, but the post office finally agreed to let me take it, after I showed them your mother's death certificate, then explained why you couldn't come in person. It took three trips."

Victoria offers him a legal-size envelope. It's certified, not reg-istered. Not an important distinction, but one that irks Gerry. An assistant should be detail-oriented. He extracts what appears to be a will, accompanied by a note from a lawyer.

"This makes absolutely no sense," he says, scanning the docu-ment. His father's name, his mother's name pop out at him, but everything else is a jumble.

"What?" Victoria is forever saying "What" and it's unclear to Gerry if she's hard of hearing or reflexively says this in order to have something to say. Whatever the reason, it's highly annoying.

"It's a letter to my mother stating that my father's will was con-tested."

"I'm sorry, I didn't realize your father had died."

"Oh, he definitely died. In September 2001. How can a will be contested almost two decades later and why would my mother care?"

Only it hasn't been two decades, not according to this letter.

*Dear Mrs. Andersen,*
*This letter serves as your official notice that the probate chal-lenge against Mr. Andersen's estate has been denied and you remain the sole beneficiary . . .*

Based on the details he can glean from the letter, his father died in early summer 2018, days before Gerry moved back to Baltimore. Had someone tried to contact his mother then? It was a confusing time, with different nursing aides coming and going. In fact, he had sacked one when he realized she sometimes took the day's mail and chucked it into the recycling bin, unopened. Did his mother even know his father had not died in 2001, as Gerry had been told?

Told by her. That was the only reason he believed his father dead. Because his mother told him, in great detail, how he had died on 9/11.

*Your father visits me. We make love in the garden.*

In hindsight, he had decided that was the first clue of her dementia. But what if—

"Victoria," Gerry says, "get my mother's executor on the phone."

THE EXECUTOR for Gerry's mother's estate is an old family friend, a lawyer who had lived on their street. Perhaps not the best way to choose one's lawyer, but no harm had come to Gerry's mother by conducting her affairs that way. Tom Abbott is a sweet, gentle man and Gerry had often wished he were his father. But even as a child he could see there was no spark between his mother and Tom.

"I think I've untangled things," he tells Gerry later that afternoon, their third call of the day. "Your father died in June and left a will, dated 2015, in which he bequeathed everything to your mother. 'Everything' isn't a lot—about two hundred thousand dollars, although she would have qualified for his social security, which was more than hers. Because his will was still in probate when your mother died, his bequest to her rolls into her estate. The money will be put in escrow and go to you when your mother's estate settles."

"Why was there a claim against it?" Not his most pressing question, not even close, but the best he can manage for now.

"Here's where it gets a little complicated. Gerry—your parents never got a divorce. Your mother could have asked for one on grounds of abandonment or adultery, but she chose not to. When they separated, in the 1970s, divorce law was far more restrictive and your father may have believed he couldn't initiate the action. Maybe he didn't want to because, without a formal dissolution of the marriage, there would be no official orders about child support. Anyway, his second marriage, as a consequence, was never legal. And in 2001, he left that woman, just moved out and on. I don't know why you assumed he was dead—"

*Because my mother told me he was.* "I'm not sure, either."

"But he had no legal obligations to his common-law wife. Kids were long grown. Then he dies and leaves what he has to your mother. His ex challenged the will. They had been together almost forty years, after all. But common-law spouses don't have standing in Ohio and, even if she did, his will is legal unless she can prove undue influence, or that he wasn't of sound mind when he made it. He was free to leave everything to your mother and now it goes to you."

"I'm not sure I want it," Gerry says. Blood money. No, not blood money. Bloodless money. *Guilt money.*

Or—is it possible that his father and mother loved each other? Is that the part of the story he missed? Is that why his first novel had hurt his mother?

"You can give it away, once it's yours, which should be by this fall. Donate to some cause in your mother's name. Maybe it's chump change to you, but it's enough to do some good in the world."

*It's enough,* Gerry thinks, *to cover my losses in transfer taxes and the like if I decide to sell this place sooner rather than later.* If he leaves this apartment once he recovers—who would blame him, who would find it suspicious? The apartment tried to kill him, after all. The floating staircase was like a mouth that tried to devour him whole, the whale to his Jonah. There would be almost a kind of poetic justice to his father's money covering the losses he would incur on all the taxes and real estate fees.

He has recorded his conversation with Tom on his smartphone, informing him, as Maryland law requires, that he is doing so. He then asks Victoria to transcribe it for him, something she grumbles about, but she is his assistant, after all.

That night, Gerry sleeps better than he has in some time. That is, he sleeps well until 2:11 A.M., when the phone by his bed rings and he picks it up and hears a female voice.

"Gerry? Gerry? I'm sorry I haven't called for a while."

"No," he says. "No, no, no." The calls had stopped after Margot, there aren't supposed to be any more calls. He had removed the recorder that the private eye recommended. The obvious answer is the obvious answer.

"We need to talk, Gerry."

The voice sounds different, or does it? Slightly more syrupy, but maybe that's his brain, struggling for consciousness. He is so foggy tonight, he feels as if he's swimming through sludge.

"Aileen!" he bellows. "Aileen!"

She comes up the stairs, moving quickly by her standards, huffing and puffing. "What's wrong, Mr. Gerry?"

"Please check the caller ID on the kitchen handset."

She grabs the kitchen phone from its cradle. "I must have dozed off, I didn't hear it ring."

*Not again,* Gerry thinks. *Not again.*

"Hey—there is a number—nine-one-seven—where's that?"

Nine-one-seven. The area code for New York, the one used by most mobile accounts. "Bring it to me, please."

She does. The number is familiar, but not immediately identifiable. He just knows he should know it. So few numbers reside in his memory now, the cost of using a cell phone, although he still remembers his mother's number on Berwick, a number that no longer rings, connected to a landline that will never ring again. This number, though—it's tantalizingly familiar. He picks up his cell phone and enters ten digits to see if it will spit out a contact.

He sees a familiar face in the little circle. Tiny as the face is, he can recognize the come-hither gaze, the coquettish affect.

"It's Margot," he says. "Someone has Margot's phone. I thought you—" He doesn't want to say out loud what he thought, that he presumed Aileen would take care of disposing of *everything*.

IT IS FOUR A.M. and the two have been sitting up, neither capable of sleep. Aileen can't even muster the concentration to knit.

"I *did*," she says for the umpteenth time. "I dropped her purse in the harbor, expensive as it was. A Birkin bag—it broke my heart to do that. A purse like that goes for thousands of dollars on the Internet. Anyway, if a phone was in there, it wouldn't be any good, even if it was in an OtterBox. Besides—"

"Besides, what?"

"Nothing."

"You didn't look through her purse?"

"Why would I?"

"I don't know."

"You want to know what I think?"

Gerry does and he realizes how unfathomable this notion would have been to him two weeks ago. God help him, he wants to know what Aileen thinks.

"She has a partner."

"What?"

"This thing that's happening to you, it takes two people, I think. Margot was in cahoots with someone—and this person has her phone."

"How, why?" Gerry considers all the times Margot lost her phone, left it in restaurants, cabs, salons. Margot was forever losing her phone. But why would some stranger then call him? "Even if there's another person involved—why continue the ruse when Margot has gone missing? Why use a phone with a number I can identify? The point has been to drive me crazy, make me look as if I'm imagining things, right?"

Aileen leaves her chair and plops herself on his bed, which he finds odd, un-nurse-like, but he doesn't feel he should protest. Still, her weight causes the mattress to shift, which gives him some discomfort in his braced right leg. *First do no harm, Aileen.* That's for doctors, but nurses should strive for it, too.

"If someone can make you believe a dead Margot is calling you from beyond the grave, maybe that would be enough to send you around the bend."

"But she didn't say she was Margot. And what's the point in sending me 'around the bend'?"

"Wasn't that the point of the whole campaign? These mysterious phone calls that no one else heard, the mysterious ghost you thought you saw, although I still don't know how that would be possible."

*It would be possible if Margot stole his badge and keys the first time she visited.* Everything is falling into place. The relief he feels is almost like, like, like—oh, never mind, Gerry hates similes anyway. He's not losing his mind. He thinks not of *Gaslight,* but of Bette Davis in *Hush . . . Hush, Sweet Charlotte,* watching the laughing conspiratorial lovers waltz and talk, waltz and talk on the verandah below her, delighting in how they turned the poor woman's mind against her. How his mother had loved that movie, which seemed to air every three months on *Picture for a Sunday Afternoon*. But between that film and *What Ever Happened to Baby Jane?*, young Gerry had been terrified of Bette Davis.

"Margot kept suggesting she had something on me. But it wasn't Margot's voice on the phone. Obviously."

Aileen nods, taps her temple. "As I said, she has a partner. Probably someone right here in Baltimore—that's the only way to explain that one call that came from a local number."

"Whom could Margot possibly know in Baltimore? Why would someone else have her phone? And if someone does—they must suspect that something has happened to Margot. They want something, but what?"

"Money," Aileen says. "Money or love. Isn't that the reason for most things people do? We can live without one, but not without both."

"Money is important only insofar as it provides for our basic needs and safety. Relative to being fed and having a roof over one's head, love is a luxury."

"Then why aren't there more good movies about people trying to be fed and putting a roof over their heads?"

"Don't be ridic—" He decides to soften his critique. "There are such movies. And books. There are great stories about man versus the elements, intent only on his survival."

"Like what?"

"Well—" Gerry finds himself struggling. He is sure that he used to give a lecture on this very topic and yet all he can think of right now is *The Old Man and the Sea,* a novel he loathes. "Actually"—wait, men are not supposed to say *actually* anymore—"there are many, trust me. But you're right, it wouldn't apply here. Margot may have wanted my love, but even Margot had to realize we were done. So, fine, money. Let's accept your theory that she and her partner want money. Do you think the partner's desire for money would trump any concern about Margot's well-being, her possible murder?"

"People overlook a lot," Aileen says, "when they're greedy."

Gerry has to concede this. Greed, lust, desire—they do lead a person to rationalize.

"Okay, but how was—how is—this elaborate prank supposed to shake money loose?"

"Margot said she knew something about you, right? Her partner would know whatever it is. The partner wanted you to recognize Margot's number, wants you to panic. They want you to see through the trick this time."

"They?"

"Well, she, now. The bill's going to come due, mark my words."

And the irony, Gerry realizes, is that now he does have something to hide, whereas he didn't before.

"What do we do?"

"Nothing. Remember your own advice—inaction is better than action. We do nothing, we wait. She'll make another move."

He shakes his head. He can't put his finger on it, but the logic of the story isn't tracking. Something is wrong. Margot was too sophisticated to think that unearthing a woman who said *Dream Girl* was her life story would matter to him. He had weathered that attempt to scandalize him already, when Shannon Little published her anemic little book. Oh, such a claim might warrant a new flurry of attention, but unless someone could prove his book had been plagiarized from another text, or stolen from a student's manuscript—no, no one would care and Margot, literary hanger-on that she was, would have been shrewd enough to know that. Besides, he hadn't *done* those things. All he had ever done was refuse to tell the world "who" the dream girl was. Magicians are allowed to safeguard their tricks; why aren't novelists?

"What do you think happens next?" he asks Aileen. "If you're right—if there is someone out there in whom Margot confided, someone who has ended up with Margot's phone and has reason to believe I know something about her disappearance—what's her next move?"

She throws up her hands. "Who knows?"

"So you're a pantser, not a plotter?"

"What?"

"Never mind."

*2001*

"ONE LAST QUESTION? And then Mr. Andersen will be happy to sign some books."

Gerry was in an independent bookstore in Bexley, Ohio. He was pretty sure he was in Bexley, Ohio. The days had run together long ago. This was the last stop of what felt like a never-ending tour and he hoped this was truly the last question he would answer for a while. If someone told him tonight that he would never have to speak about himself or *Dream Girl* ever again, he would be a happy man.

"Gentleman in the back?" the store's manager said.

"You don't seem to like men very much," the gentleman said. And Gerald Arnold Andersen Jr. found himself looking at Gerald Arnold Andersen Sr. for the first time in almost twenty years, since his father had insisted on showing up at his college graduation in Princeton. ("I paid for some of it," he said, which was not untrue, but his contributions were fitful and unreliable.) From that day on, Gerry had refused to have any relationship with his father. In interviews, he went out of his way to make it clear that he had been raised *by a single mother,* that his father was not in the picture at all. He omitted any mention of his father's bigamy out of fealty to his mother.

"My characters are my characters," he said. "I think it's somewhat naive, as a reader, to talk about whether writers 'like' their characters. That's not the point of what I'm doing. But perhaps I'm not the writer for you. I have you pegged as more of a MacDonald guy."

There had, in fact, been MacDonald novels in the house when Gerry was young and he credited his father's detective stories with ushering him over the threshold into the world of adult books. His memories of MacDonald were nothing but fond. But he was thrown off by his father's appearance and his words came out brackish, belittling. He had breached the basic etiquette of a book tour, in which the author must always be kind, no matter how ridiculous the question.

And no matter if it was asked by your wastrel father, who, go figure, had shown up as Gerry was finishing his victory lap. Ten weeks on the *New York Times* bestseller list and counting, a film option, and now his publisher was going to re-release his three previous novels in handsome new editions with covers in the style of *Dream Girl.*

Gerry Senior had to want something. But what?

Not an autobiographical book. He didn't even have the decency to buy a copy. But he lingered as Gerry signed books for the hearteningly long line of customers. Gerry's media escort, a busty divorcée who had been dropping hints about sleeping with him—lots of jokes throughout the long day about how hilarious it is that she's called an *escort,* etc., etc.—pegged his father, lingering at the back of the room, as trouble. He could sense it in her body language, how she made sure to stand in what would be Senior's direct path, should he try to approach. But his father remained where he was, his back against the science fiction section. Did anyone see the resemblance? It killed Gerry how much he looked like his father. The Andersen genes were strong—in the rare photos that show him with his father's family, you could always pick out who married into that tribe of blue-eyed blonds. His mother appeared outlandishly petite and dark in the family holiday photo taken when Gerry was not quite two. Legend had it that Grandmother Andersen had leaned over and hissed to her son: "Is she a Jewess?"

Books signed, stock signed, chairs folded, time for Gerry to make his getaway and, lord knows, the escort seemed eager to escort him. He didn't really have the energy for much, but if she wanted to do a little something in the car, that could work for him. He was a single man, unencumbered, a consenting adult.

He was about to slide through the bookstore's rear exit when he felt a tap on his shoulder.

"I guess you're surprised to see me."

Gerry shrugged.

"You seem to have done pretty well for yourself. How many copies of this book have you sold?"

A question Gerry hated, although at least the number was finally respectable. It seemed to him that only novelists were asked, in this indirect way, how much money they made.

"I'm doing fine," he said. "What do you want?"

"To see my boy, of course."

"I'm not your *boy*."

"How's Ellie?"

"Fine."

"I bet she's bursting with pride."

"She's always been proud of me, yes."

"Yeah, once you came along, she didn't really have anything left for me. When I would come home from being on the road, I felt like an interloper, like you two were the couple and I was the kid."

*Interloper.* Gerry's father had always liked to show off his vocabulary, much of it learned from the old *Reader's Digest* feature Build Your Word Power. He took the quiz very seriously and woe to anyone who dared to mark it up before him.

But had his mother treated his father like an *interloper?* Gerry didn't think so. His mother had lit up when his father walked into a room. She was a young, still quite beautiful woman when he left, yet she never dated again, and it wasn't for lack of opportunities. It was always clear to Gerry that Gerry Senior was the only man his mother ever loved. He considered that unrequited, undeserved devotion the singular tragedy of her life.

"What do you want?"

"I'm going to be leaving Colleen."

"Who?"

"My second wife."

"Down from two wives to one to none. That will be different for you."

"Maybe I'll swing by Baltimore, pay your mother a visit. It's not like I haven't done it before."

Gerry's right hand was sore from signing, but he felt his fingers clench and unclench. God, it would be satisfying to punch him, just once. "Why would I care that you're leaving Colleen? What does that have to do with me? What do *you* have to do with me?"

"You'll never be rid of me," his father said, pointing to Gerry's head. "I'll always be in there. You're *my* boy."

It was like a curse in a fairy tale. Gerry didn't believe in fairy tales. He took the escort by the elbow and piloted her into the park-ing lot. Unfortunately, his decision to touch her, even if it was only an elbow, ended up committing him to far more intimate and inten-sive acts than he had planned. Ah well, he wasn't married and if he noticed, when she plunged her hand inside his pants as they necked outside his hotel, that this "divorcée" wore a ring on the fourth finger of her left hand, what business was it of his?

"Who was that man?" she asked later in his bed, after he had tried and failed to fuck her into silence. "Back in the bookstore."

"Some run-of-the-mill crazy."

"Yeah, we see those a lot. I would have thought you were more likely to be a magnet for the female crazies. Those sex scenes in *Dream Girl*—they're pretty hot."

Were they? Gerry had intended them to be more comic than erotic. She was probably saying what she thought he wanted to hear.

"Gosh, I hope *I'm* not in your next book," she added in a tone that implied she yearned for just that.

"Who knows," he said, wondering what other novelists she had slept with, and if he would consider any of them more accomplished than himself. "Anyway, I have a very early wake-up call."

"I'm the one taking you to the airport. Should I call you or nudge you?" To her credit, she gave the old joke a curlicue of self-aware irony.

"Call," Gerry said.

*April 1*

VICTORIA IS IN AN ODD MOOD on April Fool's Day, a day
that Gerry has always loathed, finding practical jokes to be a particular kind of sadism. His father, of course, had loved them. His father's
sense of humor was so low that he had thought it funny to shake his
four-year-old's hand with one of those old-fashioned buzzers that ad-
ministered a shock. To this day, Gerry isn't much for hand-shaking.
People think he's a germaphobe, but he's simply never gotten over the
idea that something hard and electric might be pressed into his palm.

He attributes Victoria's mood to the weather. March has gone
out like a wet, cranky lion, the temperatures falling from last week's
springlike interlude, rain squalls sweeping across the city every few
hours. She isn't unkind—if anything, she is more solicitous of him
than usual, asking him twice if he's sure that a turkey sandwich will
suffice for lunch, if he's happy with his tea. She does inquire at one

point whether the detective from New York has followed up with him about Margot, but she appears to be making idle conversation.

Yet—her hands are shaking when she clears his tray and she is unusually pale. Probably love trouble. A neurasthenic type, he decides, the kind of girl—*woman*—who takes long, solitary walks at night, considers the Brontës and their heroines to be role models. He remembers a young woman in that vein whom he and Lucy had known, who was given to floaty, ankle-length dresses and outrageous hats. What a revelation she had been when they had gotten to know her better.

When Victoria comes in to say goodbye, she says: "We should probably start talking about the next phase of your care. You won't need a nurse forever. Do you think you could be comfortable without Aileen once you're able to use a walker?"

It's a day he has been yearning for, but now he's terrified of this benchmark. To move on his own again, to reclaim his body will be glorious. But—to be here, alone, in this apartment, where there are still things that can't be explained. To not have Aileen in his sight or within earshot. How will they ever be free of each other? To think that this is the person he will be yoked to for the rest of his life, not because of love or passion, but because of a terrible secret. If he were to call the detective—no, if he were to call a *lawyer,* explain the situation, and they could cut a deal—no, if he were to call Thiru—

His mind abandons all plans as preposterous. He can never confess without a horrible scandal. Imagine the first line of his *New York Times* obituary if this should come to light.

"Let's see what my doctor says. I admit, I am nervous about being alone here at night. What if I were to fall again?"

"I guess you could wear one of those bracelets?"

*I've fallen and I can't get up.* Gerry remembers being in his twenties when that television ad became famous. How he and Luke and Tara had laughed at the idea, at the poor production values. Why had it struck them as funny? Why had it struck them as improbable? He thinks of the Sphinx's riddle, about the animal who starts the day on four legs, goes to two, ends up with three. Add a walker and one could argue it's six.

So there, Sphinx. You didn't know everything. But then, neither did Oedipus.

"Let's see what the doctor advises," he says. It is four P.M. and he is counting the hours until Aileen's arrival and his nightly dose of Ambien.

GERRY WAKES UP in the middle of the night to the sound of a quarrel. *Mama never raised her voice,* he thinks. When his parents did argue late at night, he would have to tiptoe to the bottom of the stairs if he wanted to hear anything and, even then, it was difficult to make out the words.

But most of the time, he didn't try to eavesdrop, he just stayed in bed, willing himself to go back to sleep. He starts to do that now. *Maybe the Olympic swimmer has finally decided to spend a night here,* he thinks. *Maybe the sheikh is here, berating his staff.* It would be just like Baltimore to erect a luxury high-rise in which one could hear the neighbors through the walls.

And then he realizes the two voices are female and coming from downstairs. Tiptoeing is out of the question, of course. Even if he were mobile, he would be nervous about standing at the top of those stairs.

One voice is clearly Aileen's, only it sounds different from the way it usually does. Less flat, more passionate. *I did what I had to do. Don't second-guess me.*

The other voice is higher, but not as loud; her words don't carry as well. She seems to be asking questions, each sentence ending on a little wail. *Do? Do? What are we going to do?*

*I had no choice.*

*Jesus, Leenie.*

Leenie. Leenie. Gerry knows a Leenie. Knew. *"I go by Leenie. Rhymes with Deenie, like in the Judy Blume novel."*

It's as if his bed starts to float through the night sky, taking him to his past, the way the ghosts guided Scrooge through London. He is in his office at Goucher. Leenie has big thick glasses, she is round as a bowling ball. She has requested this office visit to explain why she wants to avoid participating at the next class, which has been designated a day of silence in support of LGBTQ people. He thinks that was the acronym at the time, although maybe the *T* and the *Q* hadn't yet been added.

*Leenie. Leenie Bryant.* And she had a friend in the class, they were thick as thieves, a slender girl. One so thin and one so round they had looked like the number 10 when they walked side by side.

The thin girl had been named Tory. At least, that was the name she used for her short stories, anemic little sketches that always ended with someone's suicide. "It's short for Victoria," she had told him, "but I prefer it because it rhymes with 'story' and all I want to do is write stories."

*Leenie and Tory. Aileen and Victoria.*

What is happening? Why are two of his former students downstairs in his apartment, arguing? How did one of them become his night nurse? Why had Victoria not reminded him that she was in his class when she applied to be his assistant? *I was there at the same time, but I majored in biology.*

*WHAT THE FUCK IS HAPPENING?*

He must be dreaming or hallucinating. He will start cutting back on the Ambien, the oxycodone. He will, he will.

"I'm going to tell him."

The voices stop. There is the thud of something falling, then a sound unlike anything Gerry has ever heard, as if a wild animal is rampaging. He would not want to see what's making that sound.

Footsteps on the stair, heavy and slow; has to be Aileen. *Leenie.* Huffing, puffing, carrying something cumbersome in her hand. It's the Hartwell, his first prize, a marble book on a brass base, his name and the year, 1986, inscribed on the book. The prize has sat on his desk in various cities for almost thirty-five years now, a testament to young promise fulfilled. Gerry has won other prizes since then, but none has carried the literal and figurative weight of the Hartwell.

There is something clinging to it, something dark, liquid, viscous, with pale flecks. He doesn't want to think about what's clinging to the statuette. Gerry glances at the clock. It's eleven thirty P.M., thirty minutes left of April Fool's Day. If this were a terrible practical joke, he wouldn't mind.

"I'm going to have to get another freezer," Aileen says. She puts the prize on his bedside table, goes to the kitchen, returns with a glass of water and his medication, including the calcium pill, which he usually doesn't take two nights in a row.

He takes them. Who cares if he never wakes up?

## 1986

"THIS IS SO CIVILIZED," Lucy whispered to Gerry. "None of that short-list savagery, no putting people through the suspense of it all for everyone else's amusement. Just a dinner, a presentation, and 'remarks.' I love this."

Gerry loved it, too, although he was trying to pretend he didn't. He had entertained, for a brief moment, not showing up for the dinner. Thiru had been furious with him. "You are not going to be that kind of writer," he said. "I'm not asking you to be Truman fucking Capote, running around with society types and appearing on *The Tonight Show*. But when someone gives you a prize, you are going to show up and you are going to be properly grateful. Jesus Christ, it's eighty thousand dollars—that could be a year off from teaching. Go someplace like Mexico or Costa Rica and it could be two years. You don't have to kiss anyone's ass, but you will attend, and you will be properly grateful."

He was properly grateful. He had even splurged on a proper tuxedo. In the fitting room at Hamburger's, as the tailor measured his inseam, he had been surprised, then terrified and, finally, elated, at a fleeting thought: *I will wear this tuxedo many times. I will win other awards. I will be given prestigious honors. This is only my first book.*

But, much as he would like to go away and do nothing but write, Lucy couldn't leave her teaching gig and there was no way she would let him take even a brief writing sabbatical. Lucy had no intention of allowing Gerry out of her sight for so much as an evening, which was why she was here. She had made that very clear when he reported Thiru's comments to her—how he must attend the dinner, even though it was in Mobile, Alabama, a wretchedly difficult place to fly, and a not-inexpensive one.

"You mean, *we'll* go," Lucy had said.

"I only meant to spare you a night of tedium."

"Sure."

And here she was, her arm linked through his, eye-fucking every woman who spoke to him. Lucy, who had never expressed the least bit of professional rivalry with Gerry, had suddenly become jealous of other women. It was at once incredibly erotic and a bit of a drag. He looked at her in the dress she had insisted spending three hundred dollars on in a Cross Keys boutique—three hundred dollars! She had never splurged on clothing before. It was a bubbly thing, apparently the current style. It didn't suit her. Worse, it was out of place here in Mobile, where the women tended toward a kind of era-less soap opera beauty. Big hair, low necklines, lots of sparkles.

"You can stop looking at her tits now," Lucy hissed after he greeted one of the jurors.

"I wasn't," he said, and he hadn't been. But then he had to look and—well, they were worth regarding. He had never been a breast man and, in marrying Lucy, he had figured he had cemented his preference for slender, small-breasted women.

What if he hadn't?

That question was like the fleeting thought in the dressing room at Hamburger's—thrilling, awful, wonderful. When he married Lucy, he had been "promising." Now he was beginning to fulfill that promise. This was only his first book, not his last. Would Lucy really be the last woman he ever had sex with? Of course she would, that was the promise made. He didn't believe that adulterous thoughts counted. He was pretty sure that a marriage's only chance was in each partner having a lively inner life, fantasies that could never be shared. But it had not occurred to him that professional success could nudge those fantasies closer to him, like someone moving a plate of brownies toward you when you were adamant that you were dieting. *Just have one. What could it hurt?*

The female juror, the one with the tits, had seated herself on Gerry's right. It was almost impossible to speak to her without staring into her cleavage, and he had to speak to her, he had to be polite. Thiru's orders.

Lucy, under the cover of the tablecloth, put her hand on his groin. It felt more like a threat than a come-on.

"It's funny how obscure our prize is, when it's so richly endowed," the richly endowed juror was saying. "I can't help thinking that it's about location—if our foundation were in New York or Chicago, it would be a much bigger deal. Why, the Pulitzer gives its winners only three thousand dollars and the judges are newspaper editors. Our jury is comprised of past winners, critics, academics."

"Comprises," Lucy said.

"What?"

"The correct usage is 'comprises.' The whole comprises the parts. Not 'comprised of.' Lots of people get it wrong. It's one of my bugaboos."

The female juror eyed Lucy thoughtfully. "I'd almost forgotten," she said. "You write, too."

"She's a wonderful writer," Gerry put in. "Fiction and poetry."

"Have you—"

"Have I published anything yet? Not outside of literary journals."

"She's been working on this book of interconnected stories, it's really marvelous."

"How lovely," the female juror said, putting her hand on Gerry's forearm. "You two are the loveliest couple, so perfectly matched, in brains and beauty. I mean that."

She excused herself to speak to someone on the committee about the evening's program.

"Do you want her?" Lucy said.

"What? No! What are you talking about?"

"Because you can have her. If I'm in the room."

"What are you saying?"

"I know you, Gerry. I can feel how restless you're becoming. I've been thinking—if we do these things together, we'll be okay. It's how we'll survive your . . . restlessness."

"Lucy—no, you're wrong. Ever since I've had this modest success, your emotions have been all over the place. This isn't about us, as a couple. Please don't worry. I'm not leaving you behind, in any sense."

Lucy has never looked more like Barbara Stanwyck than she does in this moment. Cool, appraising, plotting.

"Let's invite her back to the hotel with us, after the event, to have a drink. Let's see what happens."

"You're being very silly."

"What do you have to lose? If I'm wrong, or if you decide you want no part of it, we have a drink with the nice lady who helped hand you eighty thousand dollars and I can make up for being so rude to her just now. If I'm right—"

*What do I have to lose?,* Gerry thought.

*What do we have to lose?,* he thought, two hours later, when he allowed his wife first crack at those magnificent tits, the three of them giggling in the fussy canopy bed at the hotel. *Maybe this is how a marriage lasts. Maybe Lucy is onto something. What do I have to lose?*

"Just remember," Lucy said, lifting her lipstick-smeared mouth to his, "I always have to be in the room."

"Of course," Gerry promised, "of course." He bent down so his head was next to hers and they suckled at the juror's breasts like two hungry kittens.

*April 2*

"I SUPPOSE," Aileen says the next day, when Gerry has finally admitted to himself that he will be denied the solace of sleep no matter how many drugs are in his system, "you want to know what's going on."

*Does he?*

"If you must."

"I'm going to tell it in chronological order. I'm sure you won't respect that as an artistic choice—"

"No, I think that's fine, under the circumstances."

He's not sure of the time, only that he has not slept. Early morning, he judges by the light. He can hear traffic, the sounds of a city coming to life, but it's not yet rush hour.

She takes her usual seat. "Tory and I have been friends for years and roommates since we left Goucher. When she applied for the job as your assistant, she was gutted that you had no memory of her. It tore her up. We talked about what kind of man forgets someone he taught only seven years ago and we realized—the only students you cared about in that workshop were the boys and that one girl, Mona, because she was gorgeous."

*And the best writer in the class. Also, not all of the boys, only the two who were good.* But he's in no position to argue. He's literally in no position to argue. He's in his bed, incapable of walking, barely capable of holding a seated posture for more than a few minutes, and his "caretaker" has bashed in the head of his assistant, who is also her friend and roommate.

"We realized you don't *see* women unless you're attracted to them, that it was such a joke that you had gotten all this praise about some 'dream girl' who changed a man's life, that there was no way Aubrey was really your creation because she was too real, and you didn't know anything about real women. There's always been this rumor that you stole some woman's life, maybe even stole her literal story. We decided to gaslight you."

"But—how could you know I would have an accident?"

She sighs, hitches her chair closer to his bed. He can't help himself, he flinches.

"That was never the plan. It was going to be all letters and phone calls. But then you fell."

*There was a letter!* Then he realizes how silly it is to feel triumphant about being right about the letter.

"So we improvised."

"Are you a nurse in real life?"

"No, I was working as a barista at the Fort Avenue Starbucks. But you'd be surprised what you can learn on the Internet. There's a lot of information for people who have to be caretakers because someone in their family has had a fall. Most people can't afford private nurses, you know."

Is she actually resentful of the fact that he's been paying her a good wage for a job she's not certified to do? Is this some kind of boomer-millennial warfare?

"But—why—what happened tonight?"

"Victoria found Margot's phone in your office when she arrived yesterday morning. I had left it out by mistake."

"Why would Victoria call me on Margot's phone, then? It was Victoria, right?" He is hearing the voice now, pitched lower than Victoria's mousy squeak, capable of declarative sentences. How easily he had been fooled. Maybe the problem was that he didn't *hear* women.

"No—I mean, yes, Victoria was the one who usually called you, but I was the one who called the last time. I guess I left that part out. Margot's phone was in her bag. I had wiped it, it was safe, I was going to sell it to Gazelle for a little money. I don't know why I played that trick on you that night. I guess I wanted to see where your head was at. Anyway, I left Margot's phone out in the spare bedroom where I sit at night because I didn't think Tory went in there. Yesterday morning, she did."

"Yet the phone was"—what was the word she had used?—"wiped. Why would Tory even notice it?"

"It has a fancy case, a Louis Vuitton, something called the Eye Trunk. It costs almost fifteen hundred dollars new. I guess she got suspicious. At any rate, while I was here last night, she searched my room back at our apartment and she found Margot's purse. Victoria came here to talk to me and she got kind of hysterical. She couldn't be reasoned with."

*Reasoned with. Yes, it's so frustrating to argue with someone who can't be reasonable about the fact that you're covering up a murder.*

"You told me you threw the purse in the harbor."

A shrug. "Again, I thought it was a harmless lie. I had hoped to sell it online."

His head hurts so much, he has all the fogginess of the drugs without the benefit of sleep. He feels as if he is diving, diving, diving, going so deep he no longer remembers what he's looking for.

"Aileen, did I kill Margot?"

"Yes, so you should understand how accidents can happen."

An accident. How does one *accidentally* hit someone with a large, heavy piece of bric-a-brac until she's dead? It's not as if Victoria could have run into the Hartwell Prize or tripped and fallen on it. Aileen notices that he is staring at the statuette, still on his bedside table. She takes it to the kitchen sink, begins washing it. He considers asking her if she knows the proper way to clean an object made of brass and marble. He decides to stay silent.

"Maybe we should get married," says his not–Lady Macbeth as she scrubs busily.

*"What?"*

"If we marry, neither one can testify against the other. I mean, it would be in name only. I'm simply being practical. Not that different from people marrying each other so one can have a green card."

He wants to scream. Only who would hear him and, if anyone did, what would happen? He is a killer and now a co-conspirator in a second homicide. He let a woman clean up his mess and things have only gotten messier.

"I once had to research spousal privilege, for a book. It's a little more complex than most people believe." This is not true. He is basing his knowledge of spousal privilege on an episode of *The Sopranos,* which he has been watching in bowdlerized reruns on some cable channel.

"Hmmm," she says, drying the prize. "Well, it doesn't matter. Because no one's asking anything."

*For now.*

"Aileen—or should I call you Leenie?"

"Either is fine."

"Can I have my pills?"

"Yes. And at some point, I'll drive Tory's car to long-term parking at the airport, then take the light rail back into the city, paying cash."

This, too, had featured in a *Sopranos* episode, Gerry realizes. And in the local story he had researched, hoping to use it as a springboard to a novel. The man's ex-wife's car had been found in long-term parking, but at Reagan National. The supposition was that he had driven there, then taken the subway to Washington's Union Station and paid cash for a ticket on the regional train, thereby avoiding any kind of electronic trail.

Isn't it amazing the things one can learn on YouTube? Isn't it amazing the things one can learn from art?

*1999*

GRETCHEN'S MATCHING SUITCASES—no wheeled luggage for her, not when she had a set of beautiful leather bags that had been presented to her over a series of birthdays and Christmases, from ages fourteen to eighteen—were lined up in the hall outside their apartment from smallest to tallest, almost like the von Trapp children getting ready to sing.

"I'm going back to New York, Gerry," she said, "and I am divorcing you."

"Why?"

"Because I have been offered a very good job at Lehman Brothers. And because I don't like Baltimore and because you don't belong in New York."

It was the third part that hurt. What did she mean, Gerry didn't belong in New York? What was she saying about him? That he was second-rate, a *regional* writer. It was true, his novels, three so far, had all been based here. And books two and three had been a bit of a misfire. Not bad books, but not the books that people expected to follow his first book. Had Gretchen forgotten that they had met in New York, that she was the one who insisted on the move to Baltimore when she got the offer from T. Rowe Price? He had not dragged her here, quite the other way.

That said, he had liked their life in Baltimore. The enormous apartment, which cost a pittance relative to New York, teaching a single class per semester at Hopkins, plenty of time to write, while Gretchen's salary paid the major bills.

"I'd be happy to go back to New York, all you had to do was ask."

"I don't want you to come with me. Good lord, Gerry—you don't even *like* me."

She wasn't wrong. He didn't like her. She was humorless and pedantic. The only fiction she read was his, and then only grudgingly, in that way more traditional wives fraternize with a traditional husband's coworkers. The only thing they had in common was sex and even that had a kind of grudging aspect to it, almost as if she resented how much she liked it.

And yet—the idea of her leaving him was something he could not bear.

"Maybe if we went to counseling—"

"I'm not your mother, Gerry."

"You're *nothing* like my mother." Actually their stature was similar, although his mother didn't have such thick calves.

"I mean—I know you don't want to be your father all over again, disappointing woman after woman."

"Woman after woman—I didn't realize I had disappointed any women!" Okay, Lucy, but who was to blame for that?

"I can't stay in this marriage so you can prove to the world how good you are, Gerry. We're wrong for each other. It's not a crime. We have no children. Divorce is not a big deal."

Some part of Gerry's brain was arguing that it was a big deal when one spouse outearned the other ten to one and owned an apartment overlooking Gramercy Park. Gretchen owed him. Could he bear to collect? Could he afford to collect? Even simple divorces had costs, as he had learned when he and Lucy ended their marriage.

"I love you." He sounded tentative, even to his own ears.

"You did. And I loved you. But we're wrong together, Gerry, and it's been clear for a long time."

"There's someone else. You wouldn't do this if there wasn't someone else." Gretchen had been going to New York a lot. For work, she claimed, but now it was clear to Gerry what all those trips had been about.

"Goodbye, Gerry. I'll be in touch about the legal end of things."

The elevator arrived, carrying only a wheeled cart that someone downstairs had clearly sent up to Gretchen at her request. She piled the von Trapp children on the cart in a neat pyramid. *Good night, farewell, auf Wiedersehen, adieu.* She shook his hand and refused his help in pushing the cart back onto the elevator.

He ran down eight flights of stairs, but she was gone by the time he reached the lobby. There was nothing to do but to walk. It was a fine autumn night, smoky and cool. He had forgotten his jacket, but his wallet was in his back pocket. He would walk until he was too exhausted to think or feel.

*April 5*

SO A SECOND FREEZER ARRIVES, the whine of the cordless saw resumes, and Gerry wonders if a different soup kitchen will be receiving a side of beef or if that ruse was required only when Victoria was lurking about. He lives by the motto *Don't ask, don't be told*.

At Aileen's urging, he leaves a message for Victoria the first day she fails to show up for work. It is spooky to speak to Victoria's truly disembodied voice, on a phone now in her car's glove compartment, but he tries to sound as normal as possible.

Meanwhile, Leenie has sent Margot's phone to a company that buys old electronics, using Victoria's name, address, and email for that transaction. It strikes Gerry as too clever by half.

"What if there are incriminating emails or texts or calls—"

"I'm telling you, Margot's phone is wiped clean. As for Tory and me, we were very disciplined, we never communicated by text or email when we were, um, making our plans. But remember, now you have to know we were roommates. If someone comes around. You didn't know, but after Victoria went missing, I had to tell you. We hid it from you because we didn't think you would approve of an untrained person being your nurse."

This, at least, has the advantage of being sort of factual. He should have known, from dealing with nursing agencies for his mother, that Aileen's rates were too good to be true. Gerry's thrift has often been his undoing.

Aileen—Leenie—says: "I'm going to report her missing after forty-eight hours."

"You know you don't have to wait that long to report a missing person. That's a television conceit."

"Right. But 'Aileen' would believe that. I'm playing a character. Haven't you gotten that by now?"

Oh, he has gotten it. Aileen is stolid and doesn't read and doesn't get jokes. Leenie is quicker, in thought and movement. Rash, one might say. But she reads.

She also writes, as it turns out.

She says she's going to bring him her work, that she wants him to see how her writing has matured over the past seven years. He is not looking forward to it. He thinks about Roth's alter ego, Zuckerman, trapped against a mailbox by Alvin Pepler, the Jewish marine and quiz show contestant, who demanded that the writer read his critique—of Zuckerman! Roth described it as the lion approaching Hemingway, keen to provide his thoughts on "The Short Happy Life of Francis Macomber."

But Aileen/Leenie is not Gerry's character. She is very much her own character. This story, her story, is much more interesting than anything she ever put on a page when she was a student. Gerry is a secondary character, as long as he stays in bed.

And as long as he stays in bed, how can he be suspected of anything? He uses his phone to read, something he thought he would never do, but he has an urgent impulse to read Hiaasen and Leonard and Westlake, writers who could probably construct a story in which a man in Gerry's (prone) position could somehow jettison the Inconvenient Nurse while making her the singular culprit. On his SmartHub, he watches films reputed to have airtight stories; he rereads Christie, whom he adored in early adolescence, then later rejected. The number three best-selling writer in history, according to Google, and given that number one is the Bible and Shakespeare is number two, doesn't that really make her number one? The Bible has no single author and Shakespeare has no estate. What would Shakespeare do with this story and would it be a comedy or a tragedy? Some wild coincidence involving twins and eavesdropping. If only Gerry had a twin.

No, Gerry simply cannot plot his way out of this. Two women have been killed in his apartment, one by him, and he has sat here, doing nothing, while a woman carves up their bodies and takes them God knows where, possibly the very incinerator his mother used after crab feasts. He saw online that the city will be closing the facility soon and then how will people dispose of their crab shells and dead bodies?

*1990*

"ARE YOU GOING to make it to New York?"

"I don't see how I can, Tara—it's the end of semester, grades are due, I have so much to read—"

"Jesus, Gerry, all you have to do is get on a train. Three hours up, three hours back, fifteen minutes in his room."

The cord on the wall phone in the kitchen is a long one and Gerry can pace while he talks to Tara. It drives Gretchen crazy, the way he paces when he speaks on the phone, but Gretchen isn't here tonight. She has joined a book club in the building, although it seems like more of a drinking club to Gerry. Gretchen always waits to read the book until the last minute, then complains about the selection. Her club's choices are pretty middlebrow, in Gerry's unvoiced opinion, and he imagines the discussions are not of a particularly high caliber. The real emphasis seems to be on the themed refreshments. The current book is *The Remains of the Day,* which Gerry admires almost in spite of himself. Ishiguro is only four years older than he is and his third book has won the Booker! Gerry is reworking his third novel after Thiru's careful notes. He has high hopes for it, but he had high hopes for his second novel, whose reception was basically "not like his first novel." That was the point, of course.

"Will he even know I'm there, Tara?"

A long pause. "I don't know, Gerry. I thought he registered my presence, but maybe it was wishful thinking. Still, I'm glad I did it. I'm glad I got to say goodbye. I think you'll feel the same way."

Easy for Tara, living in Greenwich, to say. She hadn't required an entire day to make her visit. And she didn't have a job, just a baby. Tara was probably happy for the melodrama of a deathbed visit. It relieved the tedium of her day-to-day existence, whatever that was.

"Is it—difficult? To see him, I mean."

"Extremely. I worry it will blot out the memories I have of that gorgeous, gorgeous boy. But maybe it should, Gerry. Maybe if more people lose people they love, things will change."

"Okay, Tara. I'll go tomorrow."

He hung up the phone, called Amtrak to check the schedules. There was a seven thirty train. He could reasonably expect to arrive at the hospice by eleven, be back in the apartment by four. He could do this.

*I can do this,* he said to himself the next morning, waiting in the line at Penn Station to buy his ticket. He had never realized what an active commuting culture Baltimore had. The station was bustling and full and he began to worry that the ticket line would not move swiftly enough for him to catch the seven thirty train.

And then he began to hope that would be the case. No one could blame him for missing the train, right? It's not as if anyone were expecting him. In fact—how would anyone know if he had been there? Tara wasn't the type to check behind him, to call the hospice and inquire if Gerry Andersen had visited Luke Altmann. He remembered shaking hands with Luke that first day at Princeton. "I know—I look like a Hitler youth, but my people ran away from Germany in the 1930s." The shock of blond hair that he was forever pushing out of his eyes. Young Gerry's heart had sunk at the thought of having such a good-looking roommate. What a laugh they'd had over that later.

7:21. 7:22. 7:23. It was about to be his turn at the window.

No one really knew how this disease worked. They said it couldn't be caught through casual contact, but how could they be sure? Would he be expected to take Luke's hand? What would he say? Could Luke even hear?

7:24.

He stepped out of line and left the station just as the announcement for the New York–bound train began. He waited two days before he checked in with Tara and described his visit with the dying Luke.

"Was it hard," Tara asked, "seeing the lesions on his face?"

"Yes," Gerry said. "Very tough."

"Gerry, there are no lesions on his face."

Luke died a week later. Tara and Gerry never spoke again.

*April*

WITH VICTORIA GONE and, along with her, the framework of her Monday-through-Friday schedule, Gerry no longer knows what day of the week it is. He's fine with that.

"Gerry?"

"Yes?" He still doesn't like the sound of his name in Aileen—Leenie's—mouth.

"We need to talk."

Not about marriage, he hopes.

"Okay," he says, not looking away from his downloaded copy of *The Daughter of Time.*

"Wouldn't it make sense for you to give me Victoria's money? Without her kicking in, it's going to be hard for me to make rent and we pay rent on the fifteenth."

"How do I give you Victoria's money?" he says. "I don't have access to it."

"Her paycheck, I mean. If you're not paying her, why not pay me double?"

He almost says yes. That's how weak he is, how feeble he has become. He's not thinking things through clearly. Luckily, he sees the flaw before he agrees.

"Aileen—"

"Leenie."

God, this is exhausting. "Leenie, if anyone ever did a forensic accounting"—he thinks that's the term—"and saw this huge increase in your salary, it would be very suspicious, don't you think?"

As "Aileen," Leenie had thought physically, like Rodin's *Thinker*, all furrowed brow and bent body. Leenie stands stock-still, her chin on her hand.

"I can't make rent," she says.

"You could find another roommate, couldn't you?"

"No, Victoria's the only one on the lease. I had some credit problems a few years ago and we thought it better that way. Legally, I don't have standing. I could get in trouble if I brought another tenant in."

So she's comfortable carving up bodies and disposing of them, but worries about being hauled into rent court.

"That is a tough situation," he says, trying to sound sympathetic, "but I'm not sure how this is my problem."

"If you hadn't killed Margot, I wouldn't have had to kill Victoria."

Gerry is pretty sure there's a fallacy lurking in that reasoning, but he can't be bothered to find it. Instead he asks what he has asked before, hoping for a different answer.

"Did I kill Margot, Leenie? Did I? What really happened that night?"

She stomps downstairs, offended. She has bashed in the head of her friend, but she apparently takes great exception to the suggestion that she might have plunged a letter opener into Margot's eye.

Not that even Gerry can persuade himself she did it. Why would she have killed Margot? Did Margot, of all people, figure out what was going on and return to the apartment to confront Aileen? No, that makes no sense whatsoever.

The landline rings. Thiru.

"I've received your royalties and gone over the accounting. Any chance you'll ever surrender your love for paper checks and let me use ACH to deposit these things?"

"No—" he begins. Then he remembers that Victoria was the one who deposited his checks. He does not want to entrust this task to Aileen, does not want her to see what *Dream Girl* puts back into his coffers every six months. "Yes. Yes, I think I will change. How does one go about that?"

"I just need some basic information. Routing number, account number. Your assistant can—"

"*No.*"

"Excuse me?"

"Victoria is gone. Stopped coming to work, with zero notice. But I can give you that information now. I keep a checkbook in the drawer of my nightstand."

Gerry realizes that lying, once it has begun, never stops. He has lied to the detective about Margot and now he has lied to Thiru about Victoria. In their long partnership, he has never before lied to Thiru, although he was sometimes obscure about the infidelity that ended his first marriage. Thiru would have been scandalized, not by

Gerry's adultery, but by his ability to screw up what most men would have considered a dream scenario.

Thiru assumed men were unfaithful, he called it the nature of the beast. But all Gerry had ever wanted was to be good, *not* his father. For much of his life, he had been able to achieve this not inconsiderable goal. He considered the two episodes of adultery—the stupid fling with Shannon Little, the one-night stand when he was married to Sarah—to be forced errors. The enormous guilt he still felt about both was proof that he was not a sociopath.

"Gerry Andersen, giving up paper checks. It's almost like that Internet meme that goes around from time to time."

"What?"

"Do I need to define 'meme' for you, or this one in particular?"

"I know what a meme is, Thiru, I just don't get this one."

"I'm thinking of the one where people try to craft a message that would alert others they are in danger, while seeming neutral to their captors. You giving up paper checks—that's darn close. If you said something rhapsodic about *Wuthering Heights,* I would know for sure that someone had a gun to your head. Or if I ever saw the word 'limn' in your work."

Gerry laughs as best he can. The primary thing is, there will be no checks arriving, no record of his money for Aileen/Leenie to see. It has become all too clear to him that Leenie is very, very interested in money, especially his money.

She's going to do something stupid with the purse and the phone cover, he is convinced of it.

*1972*

THE SHOEBOX WAS from Hess at Belvedere Square. Gerry believed he knew exactly what pair of shoes it once held. Two-toned spectator oxfords with a slight heel. His mother was vain about her feet, which were small and delicate, a size six. Whenever they went shopping for his back-to-school shoes, she usually ended up buying a pair for herself, too. How the Hess salesmen loved to wait on her. Gerry knew his mother was pretty, although he tried not to think about it. But whenever he saw her calf in the hands of a shoe sales-man, he was reminded not only how pretty she was, but how she must have had her pick of men, and yet she still chose his father.

He was not looking for the shoebox, of course. Who would look for a shoebox in the pantry, behind boxes of generic pasta from the Giant? He had been looking for his mother's secret stash of choco-late, a game of sorts. She hid her chocolate; he found it, ate a few pieces; she pretended to be outraged. Then she hid it again. He wasn't snooping, not really. It had never occurred to him to spy on his mother. The only thing she had ever tried to keep from him was his father's awfulness. But his father was gone, had been gone for almost two years now.

The shoebox was light, too light to hold even a dainty pair of size sixes. Curious, Gerry pulled it down from the shelf and opened it.

Envelopes with cellophane windows. Bills. Six months of bills. He didn't know much about bills—what fourteen-year-old boy did?—but he quickly realized these were unpaid.

*They don't make money off of us. They make money off people who don't pay their bills.*

His mother had said that to him once when he was trying to understand why a simple piece of plastic could be substituted for cash, why stores would accept it. In the 1960s, there was a single Baltimore charge card, accepted by all the local department stores. He had hovered at his mother's elbow, watched the clerk press down on it with the metal machine that looked like a stapler. It made no sense to him. All he understood was his mother's pride at not being one of the people that the store made money from.

He was fourteen. He wanted to shove the box back on the shelf, continue to look for her chocolate. Instead, he sat at the kitchen table and made neat stacks of bills. She had been using a charge account at Graul's from time to time; strange, because she seldom shopped at that grocery store despite it being in view of their house. She always claimed it was too expensive. But it was the kind of store that would allow customers to have charge accounts. Bills for clothes, but all for him, and not many because he wore a uniform to Gilman. The car payment. Utilities. C&P Telephone.

It was a school day, late afternoon, the sky gray, a boisterous wind whipping around the house. When his mother came through the kitchen door and saw what he was doing, she didn't seem particularly surprised. If anything, her reaction seemed to be one of relief.

"Gerry," she said.

"Get your checkbook, Mother. And your paystubs. I can get us out of this—and make sure it never happens again."

He did, eventually. He worked out payment plans with those who were owed money, then created a household budget. He also got a job—at Graul's, as a stock boy, which meant not only did he contribute money to the household, he sometimes was allowed to take home unsellable goods—badly dented cans, cans with missing labels. His mother made a game of concocting dinners from these rejects. They were not particularly good dinners, but he admired what they jokingly called her "can-do" attitude.

And every month, he sat at the kitchen table, filling out the checks and then passing them to his mother to sign. He couldn't help noticing that his father's name was still on the account, which worried him to no end.

*April*

"I GAVE UP MY APARTMENT," Leenie says.

"What?"

"I told you I couldn't make the rent without Victoria. Besides, you have all this space here. I told Phylloh that I would be staying here until you're healed." She frowns. "She asked me about Victoria. I don't like her. I think she's nosy."

Gerry chills at this pronouncement. Time was, he would have agreed. Now he worries something might happen to her. Curvy, innocent Phylloh, who reminds him of a poppy seed muffin, which is something one's not supposed to say anymore, but can he at least *think* it? In his aging body and his aging mind, can he allow himself the thoughts and metaphors and pronouns that were permissible when he was young? Is that so much to ask?

"There's no spare bedroom," he says. "As you know, there's only my office and the little study, with the sleeper sofa."

"That's okay. I'll sleep in your bed. You're not using it, after all."

He does not like the idea of Leenie in his bed, for which he is filled with overwhelming nostalgia. One thing Sarah had taught him during their brief marriage was the importance of good sheets and linens. His bed is a basic wooden frame and he doesn't go in for all those extra pillows that have to be removed at night—what's the point of pillows that one removes every night?—but he misses his king-size bed. He wants to leave this bulky, ugly hospital bed and go back to his true love. Except—he also never wants to leave this hospital bed. It's complicated.

"Is this really necessary?"

"I told you, I can't afford the apartment without Victoria."

"Not even for another month?"

She shakes her head.

"If you must—you must." He can buy new sheets, when this is over. Will this ever be over? How does it end?

"Also—may I use your computer?"

This is even more disturbing than the thought of her in his bed.

"For—"

"I told you I'm working on something. I'd like your feedback when I'm done. Oh—and I told Claude to stop coming. I can do what he was doing. It's amazing what—"

"You can learn on YouTube. I know. I know."

*April*

STRANGELY BUT ALSO HAPPILY, Gerry sees less of Leenie now that she's living downstairs. When she does come up to
minister to him, she wears her own clothes instead of the polyester
nurse scrubs. She tends toward tight jeans and too-short tops, in
which she looks rather bulgy. She has quite a few tattoos, including
a rose on the small of her back, which Gerry sees when her shirts
ride up. He remembers a verse from a book of doggerel he read as
a child, about a "little Hindu" whose pants and shirt don't quite
reach. Good lord, what a terrible thing in retrospect, almost as bad
as Little Black Sambo. Yet Gerry still owns the tiny red Helen Ban-
nerman version of that tale because his mother gave it to him on his
birthday, with an inscription. The sight of her pretty, spiky cursive
writing fills him with so much joy that he cannot bear to jettison

the book. Should that go to Princeton? Maybe with a note about why he still owns it?

Leenie is standing at the foot of his bed, a sheaf of papers in her hand, clearing her throat to get his attention.

"I thought I would read my story to you, the way we did in class."

"Okay." What else can he say?

She clears her throat again. "It's called 'Mobius Dick, aka Great White Male.'"

"Hmmmmm."

"Please hold your comments until I finish reading."

"If I had a copy it would be easier to follow."

"Just listen."

*It was supposed to be an honor, getting in the seminar taught by Harry Sanderson. It was not so long ago that he was the flavor of the month, anointed as the face of American literature in the earlier twenty-first century. The best-selling book he published in 2001 was at once small and large—although it centered on a weekend in the life of a man in an early midlife crisis, it also seemed to anticipate the 9/11 attacks and the way the world would be reordered by them.*

*There were ten girls and two boys in the class. This was not unusual. Beardsley had been coed for almost twenty-five years by this time, but it was still overwhelmingly female. On college visits, boys would lean into other boys and inform them: "The odds are good, but the goods are odd." Yet, somehow, the two boys were the only students that Harry Sanderson seemed to care about. The two boys and the girlfriend of one—a girl named Moana who looked as if she could be the character Sanderson had described in his most successful novel.*

She looks up from the page, her face expectant. Where to begin? Seriously, where to begin?

"I notice that you are choosing names that are barely different at all from what I would assume are their real-life inspirations. Harry Sanderson for Gerry Andersen. Moana for Mona—"

"Oh, *her* you remember."

"You've jogged loose quite a few memories of that semester at Goucher. It was only seven years ago, after all." *And she was quite beautiful and also by far the best student in the class. Life is unfair, Leenie. If you haven't figured that out when you're almost thirty years old, that's a problem.* "Anyway, why such thinly veiled identities? Why not a memoir if you're going to hew closely to the truth?"

"It's a *choice*," she says. "I'm trying to make a point, that it's a very thin line between fiction and real life, that all fiction is appropriated from the lives of others, so it's better to be transparent about it. All these labels, what do they mean? Everything is fiction and everything is true. It's very meta."

Gerry allows himself an inner *Princess Bride* moment. *I do not think that word means what you think it means.*

"So why does Goucher get a pass? Why call it Beardsley? Why not . . . Groucher?"

"Because Beardsley's the name of the private school in *Lolita*."

"What does that have to do with anything?"

"Because you're my Humbert Humbert and you're going to rape Moana."

"*What?*"

"It's thematically consistent. You rape the woman whose life inspired *Dream Girl*. Metaphorically."

"*There was no woman whose life inspired* Dream Girl *and that book was almost fifteen years old by the time I taught at Goucher.*"

"But isn't there a woman with a secret you don't want anyone to know? Weren't you worried that was the secret that Margot was going to share with the world?"

There's a weird faux innocence about Leenie's question. How does she even know what Margot threatened to do? He remembers the fight with Margot, how she raked his face with her nails, the strange things she said. Victoria was here. What had she heard? What had she inferred? What had she told Leenie? He still had no idea what terrible secret Margot knew, or thought she knew, but it wouldn't have been about *Dream Girl,* because there was no secret there.

"Aren't *you* troubled by giving a Chinese American girl a name from a Disney film about a Hawaiian girl?"

"Well, later I'm going to get into how Harry, like most men of his generation, fetishized Asian women. There's going to be a lot of wordplay with Moana and 'moan.'"

*Of course there is.*

"Anyway, what do you think?"

He decides to risk honesty, of a sort. "It hasn't gotten started."

"What do you mean?"

"Put me, the reader, in the classroom. Show me the characters, let them define themselves by action and dialogue. This sounds like a dutiful summary. You're tapping on the mike, clearing your throat. You literally cleared your throat before reading. *Start,* Leenie."

Unexpectedly, she does. She comes up later that evening with more pages and they are better. Still not good, no, never good, but she is listening, trying. She's not even thirty. At her age, Gerry wasn't the writer he would become by age forty. He was better than this, he was better than this at age eighteen, but he wasn't the writer he would become. As he listens to Leenie's new pages, he finds in himself the man he was in his twenties, a serious and thoughtful reader, a man who had aspired to nothing more than a tenured position in a good writing program, a little house, sabbaticals. A like-minded partner.

Of all the women in his life, he misses Lucy the most. It had taken real effort to screw that up. If only the Hartwell juror had been more of a prude; but Lucy's instincts for willing co-conspirators were good, too good. In that brief, giddy time when they brought other women into their bed, he had felt as if he had been initiated into a vampiric cult. Sleeping with Shannon Little, outside Lucy's sight, had been the only way to break the spell, break the marriage. Lucy was making him bad and he was determined to be good. It was all he had ever wanted.

But the best thing about Lucy was that she had been there in the beginning, when his hopes were modest. He remembers the nights in the funny little duplex on Schenley Road, drinking cheap wine from the three-dollar bin at Trinacria. Whatever happened to Lucy? He thinks she's a teacher somewhere, publishing in the better journals, more poetry than fiction these days. Gerry has always had a soft envy for poets and their economy with words.

He marks up Leenie's pages and recommends books to read— Francine Prose's *Blue Angel,* Richard Russo's *Straight Man,* John Irving's *The Water-Method Man.* He doesn't like academic satires, but if she's going to attempt this, she might as well read the best. She is touchingly earnest about his advice. It occurs to him that this is all she wanted, after all, the singular focus of the writer-teacher by whom she felt ignored all those years ago. The silly campaign she and Victoria cooked up was nothing more than a bid for attention. She now has an exclusive seminar. He almost enjoys it. This, more than anything in months, has engaged him, made him feel mentally astute again. *I'm not dead yet! I don't want to go on the cart.* He feels strangely good.

Until he remembers that two women are dead.

## April

IT'S SAD, how long it takes for anyone to inquire after Victoria, and when it finally happens, it's her landlord. Leenie has told Gerry that Victoria has parents, but she's not particularly close to them, and it's been over a year since she had a boyfriend. Before disposing of Victoria's phone, Leenie signed her up for a dating app and cast a wide net, "swiping right" on the most unsavory types possible, setting up a date with one at a Baltimore bar a week after Victoria was well past the point of dating anyone. If he showed, he was stood up, but let him prove that if the moment ever comes.

Two days later, Leenie packed a bag with Victoria's clothes and drove to the airport. She left the clothes in various donation boxes in the city, tossed the suitcase in a dumpster, parked in long-term parking, dropped the keys in a sewer, and returned to the city via light rail. No one seemed to notice Victoria had shuffled off this mortal coil until the rent was overdue. For it turned out that Leenie had never paid her share to Victoria in March, something she had neglected to mention to Gerry.

Gerry and Leenie have only the two minutes it takes for the landlord to get past Phylloh and ascend in the elevator to review their agreed-upon story. Yes, Victoria and Leenie were roommates. Yes, Gerry was aware of that. But does the landlord know that? Even if he doesn't, it strikes Gerry as a bad idea to omit this information. Such a needless, heedless lie could come back to haunt them.

"Let me take care of it," Leenie says with what Gerry feels is unearned confidence. So far, Leenie's off-the-cuff improvisations have been a little too "exit pursued by bear" for him, only it's more like "exit in insulated freezer bags, body part by body part."

The landlord is a pale white bald man who looks as if he never stops sweating, no matter the weather. The seams of his blue oxford cloth shirt are damp, and there's a sheen on his forehead, which he mops with a handkerchief, almost as if he had climbed the twenty-four flights to the apartment.

"I'm sorry to bother you, but I'm worried. Victoria was one of the most responsible tenants I ever had, but she paid only part of the rent in March and now she's missing. I went by the apartment when she didn't answer my calls and it seems as if she hasn't been there for quite some time."

"I know," Leenie says. "I was her roommate until I moved in here to provide full-time care for Mr. Andersen."

"You weren't on the lease."

"I had lost a job and Victoria was kind enough to take me in." Gerry notes that Leenie is avoiding timelines. Good. "We've known each other forever. She did this, even back in college. Disappeared at times. She—well, I don't want to violate her privacy, but sometimes she thinks she knows better than her doctors what she needs. She always comes back, she's always fine."

"Have you called her parents?"

Leenie sighs. "Her parents are the last people she would turn to when she's like this. I didn't know what to do. And I didn't know what to tell Mr. Gerry"—she turns to him—"I'm sorry, I kept hoping she would show up and you would be okay with her continuing in this job again. There's so much stigma around mental illness. That's why I told you she had a personal emergency. It's true, if you think about it."

It is true and Gerry doesn't want to think about it. Being bashed in the head with the Hartwell Prize is a very real personal emergency.

The landlord looks concerned, but also confused. "I mean—I have to start eviction proceedings. I can't not enforce the lease. But she'll have some time to respond. If she shows up—"

"Fingers crossed," Leenie says, and she actually holds up her right hand, showing how she has crossed her index and middle finger. Of course, this is also what children do when telling a lie, only with their hands behind their backs.

"I could cover her rent for the month," Gerry says impulsively.

"Why would you do that?" the landlord asks.

Leenie glares at him, the same question evident in her dark eyes, but less open-ended. *You're acting like a guilty schmoe,* she seems to be saying, and he is.

"She's not here to collect her salary. If I pay the rent for the month, it gives her a chance to come back, regroup. Come May, if she hasn't returned—then, I guess, you'll have to pursue eviction."

*And Leenie will have time to go back and check the apartment thoroughly, make sure that Victoria has left nothing behind that can pose a problem. What if she kept a journal?* Gerry had always proselytized for journals with his students, showing them the miniature Moleskines he was never without.

He explains his idea to Leenie after the landlord leaves and it takes the edge off her anger.

"She didn't keep a journal as far as I know and I don't think I'll find anything, but okay. It was awfully generous of you to pay the rent."

Yet something in Leenie's tone suggests she's put out by his largesse, by his willingness to expend funds on anything that doesn't benefit her directly. He can't help noting how proprietary she seems about his money.

"The thing you said about her, um, mental illness. Was that true?"

"Yes and no. I mean, she did have episodes at school where she disappeared. She's got a prescription for Lexapro. But almost everyone's taking something these days."

"What will happen to her things?" Gerry asks. "Eventually, I mean."

"If she doesn't come back to get them, the landlord will probably just put them in the street."

*If?* Is Leenie beginning to believe her own lies?

"Now can we get back to workshopping?"

*April 15*

FOR THE FIRST TIME IN HIS LIFE, Gerry files for an extension on his taxes, which depresses him. But at least he knows the date for once because his accountant has emailed him the forms he needs to fill out and file electronically.

Although Gerry has an accountant, he refuses to have a business manager, preferring to keep his own books and do as much tax prep as possible. Thiru has always twitted him about this, but long before the world at large knew about predators such as Madoff, Gerry had not wanted anyone to touch his money. After his first marriage, he never mingled money again. The marriage counselor that Sarah insisted on seeing when he asked for a divorce had proclaimed this "interesting" in a tone that suggested she disapproved. Gerry didn't care.

But his finances are unusually complicated this year, with the sale of the New York apartment and the purchase of another one, and his mother's estate still pending, although that shouldn't affect his taxes.

*His father's estate still pending.* His mother's executor has said to look for official paperwork on that soon, but it hasn't arrived.

He glances at his almost empty datebook. It has long been Gerry's practice to jot down a few details about the day's work—words written, ideas he should pursue in revision—but there has been nothing to jot down for weeks, months. Only Leenie's work is moving forward. Maybe he could keep a record of her progress, note what he has accomplished as her teacher and editor.

April 30 has been circled in bright red, but there is no text to indicate why. A day so momentous that it required no entry, yet he has zero memory of what was supposed to happen then. It's not a birthday or anniversary of note. And then he remembers—it's the day he's supposed to start preparing to walk again, transitioning first to a wheelchair and then to a walker. Within weeks, the walker next to his bed will finally be used as it was meant to be used, not as a combination of lance and shield. Did he really push Margot? Did he really kill her? He is in his seventh decade and he has never put his hands on a woman in anything but love and passion. Well, what happened with Margot was a kind of a passion, he supposes.

Leenie comes in with his lunch, a tuna salad sandwich on toast and some carrots. The food she prepares has improved and he now realizes that those terrible dinners she forced on him were part of his punishment, his gaslighting.

"It's going to be strange," he says, feeling that he's being expansive, "when you're not here any longer."

"Where am I going?" she asks.

*Not my concern,* he thinks. "I just glanced at my calendar— I'm going to be learning how to use a wheelchair in a week. That's why I do the exercises with the pulleys, so I'll have the upper-body strength to get myself in and out of the chair."

"There's still a lot you won't be able to do."

"Of course, but eventually—I will be ready to be on my own. I think I'm going to sell this place and move back to New York."

Leenie sits in the dining room chair that now is always at his bedside, ready for their "classes" together. "No," she says.

"No?"

"I don't have anywhere to go. Even with continuing payments from you—"

*Wait, there are going to be continuing payments?* He misses a few words in his panic over the idea of what he now realizes is this inevitable and infinite blackmail.

"—and I don't want to live in New York anyway. We'll never have this much space."

*We? WE?*

"Leenie, how do you envision this ending?"

"Happily ever after." She laughs at the expression on his face. "Just kidding. But, we are in this together. Remember how you had us read *The Getaway* at Goucher, then screened the film for us? We're Doc and Carol, in a sense. But we can choose whether we're the ones in the book, who are miserable together, or the ones in the film, who are sincerely on each other's sides."

There is too much to absorb in what Leenie has just said. All Gerry can do is focus on the least important aspect, that this thick-bodied, plain woman has just cast herself as early 1970s Ali MacGraw. True, that makes him Steve McQueen, but—no, he is not Doc. He does not rob banks. He has killed no one.

Finally, in that moment, he realizes this to be true. He did not kill Margot. This woman did and left the body for him to discover, hoping he would blame himself.

"If we're Doc and Carol," he says, "the ones in the film, not the ones in the book, then we have to trust each other. That's the key difference, right? In the book, they can never trust each other, but in the film, they have each other's backs. I don't want to live out my days thinking you're going to betray me, and I assume you feel the same. Cards on the table, Leenie. What really happened to Margot?"

She thinks about this, her eyes darting around the room.

"No thinking. No stories. Talk to me."

Her words come out fast, with the whoosh of a child who has been dying to confess. "Margot returned that night, just after midnight. You're right, she took the security pass. She had been drinking, I'm pretty sure of that. I'm not sure why she came back. Maybe she planned to stay here. Or maybe she was going to confront you about what she knew. Whatever it was she knew. She let herself in and—" Her voice falters.

"And?"

"She found us in bed together."

The sentence makes no sense. Gerry has not had sex since last fall; he is keenly aware of that fact. A stupid regression with Margot when he went back to New York, but she took him unawares on a bench in a shadowy corner of Riverside Park. Obviously, Gerry couldn't have been in bed with anyone and if he could, it wouldn't have been Leenie. What is she babbling about?

"The pill I sometimes give you, the one I said was a calcium supplement? It's my own scrip for Lunesta. Combined with Ambien and your pain meds, it made you sleep really soundly. I once banged a pot right in front of your face to test it. Anyway, on those nights, sometimes, I would get in bed with you. I couldn't really spoon or hold you, and I was respectful of your body, but I would lie next to you, my head on your shoulder. Just for a little while. I didn't see the harm."

"And you killed Margot because she saw that?"

"She was yelling and trying to take photos of us. I grabbed her phone to delete it. She was scary, she wasn't going to stop. She was saying you were a pervert, that she already had evidence of how awful you were, but this was just more proof and she was going to tell the world what she knew about you and she slapped me, hard. I really did see little black shapes circling my head. Not stars, I wouldn't call them stars—"

"Please, Leenie, this isn't a time to dwell on metaphors."

"I grabbed the letter opener. I was only trying to defend myself. Whatever happened, happened."

Gerry finds himself thinking of a famous parody of passive voice. *Backward ran sentences until reeled the mind.* In the same way that Leenie became hyperfocused on describing what she saw when slapped, he finds himself thinking about that one word, *reels.* A reel can be a dance, but most people associate it with fishing. A reel is an orderly thing. It unspools, it winds up. His mind is spinning like a top, a wobbly metal top, the kind that one pumped up and down, then set loose on the world. How could Margot describe him as a pervert? They had been two consenting adults and she had been the one inclined to push the envelope, including that last time in Riverside Park. Besides, public sex didn't make one a pervert. His conscience is clear. Clearish. Even what happened with Lucy, the shameful episode with Shannon Little, the one time he cheated on Sarah—none of those things make him a *pervert* who should fear shame and exposure.

"Did she explain what she meant?"

"No," Leenie said. "Things happened pretty fast. I'm glad I took advantage of her phone being unlocked. I deleted the photos, then I reset it to the factory settings."

Imagine that being one's impulse when a woman is lying dead at one's feet. To wipe a phone and reset it.

Thinking quickly, speaking gently, he says: "But don't you see— it's safer, I think, if we don't continue, um, living together. Together, we will draw too much attention. I mean, at some point, I simply wouldn't have a nurse."

"But you could have a girlfriend. You wouldn't be the first man to fall in love with his caretaker."

He is truly nonplussed now. Also, the only such relationship he can summon up is Henry VIII and Catherine Parr and she was the one that the Tudor king did not outlive.

"Anyway, I'm glad there are no more secrets between us. Because I have something to show you."

She goes downstairs. Gerry wonders briefly if she's going to go full Annie Wilkes and hobble him, so he will remain in her care longer. But he's more terrified by the idea that Leenie wants him to get well. Wants him to be her *boyfriend*.

She comes back with pages, not a sledgehammer. He decides that's lucky for him, but he has to think about it.

"I've chucked what I was working on. I decided I wasn't going far enough. I want to write something more like Rachel Cusk is doing, blurring fiction and memoir. Or Sheila Heti."

She begins to read:

*Gerry Andersen's new apartment is a topsy-turvy affair—living area on the second floor, bedrooms below. The brochure—it is the kind of apartment that had its own brochure when it went on the market in 2018—boasted of 360-degree views, but that was pure hype.*

To be fair, she didn't say it would be *her* fiction and memoir that she wanted to blur. As she reads on, uncannily aware of Gerry's inner life and thoughts, he begins to wonder what happens to him if Leenie steals his voice.

Again, to be fair—it wasn't as if he was using it.

## 2018

"ARE YOU SO BUSY that you couldn't afford dinner at a real restaurant?" Margot asks, pulling her shawl closer around her shoulders, as if City Diner, almost too warm on this early autumn night, is making her cold.

"Diners are real, Margot. And, yes, I'm slammed for time. I went straight from Penn Station to the apartment, to make sure it was ready for the walk-through tomorrow—"

"I would have been happy to do that with you."

Gerry knew this, which was why he had done it alone. He didn't want to be anywhere private with Margot. Especially the apartment. The lack of furniture would not inhibit her.

"Then I met with Thiru. I was supposed to go to Berlin this fall, but clearly that's not happening."

She arches an eyebrow when he asks for onions on his cheese-burger, knowing that's not usual for him. She limits herself to a cup of black coffee, from which she takes only a few sips, leaving a vivid crimson imprint, then helps herself to his french fries without asking.

"So you're really gone."

"Yes, so it would seem. Once I have the cash in hand from my sale, I need to move quickly to buy in Baltimore. I think it's only a matter of time before my mother is in hospice, but—the doctors have been saying that for months—"

"We never had a proper breakup," Margot said. "We just drifted apart."

In Gerry's point of view, they'd had multiple breakups; Margot simply refused to recognize them as such. She was still squatting in his apartment as recently as a month ago. His Realtor, a formidable woman, forced her out with the co-op board's help.

"I don't see you in Baltimore," Gerry said, then regretted it. He shouldn't even raise the possibility. But he is polite, to a fault. *To a fault.* He moves quickly to change the subject. "You did forward all my mail, right? When you were living there? I'd hate to think any bills went missing."

"Of course I did. God, you were always so obsessed with your mail."

"Was I?" He genuinely didn't remember it that way.

"Your mail and your bills. Have to pay the bills on time or God knows what might happen. You're such a *good* boy, Gerry."

She was mocking him, he can tell, but he doesn't know why.

"It's a habit," he said. "One thing I've done right, consistently."

"I'm sorry," she says, offering him a sincere smile. "Walk me home tonight? It's lovely out, our first real autumnal evening."

The word *autumnal* grates—so pretentious—but it was a beautiful night and what harm could there be in a walk? "Where is home these days?"

"I'm staying at a friend's place at 102nd and West End. We can walk through Riverside Park."

He did and didn't regret what happened on the bench. Margot, with her praying mantis limbs, her voracious mouth—he counted himself lucky that he got out of this relationship without her biting his head off.

*April*

GERRY IS TRYING to wean himself from all his medication. Senses must be sharp! He cannot afford a sleep so drugged and heavy that he misses another homicide, possibly his own. Funny, it doesn't occur to Leenie to watch him swallow his pills. Maybe she believes him to be addicted by now, or at least keen for his nightly oblivion. At any rate, he holds the nighttime pills under his tongue until she goes back downstairs, eager to be reunited with her manuscript. He then takes them out and crushes them as best he can, shutting them inside whatever hardcover book is on his nightstand, sprinkling the dust on the rug. It's not as if Leenie even pretends to clean anymore. She leaves that to a housekeeper who comes every other week, the only outsider who still enters the apartment. Can the housekeeper save him? It seems a lot to ask, given that he doesn't even know her name. Carolina? Carmen? Carmela? No, that was the wife on *The Sopranos*. Anyway, her English isn't very good and Gerry speaks no Spanish at all.

It strikes Gerry that he has a very bad bargain in this fake marriage, a "wife" who provides the minimal care he needs and focuses most of her energy on her writing.

It strikes Gerry that this is who he would have been as a wife.

Although neater. He has always been a generally tidy man, even when living alone, and his years in New York made him vigilant about food waste, which attracted cockroaches and rats. From his bed, he can see the dishes piling up in the kitchen. And there is a smell. She has thrown something in the bin and not bothered to take the trash out despite the fact that it is a short walk to the utility room with the trash chute. An old television theme song plays in his head. *Moving on up, moving on up.* Here he is, in his dee-luxe apartment in the sky, and he might as well be in the ghetto.

Maybe things were better when he was taking his pills.

But he is grateful to have his senses when the phone rings at two A.M. His cell phone, though, not the landline. *Changing up the game, are we, Leenie?* He grabs it on the first ring. There is a short silence, although he can hear breathing on the other end. If ever a pause was pregnant, it's this one. He waits, wondering what he will do if "Aubrey" speaks to him again. Then he clearly will be crazy or demented, because Victoria and then Leenie played the part of Aubrey, and Victoria is dead. Then again—he never saw Victoria's dead body, he has only Leenie's word for it—

"Gerry Andersen? Is that you, *Gerry Andersen?*" A female voice, unfamiliar, definitely not one he has heard before. A slurred voice. Someone has drunk-dialed Gerry.

"This is Gerry Andersen," he says. He listens intently. Is Aileen moving downstairs? Will she try to eavesdrop? He thinks of himself as a child, stealthily picking up the heavy phone in the kitchen when his father made calls from the bedroom, the need to place one's finger on the button, then let it slide out slowly, so there would be no telltale click.

"Why didn't you answer my letters? Why did you ignore me? We could have worked something out. I didn't mean to make you angry. I only wanted what was fair—"

"Who is this?"

The voice continues, heedless and emotional. "I know I should have hired a lawyer, but I don't have money to hire a lawyer. That's the whole problem. It's a catch-22."

"I have no idea what you're talking about." He feels as if he should, though. A thought tantalizes him. *Letters, letters, what letters?* Everything started with a letter, but there have been no letters since, not according to Leenie. Has she been meddling with his mail?

The woman is weeping now. "They always say not to make ultimatums unless you're prepared to follow through. And maybe I was foolish and maybe people would think I'm the bad person in all this, but you're the bad person, Gerry Andersen. Not because—but because—because it wasn't what I wanted, it was disgusting and wrong, even if you didn't realize that. I still can't get over it and I can't talk to anyone about it."

"Who is this?"

His question prompts a wave of sobs. "Jesus, are there so many of me you can't remember? You really are a sick fuck."

He tries again, his voice gentle, his ear still cocked for any sound of Leenie. "You said you sent me letters. Where did you send them?"

"To New York, of course. Where you live."

"Lived. I've been in Baltimore since last year."

"Oh." Chagrined snuffle.

"And how did you get this number?"

A sniffle, a few ragged breaths. She is calming down. "There are online searches. I spent thirty dollars to see what I could find out about you. Got your address, this number. I thought you would respond to the letters, I really did. Once you knew—I thought you would have to do the right thing."

"Knew *what*? Who is this?"

But he has been too successful at calming the woman. She hangs up—clicks off, rather—and his smartphone can tell him only that he has been talking to Caller ID Blocked.

LEENIE DOES NOT bring him his breakfast until ten A.M. Toast and overscrambled eggs on a paper plate. Her eyes have a feverish glow that he recognizes. She is a writer who senses the finish line is close. Her hair is unwashed, she is wearing yesterday's clothes. Gerry remembers the sensation, although he never forgot to take a shower no matter how well his work was going.

"Did I hear you talking to someone last night?" she asks, her voice casual. Too casual.

"Maybe I was talking in my sleep. I used to do that, or so I'm told. In fact, I was teased for having long, mundane conversations in my sleep."

"I did notice that."

He suppresses a shudder at the reminder that she has been in bed beside him. How many times? Just the once? Every time she gave him the "calcium" pill?

"When my book is finished," she says, returning to the only subject that interests her, "will you show it to your agent?"

"Of course. Although I've been giving this some thought." He has not. "Thiru might not be the best agent for you. His taste is old-fashioned. I think what you're writing is more commercial. You need one of those young agents who knows how to create a sense of excitement around a project."

Her face darkens. "You don't think I'm good enough. You don't think I belong with an agency that represents Nobel laureates and Pulitzer winners."

"Oh, God no, that wasn't my intent at all. And Thiru doesn't have a single Nobel winner in his stable." If he did, Gerry's not sure he could take it because then that writer would inevitably be Thiru's favorite, or at least the one on whom he lavished the most attention. "I think this book has the potential to create a lot of excitement, maybe even go to auction."

He suddenly realizes that this book, with certain revisions, could be his alibi *and* his SOS. If Aileen keeps going down this autofiction path, maybe he can steer her toward making a full confession. Of course, there will be the unfortunate truth that he believed himself to be Margot's killer and allowed Leenie to cover up for him, but—he was at her mercy, drugged and addled. If Thiru were to read such a book—

"You know what? Thiru should be our first choice. But we'll have to prod him to have more commercial instincts, to see the book's potential. Toward that end, I do have one suggestion. I think we need more of Gerry's inner life, but it should be dreamlike, almost off-kilter. I could even give you some prompts about his past."

She nods judiciously. "That could work."

As she heads downstairs to write—goodness, she has lost weight, she must not be eating at all—he calls after her, his voice casual. "Leenie, when you went through Margot's purse, were there letters for me?"

She stops at the top of the stairs. How he wishes he could push her. That would solve all his problems. Give the staircase another human sacrifice and maybe he'll be allowed to go free.

"Letters? No. Why do you ask?"

Not: *No, there were no letters.* But an echo, a denial, and then: *Why do you ask?*

"I still think about her claim that she had something on me. I thought maybe she wrote me, then decided to visit instead. It's such a mystery, what she thinks I might have done. Because I've been lying here, reviewing my life, and, until Margot died, I can't imagine anything I've done that would rise to the level of being a credible threat against me."

Leenie smiles. "I hope I can say the same when I'm your age."

It doesn't seem to occur to her that she can't say the same *now*. She has murdered two women, one of them her friend for almost a decade. Yet she's the one who sleeps soundly, depleted by her work, while Gerry crushes his pills and stares at the ceiling, trying to figure out how this all ends.

## 1970

GERRY WAITED for his mother in the kitchen. *I am the man of the family,* he said to himself. He knew it was an odd thing for a twelve-year-old to think, but it was true as of today. *I am the man of the family.*

His mother arrived with the groceries. She looked so pretty and happy. He didn't want to upset her, but she had to know.

"Where's your father?" she asked.

"Gone."

"Gone? He wasn't supposed to leave again until Tuesday."

"Gone forever, Mom. I sent him away."

"You— What— Gerry, please make sense." She turned her back to him and began unpacking the groceries, but her hands were shaking and she put the milk in the pantry, on the shelf with the canned soups.

"He has another family, Mom. An entire family—a wife, two daughters. I heard him talking to them on the phone."

"He called during the day? With the rates at their highest? That doesn't sound like your father."

"*She* called. Person-to-person, collect. There was some sort of emergency. I think one of the"—he needed a moment not to find the right word, but to find the courage to say it—"daughters broke her arm? I didn't hear all of the conversation, but I heard a lot. I heard enough."

"You were eavesdropping, Gerry? I've told you time and again not to do that."

"Mom, he has another *family*."

"I'm sure you misunderstood. Your father has always been a magnet for women who need someone strong to lean on. Are you sure he's not just out, wiring her money or . . ." Here, his mother's imagination faltered. She had finally run out of excuses for her husband.

"He's gone, Mom. He packed all his clothes and put them in the trunk of his car, then left. He's going to wherever *they* are."

"No," his mother said. "He'll come back. He always comes back."

"I told him we don't want him to come back. I told him he had to choose. He chose them."

He did not tell his mother how triumphant he had felt when he laid down the law to his father. And that he was not altogether disappointed when his father elected to leave, if only because it confirmed what he knew.

"Oh, Gerry, what have you done?" His mother walked slowly out of the kitchen, then broke into a run. Her bedroom was over the kitchen and he could hear her sobbing.

He rescued the milk from the pantry, found the Sealtest ice cream—his favorite, chocolate chip—still in the grocery sack and stowed it in the freezer. He put everything away, rinsed out his glass and put it in the dishwasher.

*We'll be better off without him,* Gerry told himself. *She'll see.*

*April*

GERRY IS LOOKING at his checking account online. There is more money than he expects—not just the electronic royalties deposited by Thiru's agency (why did he resist this for so long?) but also an electronic deposit of $215,000. Foreign payments? Foreign money is forever dribbling in. Sometimes gushing in. The Germans love his work.

Wait—a payment for $9,500 went out the next day, via something called a Zelle P2P payment. It takes him a while, but he finds the site within the site where he can view his Zelle activity. There is only the one transaction.

The recipient was one Aileen Rachel Bryant.

"Leenie," he brays. Then, in the tone of a parent who wants his child to know how much trouble she is in: "AILEEN RACHEL BRYANT." He's not even sure how he knows her middle name. Oh, wait—IT'S THERE ON THE ZELLE PAYMENT SHE MADE TO HERSELF.

She takes her time and is all sweet innocence when she arrives at his bedside.

"Is something wrong?"

"How did nine thousand, five hundred dollars of my money go from my bank account to yours?"

"Oh, I used Zelle. It's like Venmo or PayPal but—"

"I'm not asking how"—okay, he did, in fact, ask how—"I am trying to understand who moved that money and why."

"I moved it. On your computer, the one I've been using—you saved all your passwords, so I can access lots of things."

Lots. Of. Things.

"Why did you feel"—he decides to choose his words carefully—"you should transfer this money?"

"I've been working so hard on the book and, even if it does sell, it will be a while before I see any payment."

"But—you have your nursing salary. Not to mention free room and board here."

"Not forever. You made that clear. We won't be together forever."

"It's safer that way, don't you think? Leenie—we have to go our separate ways. We're not Doc and Carol."

"We could be."

He thinks of Thompson's Carol, he imagines the cinematic Carol. Two very different creatures, but both alluring. What does one say to an unbeautiful woman? He has no idea. Unbeautiful women have never interested him much. There is no democracy in sexual attraction and there is not, in his estimation, a lid for every pot. There are many, many lidless pots in the world, although most of them, Gerry would wager, are men. Aileen can find a man, if all she wants is a man. But she cannot have him. Even her burgeoning talent has not made her attractive to him, and that is the ultimate unfairness. Gerry, at sixty-one, is desirable because of what he's accomplished. Aileen, at twenty-nine, now showing glimmers of ability, will never write her way into a man's heart. Gerry didn't make the rules. The rules made him.

"I'm sorry, but that's not an ending I can envision."

"Okay, then," Leenie says. She walks over to the bed, picks up his cell phone, disconnects the landline, grabs his laptop. Luddite Gerry, antisocial Gerry, anti–social media Gerry cannot believe how hard his heart is beating at the loss of these things. They are his only connection to the outside world, after all.

Leenie says: "Once my book is finished and under contract, we'll say goodbye."

Gerry knows how Leenie says goodbye.

*April*

**ONLY A NAÏF** would try to buy time by switching up and giving Leenie a harsher critique. Gerry is not Penelope, he's not going
to tear up the weaving every night. He goes the other way, praises
things that could be improved, swallows his revulsion for cheap plot
devices, Leenie's Achilles heel. It's all good. It's all fine. The sooner
he can get this book to Thiru, the sooner he will have a chance
to be free. In his editing sessions, he makes tiny suggestions that
would seem to be inconsequential, but Thiru will know, Thiru will
see through it, as he once joked. Thiru knows Gerry doesn't care
what the *Oxford English Dictionary* says, he's sticking by the old
meanings of *literally* and *hopefully*. Thiru knows all Gerry's bugaboos, to use that peculiar word that Lucy loved. Gerry has been
fighting New York copyeditors for almost forty years over the word

*rowhouse.* What Baltimoreans have joined together, he would retort in the margins, let no copyeditor tear asunder.

All he has to do is sell Leenie on one small change.

"When we submit your book," he says, "let's do it under my name."

She puffs up like a cobra, ready to strike. "Are you trying to steal my work?"

"No! I'm trying to get you the attention you deserve. If this book goes out as the work of a twenty-nine-year-old unpublished woman, even with my endorsement, it will be read with—skepticism. Maybe even as a kind of fan fic. If we submit it as my first piece of autofiction-slash-memoir, it will be taken seriously as a significant departure for me. The reveal of its actual authorship, the fact that I authorized this but did not write it—ta-da!"—he mimes a magician's sleight of hand—"will knock people on their keisters."

He's not sure why he uses a vaudeville word such as *keister,* but it feels right.

"It will be like the reverse of that writer who submitted Jerzy Kosinski's *Steps* under a fake name, only to have it rejected by every major publishing house. Everyone will want this book. When we reveal the ruse, that you are my student and wrote this with my permission and approval, they'll only want it more."

He watches Leenie trying to absorb this idea. She's no dummy. She's suspicious of him. But it has never occurred to her that he is planting land mines throughout her book so that her beloved manuscript will save *him,* that Thiru unwittingly showed Gerry how he could signal his distress by mentioning what words and themes would arouse his concern should Gerry ever use them.

Maybe they are more like Thompson's Doc and Carol than they realize.

## 2008

GRETCHEN HAD TAKEN to drunk-dialing him late at night.

"I see you're dating again," she said without preamble. "I hope you realize it's on *Page Six* because of her, not you. She's the famous one."

"Yes, it's her only drawback."

"Tell her to get a prenup," Gretchen said.

"We had a prenup. At your insistence. You were so worried about protecting the apartment, your income."

"No, no, that wasn't it at all. I would have split everything fifty-fifty, but you didn't want to share the proceeds from your work. I supported you. You wrote *Dream Girl* on my dime; I was your venture capitalist and I didn't get any return on my investment."

"Rewrite history however you want, Gretchen."

Life had not been kind to Gretchen. She had been working at

Lehman Brothers when the crash came. Now she was unemployed and bitter.

"Look, between us—who was Aubrey? I know you had to be fucking someone while we were married."

"I was faithful to you, Gretchen, which isn't something I'm sure you can say. There is no Aubrey. I made her up." An old complaint from James M. Cain floated into his head, Cain's rejoinder at being accused of imitating Hammett. *It really doesn't work that way.*

"Tell me the truth, Gerry."

So he did. He shared with Gretchen the story he had never told anyone, not even Thiru. He told her the identity of the Dream Girl.

*April*

"I DON'T KNOW HOW TO END IT," Leenie says.

"Endings are hard," he commiserates.

"I feel as if something *big* should happen." She mimes an explosion with her hands, makes fireworks noises with her mouth. Gerry shakes his head.

"If I may offer an observation—you have always been a bit enamored of deus ex machina."

She glares. "I am the *deus* here, in case you've forgotten. Therefore, I am entitled to my machinations."

For some reason, this reminds Gerry of that bridge in Trenton, the one that can be glimpsed from the train: TRENTON MAKES, THE WORLD TAKES. She sounds put-upon, as if no one can understand what she has suffered. *Congratulations, Leenie, you're a real novelist now.*

He gentles his tone. "It's obvious in the text that 'Leenie' is the mastermind. Not Victoria. Don't start getting hypersensitive. I'm simply advising you to remain true to your characters. Nothing can happen now that hasn't been prepared for. As writers, we must stay within the reality we've created."

In her book, she has reached the point where she has started moving his funds and taken his electronics away. She has not bothered to imagine how dreary this is for him. He rereads favorite books, watches CNN. He cannot imagine reading something new right now, the single most compelling argument for the possibility that he is already dead and this is his singular hell.

She slumps in the chair near his bedside. "I haven't always been truthful with you."

Where to begin? What could be left?

"Yes," he says, then decides to dare a joke. "It's sort of the basis of our relationship."

"You asked me if I found letters in Margot's purse."

He waits.

"There was something and I need to tell you. But I just can't figure out the right way."

He is not without fear. Leenie's habit is to "write" herself out of a tough situation with an act of violence. A letter opener to the eye, a statuette to the head. He glances around the room to see if there are any heavy, lethal objects close at hand.

But she can't finish the book without him. She cannot sell the book without him. He is Scheherazade, forestalling the inevitable. As long as the story's fate is pending, she has to allow him to live.

"I trust you, Leenie. You'll do the right thing. You'll come up with something clever."

It almost makes him feel bad, how her round face brightens from his praise. But he's trying to survive. Where on Maslow's hierarchy of needs does one find storytelling? Technically, he supposes, it's near the narrow top, a part of self-actualization. Yet it feels as if it's the entire foundation to Gerry, as if even the basics of water, food, and shelter rely on one's ability to make sense of the narrative of one's life.

*April 29*

IT IS GERRY'S LAST DAY fully immobilized. Tomorrow, the doctor will visit, assess his healing. The brace will not come off even if he gets a good report, but he will start learning how to heave his body into a wheelchair. He wonders if he will, in fact, get a good report. Leenie was sure she could replicate the exercises that Claude gave him, but who knows?

It's like living in a sensory deprivation tank. He knows the weather only because CNN keeps the temperature in the corner of the screen; today is forecast to be in the eighties, unusually hot for this time of year. But there is no weather in the apartment. Sometimes, at his request, Leenie will slide open the doors to his terrace. His terrace. A place where he has not passed a single hour, given how cold it was when he took ownership of the apartment. He had imagined himself sitting there in the evenings, watching the sun go down over Baltimore, maybe having an occasional glass of cognac, an indulgence he picked up during the Margot years. Margot liked to drink and she didn't like to drink alone, so, Margot-like, she had bullied Gerry into accompanying her. He also had wondered if he could put the rowing machine on the terrace when the weather was fair, perhaps with a protective cover.

The rowing machine. He glares at it. *You are the source of much of this.* Able-bodied, he never would have been tyrannized by those two young women; their scheme would have fizzled quickly. They were insane if they thought their gaslighting campaign would result in much of anything. There was no Aubrey. Why can't people believe that? He remembers how disappointed he was to discover that Roth had based Brenda Patimkin on a real woman. Are there any pure acts of imagination? Outside his mother and himself, Gerry has never used real people in his work. What's the point? It's a slippery slope, in his opinion, that quickly leads to a trashy roman à clef guessing game; you might as well be Jacqueline Susann.

Deprived of his phone and laptop but allowed his hand weights, he picks them up and does a few half-hearted biceps curls. He actually has to be careful about overdoing it. His muscles are sore, his shoulders achy. He has built up quite a bit of upper-body strength, which he will require in the next stage of his healing.

Leenie has gone out on some mystery errand. He tries to think of a way to take advantage of her absence, but his imagination fails him. If he could unbrake the wheels on the bed—but that would put him in danger, would it not? Once the wheels were unlocked, where would he go, how would he control it? Even if he could find a way to steer the bed, it's too wide to allow him passage to the kitchen, where the nearest phone sits, and he would have to risk sliding past the chasm of the staircase.

And should he make it to the phone, whom would he call, what would he say? *Help, I'm being held hostage in my own apartment by a woman who has killed two women, crimes in which I am an accessory after the fact.* If only he had insisted on calling the police upon finding Margot's body. But he had been so doped up and confused, and Leenie out-thought him. *That* day. Now that he continues to crush his drugs in the hardcover books he is allowed, he stays sharp, and Leenie doesn't suspect a thing. It's not like she's ever going to look inside his books, or clean closely enough to see the residue on the table, in the sheets, on the carpet. God, the smells in his apartment. That's one sense he wishes he could be deprived of, his sense of smell.

About an hour after she left, Leenie returns. He can hear voices; someone must be with her. Is today the day for the doctor's visit? Has he screwed up the dates yet again?

But the person who enters the apartment with Leenie is a woman who appears to be about her age, wheeling a small carry-on suitcase. Blonde, with a familiar face, or maybe it's simply a generic one. Conventionally pretty, what people used to call corn-fed.

"I guess you remember Kim Karpas," Leenie says. "Normally, I'd let the two of you get reacquainted privately, but I don't have the luxury of allowing you to have privacy. After all, I need to know how the story ends."

The woman's confusion is evident; she looks to Leenie, then to Gerry in the hospital bed, back to Leenie. "But he emailed *me.*" Turning back to Gerry. "Right? You said you wanted to do the right thing, that by buying me a plane ticket—first-class, yet—you hoped you could prove how honorable your intentions were. That you would come visit me if not for your injury, but if I wanted the money, I would have to travel to Baltimore and talk to you, figure out how that could be arranged."

*Kim Karpas. Kim Karpas.* Does he know a Kim? *The money.*
*What money?* Gerry closes his eyes and sees a cat staring at him, a
cat from the cover of a book. *The girl from the bar in Columbus that*
*time. Why is she here? How did Leenie find her?*

"I guess I have to *reintroduce* you in a sense," Leenie says, almost
chortling, she is that delighted with herself. "Kim, I have to confess,
Gerry never got your letters. You sent them to his New York address,
where an old girlfriend of his read them. I guess it was her plan to
use them to make trouble for Gerry, but now they're in my possession. Quite a tale you spun, I have to admit."

"It's not a tale," says the woman. Kim. "It's *true.*"

"Oh, I don't doubt a word of it. He basically raped you in that
hotel room, which would have been bad enough under any circumstances—"

"Rape!" Gerry yelps. "I invited you up to my room and you came.
What followed was absolutely consensual. If I recall, you were the
one who had the condom, you were the one who chose to have in-
tercourse, you were—"

She is one of those pale blondes who flushes bright pink when
emotional. "I tried to say no, but you ignored me. And, given the
circumstances, I was so overwhelmed. You weren't going to let me
out of there unless I, um, reciprocated in some fashion, so I chose
the easiest, fastest way."

"The *circumstances*? You were, are, an adult woman who went
to a man's hotel room and didn't seem to mind at all when things
went the way they usually do in a man's hotel room after a couple of
drinks in a bar. In fact, it was my impression, in hindsight, that you
were looking for me, you came to that hotel hoping to find me. I'm
not going to have this turned into some sort of 'Me, too' moment."

"Yes, I was hoping to meet you, but—not for *that.* I wanted to see you, to get some sense of you, but I used a fake name just in case. I had wanted to be a writer, too—"

God, was there anyone left in the world who didn't want to be a writer?

"You had loomed so large in my life, ever since I was a teenager. I read everything you wrote. Granddad would say, 'It's right there on your DNA. If your uncle can do it, so can you.'"

Granddad. Uncle. *What?*

Leenie smiles, pleased with her handiwork. She literally rubs her hands together in delight. "Kim is the daughter of your half sister, Gerry, the family that was cut out of your father's will. They contested it, but they had no grounds—your father was within his rights to leave everything to your mother. So Kim's mother, her grandmother, her aunt—the family your father actually lived with and supported for much of his life—they're out in the cold and you're going to get money that you don't even need. Kim's grandfather always said she would inherit enough to pay off her college debt. A good man would help her out."

Gerry sees himself as a boy, playing with his father's sample case, pulling a long blond hair from one of the little chairs. Had it belonged to this girl's mother? He sees himself picking up the phone, oh so stealthily, listening to his father speak first to his other wife, then to his daughters, comforting the one who had broken her arm. Was that this girl's mother? It was the way his father spoke to the girls that hardened Gerry's heart, the tenderness and sweetness, a tone he had never known. Maybe fathers were different with daughters than they were with sons, but Gerry felt in that moment that he knew where his father's heart lay and that was why he ordered him from the house on Berwick Road, all the while hoping his father would say, "No, it's a horrible mistake. I choose you! I choose you!"

He sees himself with this woman in the hotel room. *His niece.* His stomach roils, yet surely she should be the one who is held accountable. It was consensual, he's not responsible for her regrets. He didn't *know*. It's not as if he were some paternal figure who had watched her grow up. He didn't even have an inkling she existed.

Then again, Oedipus also was wholly ignorant of his relationship to Jocasta, and the gods didn't spare him.

Gerry thinks quickly. He has to get one of the women in this room on his side. He has to get the *right* woman on his side, even if that means saying things he doesn't believe.

"Leenie, this was cruel of you. You shouldn't have lied to this young woman to get her here under a false pretext. You should have told me about her letters, what they said. I would, in fact, like to do the right thing."

He is struggling to keep his voice even, calm. He wonders what part of the saga Margot planned to make public if he continued to deny her request for financial assistance. The niece part was icky, but the #MeToo aspect was probably more of a news hook. The one-two punch—surely there was a salacious gossip site that would have enjoyed telling the story, which would then allow more traditional media to report on it with that disingenuous stance of reporting on the story's existence, not the story itself. But was this going to be part of Leenie's novel? Was this the climax?

*I have to win this young woman over. She's my only hope. I have to say whatever will keep her here long enough to save me.*

"Kim, I am so sorry for the pain the men in my family have caused the women in your family. First my father and now me. I cannot begin to find the words for the injury done to you."

"Thank you," she says stiffly.

"We do need to talk. Leenie, would you take Kim's suitcase downstairs and maybe fix us a light snack?"

"She won't need—" Leenie interrupts herself, but Gerry takes note of her words. She was about to say that Kim would not require a room here. Has Leenie secured a reservation for her elsewhere? Or is Kim going to be sacrificed for Leenie's story before the day is through? "Fine, I'll take it downstairs."

Gerry indicates the chair by his bed, the Leenie chair, as he thinks of it. He glances at his bedside table. One thing Leenie has not thought to take from him is his Moleskine notebooks and astronaut pens.

"Tell me about your mother, my sister," he says. "I know nothing about my father's other family."

Not surprisingly, she looks confused. Her confusion is only heightened when she reads Gerry's scribbled note to her. *Leenie is dangerous. She will try to harm you. Pay attention to what I write, not what I say.*

"I hope it's okay if I take notes," he says, wanting to set up a reason for having the notebook in hand when Leenie returns to observe them.

"Um, sure. My mom—she's like her mom. She's really fun, outgoing. Bubbly. My sister, too. I always wished I had that personality. I was the family bookworm. I wanted to write, so I got an MFA. But all I ended up with was fifty thousand dollars in debt."

"I have an MFA myself, but I've begun to think it's a bit of a *racket.*" He writes: *Unlock the casters on the wheels, quickly and without drawing attention to what you're doing.* "Oh, I've dropped my pen. It's rolled under the bed. Can you get it for me?"

She's catching on. She's quick, now that she's gotten her bearings.

Leenie has climbed the stairs and is in the kitchen, grumbling to herself. The "snack" that she puts together for them is two cans of LaCroix and a plate of crackers. No spread, no cheese, not even peanut butter, only crackers. She places the plate on the wheeled tray that Gerry uses for his meals. He positions it carefully so it sits between him and his guest, not across the bed as it normally would be.

"You know, Leenie, you're right, Kim shouldn't stay here. After all, you're using the master bedroom and the study has only that sleeper sofa, which is bound to be uncomfortable. Besides, Kim probably doesn't want to stay under my roof, and who could blame her? I'm going to get her a room at the Four Seasons."

"The Four Seasons," the women say in unison. Kim's tone is awed, while Leenie is clearly disgruntled. She really does hate it when he spends his money on anyone but her.

"Yes. Would you go back downstairs and get her suitcase?"

*"Now?"*

"If you could."

As soon as her back is turned, he writes: *Position the bed so it's facing the stairs and when Leenie is almost to the top, push it as hard as you can toward the stairs, then get the hell out of here.*

She looks skeptical, scared, and who can blame her? Gerry scrawls: *She has killed two women. She will kill you. GET OUT OF HERE.*

He adds: *Hand me the walker.*

Bump, bump, bump. Leenie is dragging Kim's suitcase up the stairs as if she wants to punish it. Perhaps she is disappointed because her orchestrated surprise did not deliver the big scene she was hoping for. Well, Gerry tried to warn her about her instincts.

*"Now."*

She's strong, his niece, he'll give her that, but it's on him to get the job done. He uses his aspirational walker like an oar, pressing hard on the floor, awkward and unwieldy as it is. He may never use his upper-body strength to transfer himself to a wheelchair, but he's making good use of it now. He needs only two, three hard pushes to take advantage of the trajectory that Kim has started. The bed sails forward, catching Leenie at her midsection as she crests the stairs. She tries to throw the suitcase at him, but her reflexes are slow, her aim off, and it caroms to the side. The bed knocks her backward down the floating staircase exactly as Gerry planned.

What Gerry has failed to anticipate is that the bed keeps going, accelerating, a runaway chariot straight out of *Ben-Hur,* rolling over Leenie's body—oh, the terrible cracks and squishes, he has never heard noises such as these, his intention was only to knock her out, not flatten her—then hitting the wall opposite the staircase with enough force to catapult him out of the bed and—

*1999*

GERRY WALKED. He had been walking every night for hours, ever since Gretchen left. He didn't miss her, but he was angry, offended. How dare she leave him?

He did not have much affinity for nature, preferred New York City above all cities, but late April was the one brief season when he liked the outdoors and Baltimore. The weather still had a cool sharpness, while the air, at least here in North Baltimore, smelled of blossoms and soil. He walked through the Wyman Park dell. He walked to the sculpture garden at the BMA.

Mostly, he walked along the path through Stony Run that led, eventually, to Cold Spring Lane and Alonso's.

He did not miss Gretchen. He had not loved her. She was right, he didn't even like her. Gretchen had been a rebound. Not from Lucy, but from New York City in general, his anxiety over Luke's diagnosis, Tara's decampment for the suburbs. Gretchen had been a safe haven. Marriage had been designed as an institution of safety, an economic proposition. In his second marriage, Gerry had been a Jane Austen female, mating for security. He had felt he could not risk another Lucy, who had seemed so sensible and right but had always had that wildness, and it was, he realized, the wildness that drove him away. You couldn't write the kind of poems that Lucy wrote if you weren't a little kinky, he had decided, but it was not a lifestyle that worked for Gerry.

And then Luke died and Tara stopped speaking to him and he was left with Gretchen. No, he didn't miss her. But he resented the fact that she had lured him back to Baltimore, then abandoned him. That wasn't fair play. Neither was the prenup, in which Gerry had agreed to waive any claim on the Gramercy Park apartment. Gretchen was selling it now, planning to move downtown.

The park was full of children tonight. Gerry did not want children and, in the end, women almost always did. That had to be the reason Gretchen left. But the best way not to become one's father is to never be a father at all. He had tried to be kind and faithful to his romantic partners and, for the most part, he felt he had been true to his own standards. He had been faithful to Gretchen, no small thing. Gretchen had started out as a most provocative bed partner; the contrast between her suited daytime self and the wanton body in bed at night had heightened his attraction to her. But she seemed less and less interested in him as her paychecks rose and his earnings stagnated. She did not respect him. By the time she left him, their sex life had long been dead.

He suspected she had a lover, up in New York. He didn't even care.

Alonso's was quiet tonight. The bar had been renovated recently, updating the dark, homely little tavern into something sleek and modern, much to Gerry's disappointment. He preferred its original incarnation. He and Lucy had lived half a block from here. They had doted on its horrible pizza, pizza so bad that he craved it still. They had eaten the too-salty mozzarella sticks, tried to wrap their mouths around cheeseburgers almost as large as their heads. Then they would go across the street to Video Americain, take home one of the staff recommendations. Gerry still stopped into Video Americain on his walks, still heeded the staff recommendations. Last week, he had watched a film called *Funny Bones,* which had surprised him because he realized, in the final minutes, that he didn't know if he was watching a comedy or a tragedy. *See, art can do this,* he'd said to Luke across the void. *It is possible to create a story where people aren't sure what happens next.*

He spoke a lot to Luke, in his head.

As he sat at the bar, drinking the first of the two beers he allotted himself, he became aware of a couple sitting across from each other in a booth. The woman was twentysomething, a mix of ethnicities; he had never seen anyone like her—Asian, yet freckled, her skin a warm olive cast. Not beautiful, something better. One would never tire of looking at that animated, lively face.

The man across from her could have been Gerry. Forty, give or take, full head of hair, Waspy. The couple's eyes were locked on each other; no one else existed as far as they were concerned. The man would speak; she would laugh. And yet, they did not touch. They were conspicuously *not* touching. It was an act of propriety, an attempt to convince those who saw them that this was a friendly meal, nothing more.

It was one of the most erotic things Gerry had ever seen. It was another one of Luke's *before* moments. These people had not slept together yet. The woman was trying to decide if she would sleep with this man. It was her choice, not his. The wheel was spinning, spinning, the ball was bouncing. Where would it land? Who was this woman? She was a fantasy, an apparition. The man opposite might as well have conjured her for the express purpose of torturing him. She might sleep with him, but she would never be his, she would never belong to anyone. She was quicksilver, a treasure that would flow through a man's fingers.

Then, in an unguarded moment, she took a french fry from the man's plate and ate it. Gerry realized he practically had a hard-on. There was nothing arch or sensual about the act; a french fry is technically phallic, but it is a limp phallus, especially in a place like Alonso's, crinkle cut and undercooked. No, it was her *assumption* that the man's food was hers to take. She would take what she wanted from this man, then move on. Not in a mean, avaricious way. She was not a gold digger. She wanted this man for her own pleasure, nothing more, and she would offer pleasure in return. She would be generous and wholehearted, but she could never be possessed.

Gerry would give anything to know a woman like that.

He paid for his first beer and left without having a second. He had to get home, he had to write. Fuck the maximalists, the Tom Wolfe imitators, the worst of whom was Tom Wolfe these days. Last fall, Alice McDermott had won the National Book Award over Wolfe and some people had tried to make it a literary scandal, claiming Wolfe was robbed because of political correctness. No, McDermott was showing the way with her human-scale stories, but she was too modest to make a case for herself. Gerry would write a piece about where fiction should go and then he would show everyone.

*He would show everyone.*

The wheel spins, the ball bounces, bounces, bounces. Where will it land? Will you get the girl? Will your name be read from stages, the recipient of important prizes? Will your name be remembered? How will it be remembered? Will you be remembered at all?

Everything is in the *before* moment. That's where life is richest, in that moment of possibility and antici—*say it,* the audience screamed at the screen—*pation.* That's what Luke had been trying to tell Gerry.

And then the ball finds its slot and the story ends even as it begins.

*September 27, 2019*

"I HAVE TO ADMIT," Thiru says, "it's not at all what I was expecting. Talk about mixing low and high—and autofiction yet."

"But you like it, right? And you'll set up an auction?"

"Ben will be hurt that he's not being allowed first crack, but—yes."

"He has no right to feel he is owed *this* book."

"Quite right. Look, I have to know—the thing about Columbus, the sex. Did that really happen?"

"God, no. It is *fiction*. Almost none of this happened."

"Well, a hospital bed did roll right over that nurse, killing her. And Margot Chasseur remains missing, as does the assistant. They found her car at the airport, right?"

"That part I can't speak to. I just hope the ending works, given the circumstances. That it matches up with everything that came before it."

"Oh, yes. I mean, the voice is different, but that's the point, right? Gerry Andersen writing in the voice of his insane nurse, pretending to be her, then editing her. I love how *lurid* it all is. Anyway, I'll submit to five editors in the first round. I think women will vibe more to the material."

"How quickly do you think this will go?"

"Oh, I'll sell this in less than a week. It's Gerry Andersen's last book, written in collaboration with his niece. I mean—I know you wrote only the last bit, but there's no harm in pumping up your contributions. And including an author photo of you—that won't hurt. No, that won't hurt *at all*."

Kim smiles, lowers her eyes with pretend shyness. Is Thiru flirting with her? How unprofessional. Can these old tigers ever change their stripes?

"Thank you, Thiru. I know I'm in good hands here."

"I'd like to push for a two-book contract. Do you think you have another book in you?"

"Maybe. Let's see what they offer for just the one, then talk."

Kim leaves Thiru's office. It's a splendid September day, the platonic ideal of fall, perfect for walking. Good thing, because she is staying with a friend near Fort Tryon Park and she can't afford a cab. But she will be able to take cabs, and soon. For now, she will walk until she tires, then hop on the subway to complete the trip.

The day that Gerry died—her first and only instinct was to get *out* of there, away from those crazy people. She had grabbed her suitcase, made sure the door locked behind her, and left the building through the parking garage, which was how Leenie had brought her in, come to think of it. Had Leenie really intended to harm her? Why had she invited Kim to Baltimore, hiding her identity—and true intentions—behind Gerry's email address? Where were the letters that Kim had written to Gerry last year? Kim sat in a small park near the apartment for almost an hour, trying to figure out what she should do.

Finally, she returned to the building and presented herself to the front desk, announcing she was Gerry Andersen's niece from Ohio and he was expecting her. After all, he had bought her the ticket, had he not? When no one answered the front desk's call, she insisted that someone go upstairs and let her in. *He was expecting her, he was confined to bed because of an injury, maybe something had happened.* The put-upon woman at the front desk finally agreed to send a custodian up with Kim.

She let the poor man discover the bodies at the bottom of the steps, quickly pocketing the Moleskine notebook that Gerry had thrown to the floor. She had tried, as unobtrusively as possible, to snoop for her letters, but she didn't find them, not that day. Later, when she was allowed back into the apartment, she unearthed what must have been Aileen's hiding place, a duffel bag deep in the master bedroom's walk-in closet, overlooked by the blessedly lazy detectives. The duffel was full of objects; Leenie was quite the magpie, stockpiling shiny things and rare first editions. Here was the Birkin, the phone case, and, yes, Kim's letters. She understood why Leenie had kept Margot's things, which were beautiful and exquisite, but Kim had no problem tossing them in a dumpster outside a nearby construction site. As for her letters, she shredded them.

There also was a manuscript, but Kim had read that already, having discovered a copy on Gerry's computer. It surprised her that the computer was of no interest to the homicide detectives who had investigated Gerry's death, how uninterested they were in motive or reason. But that was to her benefit, too, as it never occurred to them to request the elevator tapes that would have shown her arriving with

Leenie earlier. For them, the scene was all physics and sequence, trajectories and blood splatter. Aileen was clearly killed first, her larynx crushed by the bed. Gerry had suffered a fatal head injury when he was thrown from the bed to the floor. Scuff marks on the upper floor, the walker lying on its side—that indicated how he had managed to move the heavy bed.

Oh, they had spoken to Kim at length, and it had been hard not to demand a lawyer, but she assumed insisting on one—lawyering up, as they said on TV—would be suspicious. Luckily, the truth was more or less on her side. She had arrived that afternoon from Columbus, on a ticket paid for by her uncle, who had only recently come into her life. Email supported that. He wanted to discuss her grandfather's inheritance with her. Why had it taken her so long to arrive at the apartment from the airport, which was only a twenty-minute drive? She said she had tried to use public transportation and screwed up horribly, ended up walking a good portion of the way. She was proud of that invention—if police really did check her cell phone's GPS and determined she was in the neighborhood, it would be consistent. She knew all about cell towers from one of her favorite true-crime podcasts.

Ultimately, the police ruled it a homicide "abated by death" and a state's attorney closed the case: a man had killed a woman, accidentally killing himself in the process. "Weirder things have happened," one of the detectives told Kim when she followed up. "You should see this Wikipedia page on bizarre deaths." No one could figure out why he had killed her, or if it had anything to do with his missing girlfriend and assistant. Again, the *why* of it was of no interest to the detectives. It was speculated that Gerry had been paranoid and possibly delusional after his fall in January—consulting a private detective, then a neurologist. It appeared that he had been taking some medications that were not prescribed, possibly in dangerous combinations, although tox screens showed nothing and an autopsy found that the only damage to Gerry's brain was from the injury that killed him. If Gerry had lived to see how his death was treated by some Internet outlets, he would have killed himself.

Kim felt she was doing Gerry a favor of sorts when she finished the manuscript she found in his computer. Giving him the last word, rescuing him from being a morbid punch line, another bizarre death logged on the Wikipedia page of bizarre deaths, a terrible thing Kim wishes she could unsee. She is especially haunted by the little boy whose head got stuck in the floor of a rotating restaurant. Why had the detective told her about that list? God, men can be awful.

She wrote far more of the book than she let on to Thiru. The memory of Columbus, the night in Gerry's hotel room—that wasn't in the original, an omission she found hurtful. How could the worst thing that ever happened to her not be one of *his* pivotal memories? She added other scenes as well, invented memories that she felt softened him. When she was finished, she realized she finally had some empathy for Gerry Andersen. She had expended so much energy, for so long, on hating him, but he might have saved her life and sacrificed his own in doing so. Not intentionally, perhaps, but he had believed himself brave, he had seen himself as a hero, and that had to count for something.

A two-book deal. It's not enough. It's too much. Kim doesn't lack confidence. She can write another novel. She wrote one in her MFA program. She wrote and revised much of *The Floating Staircase*, a title about which Thiru is dubious, but Kim has been gently insistent that the book be submitted with that name, claiming it was Gerry's choice. She simply doesn't know what *she* wants. She remembers Gerry's image of a wallet on a sidewalk, tied to a string, assuming that was Gerry's image and not Aileen's. She is not quite thirty. She doesn't want to spend her life chasing wallets on strings. During the weeks she lived in Gerry's apartment, readying it for sale, she found that the shelves full of his titles in various editions and languages exerted less power and charm with each passing day. It was, she supposed, like living near a beautiful vista, a mountain range, or an ocean. At some point, you stop noticing.

She has reached the northern edge of Central Park and the sun has disappeared, the wind is kicking up. The sky to the west looks dark, as if a storm might be coming in. She descends into the subway, a tune bouncing in her head: *You must take the A train*. That doesn't sound like something she would be thinking, she's not even sure how she knows that song, although she thinks she has heard Lin-Manuel Miranda sing it, but why would *Hamilton* mention the A train? Maybe it's Gerry's voice she's hearing. Maybe Gerry will be with her forever, whispering in her ear, filling her mind with his old-man concerns and crotchets.

Good lord, how does she even know the word *crotchet*, so weird and old-fashioned, not something a thirty-year-old would say? Has she become Gerry Andersen by writing about him? She certainly didn't bargain for *that*.

# AUTHOR'S NOTE

*And now perhaps we begin to see?*

This is the way I always remember the last line of *Portnoy's Complaint*. I always get it wrong. The psychiatrist asks Portnoy, clearly rhetorically, if he is ready to *begin,* not see. At any rate, Gerry Andersen is beyond therapy at this point.

If you want to play the game of figuring out who Gerry Andersen is, check out the author photo on this book. We are about the same age, creatures of Baltimore, formed by many of the same small experiences, none of the large ones. This is a book about what goes on inside a writer's mind and it is, by my lights, my first work of horror.

Over the past few years, I have begun repurposing books that are beloved to me, trying to figure out how to further the conversations they began in my head. Stephen King's *Misery* was clearly an influence here, but so were Roth's *Zuckerman Unbound* and Margaret Mitchell Dukore's *A Novel Called Heritage*.

But I think this novel was largely birthed in the living room of a now razed St. Petersburg, Florida, bed-and-breakfast, where the faculty at Writers in Paradise met for one week in January for fifteen years to drink and talk, talk and drink.

I had the usual support of "my" publishing team, people I have named often and will not try to list here as I will almost certainly forget someone. I had the support of my family as well and many friends, both in real life and on social media platforms. In fact, it was via Facebook that Martha Frankel put me in touch with Joe Donahue, who was extremely helpful in his description of healing from a bilateral quad tear. My neighbors who happen to be doctors, Joyce Jones and Andrew Stolbach, also offered assistance. And, sometimes, food and alcohol.

Two Baltimoreans bid on the right to have their names used in this book, with their contributions going directly to my daughter's school. Thank you, Thiru Vignarajah and Sarah Kotula.

When I began this book in 2019, my desire was to set it in a time I call nowish, but the pandemic forced my hand. It's odd to feel nostalgia for the life one was living when a book project began. By the time I finished this novel, my daughter was "distance learning" at home, which meant that I had to get up at sunrise to do my allotment of pages. This was exactly how I wrote twenty-plus years ago, when I still had a full-time job.

You know what? I liked it.

*Laura Lippman*
Baltimore, 2020